W9-BKJ-771

Dreyland

SOVO RIDGE

ZEBARA

Landfail

PERRICCI MOUNTAINS

Rebit's Sound

TAROK ISLAND

Dairneholm

RHOMBOO ISLAND

SAGURIA

Outpost

Chrisherna Sea

TELARNO RIVER

ISLE OF URSINA
(Cora di Schola)

VELT

Therian Marshes

FOREST OF NULL

Grandia Sea

cave

mirabear hive

Shark's Teeth rocks

Pirates!

KATHERINE APPLEGATE

illustrated by
MAX KOSTENKO

HARPER
An Imprint of HarperCollinsPublishers

for Michael

The first and greatest victory is to conquer yourself.

—Plato

endling

noun ~ end•ling ~ \\`en(d)-ling\\

1. the last living individual in a species,
   or, occasionally, a subspecies.
2. the official public ceremony at which
   a species is declared extinct; a eumony.
3. (informal) someone undertaking a
   doomed or quixotic quest.
   —*Imperial Lexica Officio of Nedarra*, 3rd edition

CONTENTS

PART THREE: DESTINIES

PART FOUR: CHOOSING COURAGE

1
Feel Fear. Choose Courage.

I'm not brave. Not bold. Not a leader.

I'm not remarkable in any way, to tell you the truth.

Unless you count the fact that I may well be the last member of my species, the dairnes.

An endling.

I can tell you what bravery looks like, though.

Bravery is single-handedly fighting off a horde of venomous serpents in order to save a dairne pup and her little wobbyk companion.

I was that pup. And my savior was Kharassande Donati, my human leader and dear friend.

I would like to be as daring as Khara, as certain, as fair. But leaders like her are born, not made.

My father, a brave and brilliant leader himself, loved wise sayings and proverbs. He used to tell me and my seven siblings, "Feel fear, choose courage. That's what makes a leader, pups."

Well, at least I've perfected the fear part. I am deeply acquainted with the many symptoms of terror: the rippling fur, the icy blood, the frantic heart, the unsheathed claws.

My fellow travelers—Khara, Tobble, Renzo, and Gambler—tell me I am braver than I know. And I have, I suppose, surprised myself sometimes these past few months.

But my little moments of bravado aren't evidence of real courage. They're evidence of good acting. If you ask me, pretending not to be afraid is not the same as true fearlessness. No matter what my friends say.

My strong, loyal, fierce friends. How I love them all! I've lost count of the times they've kept my spirits high on our quest to find more dairnes.

We know the odds are long. Just months ago, my entire pack was wiped out by soldiers—soldiers commanded by the Murdano, the despotic ruler of Nedarra, my homeland. And my pack was hardly the first. All over Nedarra, our numbers have slowly dwindled.

I alone survived that brutal day. Me, the lowest-ranking member. The runt. The least useful. The least helpful.

The least brave.

Although I cling to hope, I fear that I may never see another dairne. It's a dread that stuns me with its ferocity at odd moments, then dulls to an ache, one that throbs like a broken bone, badly healed. A fear I've grown accustomed to, one that travels with me day and night: my ugly, inescapable companion.

Still, it's the new fears, the unexpected ones, that take their biggest toll on me.

Sometimes they come in the dark of night, silent and bloodthirsty.

And sometimes, like yesterday, they circle the skies, lovely, graceful, and deadly.

2
Razorgulls

All morning, we'd been heading toward icy peaks towering in the distance beyond the Nedarran border—toward our uncertain future, toward my flimsy hopes.

We'd already been walking for three hours, and it had been tough going. It was cold, and gray clouds encircled the mountains, groping for the peaks. Our breath hovered before us like ghosts from our tangled pasts.

The unforgiving cliff face we'd been following had widened out into a patch in the shape of a stubby triangle, and we decided to rest there. Snowy clumps dotted the area, and the vegetation was limp and brown. On two sides of the triangle, soaring cliffs rose hundreds of feet high. The remaining side was open to the sea.

As soon as we paused, a large group of birds sliced through the clouds, wheeling and darting. There were hundreds of them, moving in perfect formation like well-trained soldiers.

"Razorgulls," Renzo said. "Keep an eye on them. They have beaks like knives. And they'll steal anything they can get their claws on."

"Kindred spirits, then?" Khara teased. Renzo was an accomplished thief.

"*I* had to learn my skills," Renzo said. He patted his odorous dog, Dog, who was sniffing stones with great studiousness. "With razorgulls, it's pure instinct."

"They're rather pretty," said Tobble, the little wobbyk who'd become my closest friend. He had foxlike features in a round face, with a protruding belly, huge oval ears, and wide, dark eyes. His three tails, newly braided—an important rite of passage in wobbyk culture—were tied at the end with a strip of leather.

We watched, mesmerized by the way the red-and-gray birds wheeled and swirled, circling like debris caught in a whirlwind. "They congregate near mining areas and villages," Renzo said. "When they snatch a purse or satchel filled with gems, they head south and unload it on pirate ships. In return, the pirates give them fresh catch." He shrugged. "As a thief, I have to admire their style."

"Why not just fish for themselves?" I asked.

"The same reason pirates don't work as farmers and

merchants," Renzo said. "Thievery is much more entertaining."

"I'd hoped to pause and eat here," Khara said, surveying the area. "You think it's safe?"

"Safe enough," Renzo said. "As long as we don't let our guard down. And we do need some rest."

"I wouldn't mind a little avian snack," said Gambler, following the razorgulls with his pale blue felivet eyes. A sleek black catlike predator, Gambler had delicate white facial stripes and not-so-delicate deadly claws. "Or just about any kind of snack. Think I'll explore this meadow and see what I come up with."

"We'll have food ready when you get back, Gambler," Tobble said, and my stomach whined energetically. (Dairne stomachs do not rumble. They whine, which to my mind is much more dignified.)

"Thank you," Gambler said, "but I'm hoping to find something better than biscuits."

"We have a bit of dried cotchet meat," Tobble offered.

Gambler nodded. "Dried means dead. Not the felivet way, Tobble."

Tobble, who doesn't eat meat, wrinkled his nose, and Gambler took off, moving in his distinctive feline way, which seems simultaneously leisurely and quick.

While I collected twigs and sticks, Tobble unpacked our cooking gear. Soon we had a small fire going, and he was singing under his breath as he retrieved herbs and a small pan.

Tobble had turned out to be the best cook among us. Renzo was good, too, especially when he deployed the little bit of theurgy—magic spells—he'd begun to learn when he'd turned fifteen this year. It didn't amount to much, though: a cold stew turned hot, a bland vegetable seasoned. One night he'd tried to impress us by popping tallin kernels. They'd turned into little fireflies and floated away on the breeze.

They were impressive, all right. Just not edible.

"Theurgy," Tobble had grumbled as we watched the fireflies head skyward like baby stars. "A good cook doesn't need magic." Right then and there, he'd whipped up a batch of kitlattis—a biscuit-like confection that his great-great-great-grandmother had taught him to make. It was like eating little clouds, if clouds tasted like honey.

Wobbyks like Tobble didn't perform theurgy. Only the six great governing species—humans, dairnes, felivets, natites, raptidons, and terramants—did. (Although I'd rarely seen dairnes practice it. We were too busy trying to survive.)

"We'll have hot tea in a jiffy," Tobble announced.

"Thanks, Tobble," I said. "I'll tell Khara and Renzo."

I joined the two of them near the meadow's edge, where they were staring out to sea. "More razorgulls," Renzo said, pointing.

We watched them swoop. "They don't seem to be getting any closer," I said.

"I've never seen birds move with such precision," Khara said, brushing away a stray lock of wavy, dark hair teased by the wind. Her eyes were dark and thickly lashed, intelligent and wary. As was often the case, she was dressed in simple peasant clothes like a poacher, her former occupation, the color just a shade lighter than her soft brown skin.

At times, Khara found it easier to pass as a boy on her journeys. Apparently, some humans have limited expectations when it comes to the abilities of females. I don't understand why. In the dairne world, females and males are treated equally.

Or perhaps I should say "were."

But then, there's much about human behavior that I find baffling.

Hanging from Khara's side was a rusty blade. It was a most pathetic-looking weapon, but we'd all seen that blade in action and understood its hidden powers. That bent sword was the Light of Nedarra, a weapon with an illustrious history.

"How far do you think we can travel before dark?" Khara asked Renzo.

Khara was our leader, but for this part of the journey, Renzo was guiding us, since he was the only one who'd ventured into this mountainous part of Dreyland, one of two countries bordering Nedarra.

He glanced behind him at the looming cliffs. "Hard to

say. Terrain will just get more treacherous. And it looks like it may snow."

"Let's stick to the plan as long as we can," Khara said with a determined nod.

That plan, uncertain though it was, involved heading north and skirting the coastal mountains, in the hope of sighting a moving island called Tarok. We'd considered trying to search by boat, but we didn't have the resources to pay for even the humblest craft. And there were few available, in any case. This frigid time of year, even pirates kept their distance from the rocky coast of Dreyland. The tides were perilous, the ice floes unpredictable.

Why a sentient island like Tarok would head north, we didn't know. But what we did know, what kept my heart alive on dark nights, was a legend about a colony of dairnes who'd once lived there.

I still recalled the poem about it, the one I'd had to learn as a young pup:

Sing, poet, of the Ancients who dared forth—
Brave dairnes, o'er mountains treacherous and cruel,
Who crossed the frigid waters of the north
To Dairneholme, living isle and floating jewel.

It had seemed impossible. And yet, after much travel and pain, I'd caught sight, just days ago, of what appeared to be a fellow dairne on the island, gliding from treetop to treetop.

At least, I *thought* I'd seen one.

My stomach whined again. "Tobble says there'll be hot tea in—"

I stopped midsentence, silenced by the whirring sound of wings.

The razorgulls had changed course with startling symmetry, moving like angry bees heading for a target.

My heart tripped as my old, unwelcome friend—fear—returned.

We were the target.

3
Attack from the Sky

"They're coming this way!" Renzo snapped, moving even as he spoke.

"Byx! Tobble! Flat on the ground!" Khara yelled, drawing her sword.

"Grab a torch instead," Renzo said. He dashed for Tobble's little cooking fire and snatched up a burning log. "They hate smoke."

Khara sheathed her sword and took up a sizzling stick.

Tobble, sensibly, decided to lie down flat as ordered, but I wasn't willing to let Khara and Renzo do all my fighting for me, though I doubted I'd be much help.

I found an unburned branch and thrust one end into the flames. Grabbing fistfuls of damp grass, I threw them on the fire. Bitter-smelling gray smoke twirled skyward.

I waved my own feebly burning torch, coughing as the wind veered, and returned to stand with Khara and Renzo.

The birds were no longer a dark whirl. They were hundreds of missiles flying straight at us.

They hit us like a hailstorm, slamming into chests and heads, striking with the cruel beaks that had given them their name. In seconds I was cut on both arms, narrowly avoiding a slashing attack that would have opened my neck. I heard Dog yelp in pain as a razorgull sliced through his fur.

My heart galloped in my chest. The gashes on my forearms burned, and I glanced down to see pearly blood oozing from the wounds.

"No!" I screamed, thrusting the torch upward, flailing blindly.

The birds were not giving up. The nearest razorgulls flew away, but swiftly turned to come back at me from behind. I spotted Khara, Renzo, and Tobble through a tornado of wings, yelling creative curses, arms windmilling to no effect.

As we bled and retreated, putting the smoking fire between us and the birds, they seemed to be everywhere at once, squawking and slashing. They concentrated their efforts on our bags and pouches—no doubt hoping for coins—but attacked any part of us they could reach.

"To the cliffs!" Khara yelled.

I understood her reasoning. We were being barraged from every direction. At least if we hugged the rock wall, the birds could only come at us from the front and sides.

I tapped Tobble on the back of his head and said, "Come on, get behind us!" As if that would somehow keep him safe.

Already I was exhausted from swinging the torch, and it had dulled to a mere flicker. When Khara's torch died completely, she tossed it aside to again draw her sword, but lost her balance and stumbled to the ground.

In an instant, she was completely concealed beneath a blanket of piercing beaks.

"Aaaahhhh!" Tobble screamed. He raced for Khara and leapt into the pile of birds, scratching, kicking, and yelling, "Leave her alone! Leave her alone!"

Not for the first time, I witnessed the shocking sight of a wobbyk enraged. Enraged and fearless.

Renzo and I joined the fray, scattering enough of the crazed birds for Khara to shake herself free. She scooped Tobble up to ride on her shoulders, and the four of us, along with Dog, abandoned all dignity and scrambled for safety.

"Over here!"

Gambler! I couldn't see him through the feathered storm, but I heard his voice and pushed myself forward, trying to ignore my stinging cuts and the shrill and menacing squawks of the birds.

I hit a rock wall and twisted around to put my back against it.

"Follow my voice!" Gambler cried from somewhere to my right.

I edged along the cliff, batting uselessly at my attackers. My left foot caught on a sharp boulder and I landed hard on my back, the wind knocked from my lungs.

A massive paw reached out. Huge black claws hooked carefully around my scabbard and pulled me close.

"Thanks, Gambler!"

I scooted past him as he snatched birds in midair with felivet speed.

Khara pushed through, trying to join me. "Renzo!" she cried, her voice hoarse.

"I see him," Gambler said.

The great felivet plowed straight into the bird cloud, slashing and batting with nearly supernatural speed and accuracy. He caught one unfortunate bird, which promptly disappeared down Gambler's gullet. Lunch. Razorgull blood streaked the side of his jaw and the birds swirled away as they considered this new threat.

Gambler found Renzo on his knees, still swinging his torch, blood streaming from a dozen cuts.

"Grab my neck!" Gambler yelled, and Renzo didn't need to be persuaded. Dragging Renzo along the ground, Gambler joined us.

In a flash, as quickly as we'd been besieged, we were free of the birds. I took quick stock of my surroundings. We'd backed into a narrow crack in the rock face: no place for creatures with wings. The opening was closed at the top, and the only light came from the opening onto the meadow. I could see razorgulls patrolling back and forth, waiting for us to return to battle.

"There's a cave," Gambler said. "Come."

We followed, trailing blood on the stone floor, our only light the guttering flame of Renzo's dying torch.

At last we found a wide space with boulders where we could rest. There we took turns bandaging each other's wounds, while Dog attempted, unhelpfully, to lick them.

"So," Khara said as she wrapped a cut on Renzo's forearm, "back to the birds, or on into darkness?"

"Darkness," we all said at once.

"Well, that was easy," Khara said. She took Renzo's flickering torch and we headed off into the cold and endless blackness.

4
Good Little Doggie

Deeper and deeper into the cave we went. The torchlight faded to a weakly glowing ember and we stumbled at almost every step. Gambler's sight was far better at night, but even he could not see in absolute darkness. We tried to feed the flame, but the only fuel we could find was damp moss coating the walls and floor. The instant the torch died, we would be completely sightless, feeling our way far below the reach of the sun.

"I sense open space ahead," Khara said. "The air is different."

"Yes," Gambler agreed. "But without light . . ."

I, too, could tell the air was growing less stuffy. I smelled something familiar yet strange: water. Not salt water. Not clear spring water. This water had a scent of strange minerals, of marsh and mushrooms.

The torch sputtered and died, plunging us into a black void. I held my hand an inch in front of my face and saw nothing. It was a strangely suffocating feeling, losing a sense so completely.

"I can see a little," Gambler said. "Byx, take hold of my tail. Everyone else join hands with each other."

We crept forward hand in hand, or hand on tail, moving with all the speed of moonsnails. For two hours, maybe more, we were in a place without time. As we inched along, we complained about our bandages and pain, trying to distract ourselves from the crushing terror of being far underground without so much as a glimmer of light.

When we ran out of complaints, Tobble sang an old tune about giant mudworms, a great fear for wobbyks, who live in underground tunnels.

The chorus was gruesomely appropriate, and soon we were all singing along with him:

When wobbyks doze in slumber sweet,
The mudworm knows it's time to eat.
It dines on tails. It gnaws on paws.
(The mudworm doesn't care for claws.)

"Have you ever seen a giant mudworm, Tobble?" I asked.
"Once," he answered. "When I was just a kit." He

shuddered, and I felt his big ears tremble like leaves in a breeze. "And believe me, once was plenty. They are giant and slimy and always hungry."

Our voices were growing hoarse when Gambler suddenly stopped. "It's lighter ahead!" he reported. "There must be a way out!"

He was right about the light, wrong that it was sunlight. We soon realized that the walls of the cave were emitting a faint golden light. After total darkness, it was welcome indeed.

Gradually our eyes adjusted and we could see well enough not to trip every second step. The feeling of openness grew, too. We rounded a bend in the tunnel and saw a circle of aqua light ahead. It seemed dazzling but was probably no brighter than the light of a crescent moon.

The tunnel ended a hundred feet or more above the floor of a great cavern. We gazed in awestruck astonishment at a scene that defied imagination.

The cavern wasn't big. It wasn't even huge. It was vast.

The entire Nedarran royal capital of Saguria would have fit comfortably in the immense space. Above us, an impossibly high ceiling bristled with rocky spears. The floor of the cavern had its own version: a forest of rock daggers pointing upward. The projections on the floor formed a ring at the edges of the most startling feature of the cavern, a lake with dark water so perfectly undisturbed it looked like polished black glass.

"I see fire," Renzo said. "All the way across the lake, to the right. Maybe several small fires."

"And I smell them," I said, testing the air.

We clambered down the steep descent, then set off on a strange and difficult march. The only way around the lake involved passing through clusters of oddly shaped stalagmites. Some looked like squat beehives. Some resembled a knight's spear, tapered and smooth. Others reminded me of huge candles, melted into grotesque forms.

But no matter their shape, all were capable of inflicting a cut or a bruise, and in our already bloody condition, it was tough going.

When we finally reached a narrow black sand beach, we collapsed in a heap.

"Should we look for kindling and try to build a fire?" Tobble asked, examining a bloody bandage on his left foot.

Khara shook her head. "No. Not until we find out who or what started those fires across the lake."

"Does anyone need fresh bandaging?" I asked.

We'd used up all our cloth strips and had nothing left to bind our wounds but some bitter-smelling lammint leaves I'd collected earlier. Lammint leaves are known to be medicinal, but between us we had so many shallow cuts from the birds, and so many scrapes and bruises from the stalagmites, that it was almost pointless. My whole body was a living bruise highlighted with a dozen stinging cuts.

I crushed up some lammint leaves and passed them to my friends, who pressed them to the new wounds they'd acquired in the cave.

"I'm really sorry," I said.

"Sorry for what?" Renzo asked.

I pointed to the bandage on his arm. "For that." I waved my hand. "For all of this. You wouldn't be hurt if it weren't for me."

"Byx," Renzo said, eyes locked on mine. "That's a path you can't allow yourself to take. We're in this together. All of us."

"Renzo's right. We're all committed to this mission. If there are dairnes still alive, Byx," Khara said, "we are going to find them."

I nodded. But it was hard to shake the feeling of responsibility. Here we were, in the middle of nowhere, bleeding and bedraggled, just because I thought I'd seen another dairne. Because of one brief, heart-lurching sighting, my new pack of friends was willing to risk everything.

I'd grown used to difficult choices lately. But difficult choices were easier when your friends weren't involved. And the worst part? Even if we did find more dairnes, we weren't sure if we could ever safely return to our homeland. The Murdano wasn't exactly happy with us at the moment. Not happy, as in he'd be delighted to see us all dead.

He'd sent us on a mission to find more dairnes, hoping he could capture a few, then kill all the rest.

The Murdano had his reasons, vile though they were. Because dairnes can tell when someone is lying, we can be quite useful to those in power. On the other hand, too many dairnes could present a real threat to someone like the Murdano. The truth can be a dangerous thing. Especially if you're a liar.

It is, as my packelder, Dalyntor, used to say, our "burdensome gift."

We had, of course, decided not to fulfill his mission. And now, for all we knew, we were being chased by the evil despot's soldiers.

I sighed—louder than I'd meant to—and Dog padded over, tongue dangling, tail wagging incessantly. His fur was streaked with blood, but he seemed as giddy as ever.

"He wants to be sure you're all right," said Renzo, who, for some reason, believed Dog could do no wrong.

I managed a tolerant smile. I have mixed feelings about dogs.

I know it's wrong. My parents taught me to treat all species with respect. But just for the record, allow me to make this one thing clear: I am *not* a dog.

Unfortunately, I am regularly mistaken for one. Far too many strangers have stroked my head and cooed, "Good little doggie." (Clearly, humans are not the most observant mammals. It's perfectly obvious I'm not a doggie, good or otherwise.)

To begin with, dairnes have glissaires, fine membranes that allow us to glide, batlike, through the air. Not for long distances, alas. But floating high above the world, even for just a few seconds, is a joy no mere dog will ever experience.

We also have hands, complete with opposable thumbs. They are every bit as clever as human hands. And far superior to clumsy and unreliable paws.

Moreover, we can use human language skillfully—better than many humans, in fact. When a dog, on the other hand, wants to communicate with people, there are limited options. Basically it comes down to three choices: bark, beg, or bite.

Here's another advantage to being a dairne. Unlike dogs, we have pouches on our stomachs called "patchels," convenient for carrying items. Once upon a time, I used mine to hold small treasures: a glistening sunstone, a ball for tossing with my packmates. These days, it held just a few things, including a map that might or might not hold my destiny in its pale scribblings.

But that's not all. Dairnes aren't just better designed than dogs. We behave better, too.

We don't go mad with glee at the glimpse of a zebra squirrel.

We don't roll on our backs in humiliating appeals for a stomach scratch.

We don't sniff impolitely at the backsides of passersby.

Dogs are, in a word, rude. And yet every village seems to be crawling with them, in all shapes and sizes. Some are as hulking as rockwolves, some not much bigger than well-fed mouselings.

So many dogs.

So few dairnes.

My father, may his heart shine like the sun, had another favorite saying: "A dairne alone is not a dairne."

He meant that for my species, the pack is everything. To be without them means ceasing to be who we are meant to be.

I used to groan at my father's sayings. All my siblings and I did. But I would give anything to hear him speak just one more time. Oh, to hear him say my name again!

But that will never be. I'll never see my pack again, or my family. In fact, though I cling to hope like a sputtering torch in a dark cave, I know I may never see another dairne, no matter how far my friends and I travel. No matter how hard we search.

I watched as Dog licked my hand, depositing an

unappetizing layer of slobber in the process. "You're a good little doggie," I said, and his tail went into a frenzy.

I suppose they're not so bad, dogs.

And I need all the friends I can get.

5
A Felivet's Fear

After far too brief a rest, Khara stood and stretched.

"Let's get moving," she said, and with a bit of good-natured groaning, we soldiered on. Ten minutes later, the beach ended at a cliff face that extended all the way to the ceiling of the cavern, cutting us off.

My heart fell. There was no way forward.

"Uh-oh," Tobble murmured.

I found myself entertaining terrible visions of the five of us wandering pitifully through stalagmite forests until we died of hunger.

"I'll take a look," Renzo offered.

He waded into the water, inching alongside the wall of rock. He was waist deep when he turned to us and yelled, "There's a submerged ledge. We might be able to follow it around to the far side."

"Tobble," Khara said, "you can ride on my shoulders." She knelt down and Tobble hopped aboard.

"Come on, Byx," Renzo urged. "Time for a piggyback ride."

I glanced at Gambler. He was pacing back and forth, staring intently at the water.

"What's the matter, Gambler?" I asked.

"Water, that's what's the matter," he muttered. "We felivets don't mind a stream or a puddle. And despite what people say, we can swim. But large bodies of water? You don't know what may be under the surface."

"You're too big to carry," Khara said in a gentle voice.

"I know!" I don't think I'd ever heard Gambler sound quite so irritated. "I *know*. I know I have to do it."

I frowned at Gambler in disbelief. "Are you afraid?" I said.

The thought seemed preposterous, and I meant my question as a joke. To me, Gambler was the epitome of bravery. This was a felivet who had single-handedly attacked a fearsome Knight of the Fire and lived to tell the tale.

"Not afraid," Gambler snapped. "It's just . . . I don't like water."

"I'll go first," Khara said. "If there's anything with an appetite for meat under the water, I'll just let them have Tobble."

"Hey!" Tobble objected.

"I'm joking," Khara said, winking at me.

But she wasn't joking about going first. "It's freezing!" she complained as she stepped in. Cautiously Khara made her way, deeper and deeper, until she found the underwater ledge and eased along it. She kept one hand on the cliff face, the other held out for balance. With Tobble on her shoulders, she looked like a human who'd grown a very strange second head.

Khara and Tobble moved out of sight as the cliff face curved, but after a few minutes she called, "It's clear!"

"Hop up, Byx," Renzo said, crouching a bit.

I shook my head. "Thanks, but I'll ride on Gambler's back. I've done it before."

I didn't want to imply that Gambler needed support. Felivets are the most solitary of species, and I knew he wasn't a creature who'd welcome assistance. But I wanted to help, if I could.

Renzo took the hint, nodded, and set off after Khara.

"Our turn, Gambler," I said.

Gambler sent me a glare that once upon a time might have caused me to drop dead from sheer terror. But I knew I had nothing to fear.

I hopped atop his powerful back and said, "Let's go."

Gambler, of course, couldn't walk on the submerged ledge. He had to swim.

He swiveled his huge head and looked at me. Then he slipped into the water as silently as a hawk through clouds.

We moved effortlessly, it seemed. But having ridden on his back once before, I sensed his fear. His muscles were tensed, his breathing strained.

It made me wonder about Gambler. He was mighty, he was wise, he was the last creature you'd ever want to have to fight.

Was it possible that even he experienced fear the same way I did?

Finally, we climbed out of the water onto an area of wide shale stones. I jumped down so that Gambler could shake himself dry.

"Thanks for the ride, friend felivet."

Gambler sneered and tried to look angry, but his pride was obvious. He'd done it. After a moment, he even gave me a slight nod of acknowledgment for my supporting role.

The others were waiting, soggy and shivering. "That definitely looks like a village," Renzo said, peering at two distinctly separate blazes.

"I think I see . . . I don't know, not humans, but something moving around the flames." Khara sighed and shared a worried look with me. "What do you think, Byx? It looks like the only two options are the way we came, or forward to whatever those creatures are."

I was quite sure Gambler wouldn't be anxious to swim back. And none of us wanted to risk the cliffs and the birds again—if we even found our way through the blackness.

"Let's see who they are," I said, sounding more certain than I felt.

The shale was slippery, covered with patches of dark blue moss, but it was a walk in a meadow compared to much of what we'd dealt with.

We were perhaps a quarter league from the village when a shrill alarm assailed our ears.

Brrreeeeet! Brrreeeeet!

It was some kind of horn. Two alarming bleats, then nothing.

We looked at each other, waiting, not sure what to do. Before we could decide, the lake beside us erupted in froth.

A dozen or more creatures exploded from the water with such force that they flew through the air before settling into a line between us and the village.

I knew what they were. We all did.

"Natites!" I cried.

6
Lar Camissa

Natites are one of the governing species of Nedarra, but they're found in many lands. They come in a variety of colors, sizes, and body types. But even knowing that, these seemed like extremely unusual natites.

For one thing, natites tend toward shades of blue and green, but these creatures were colorless. Their skin was slick and translucent, their arteries and veins visible just under the surface. I even caught a glimpse or two of internal organs.

Like most natites, these were water-breathers with multiple gills. But their most startling feature, after the disturbing translucent flesh, was their enormous eyes. Shimmering gold with an oblong black iris, they were, taken together, nearly as large as the natite's head. Mounted on stubby but moveable stalks that jutted from the back of their jawbones was a second set of eyes. These were eerily luminescent, casting a green light that framed their heads.

I shuddered. It was the same reaction I'd had the first time I'd seen a natite, but in comparison, that creature was tame-looking indeed. These looked more like creatures of theurgy than mere flesh and blood.

They were armed, too, with strange implements. I saw stone axes, chipped flint blades, and primitive but effective-looking lances, along with flails: rocks on ropes, strung like giant pearls.

Khara held her hands up, palms out, to show she wielded no weapon. Tobble, Renzo, and I mimicked her. Gambler, of course, could not do the same, so he opted for the felivet version, slightly lowering his head and sheathing his claws.

"We mean you no harm," Khara said.

The natites said nothing. They just stood there, like a soggy wall between us and the village of twenty or thirty roofless huts made of piled stones.

I scanned the village. The cluster of huts extended over the water in part, with stone piers bearing a few more homes. This was not surprising, since natites were creatures of the water who could also walk upon the land. At the farthest inland reach of the village, a stone fence corralled a dozen white slugs the size of ponies.

Once again, I shuddered.

"Listen, please," Khara said. "We are lost and intend you no harm."

Silence from the natites, but I had spotted something. "I think some kind of village elder is coming," I whispered.

A group of six natites approached from the village. One sat imperiously atop a huge, undulating slug. In another place and time, it might have been a comical sight. But I sensed our lives were in this natite's hands. Laughter was the last thing on my mind.

Once they'd arrived, Khara again explained that we were lost, passing through, and meant them no harm.

One of the newly arrived natites spoke in heavily accented Common Tongue.

"Behold Lar Camissa, Queen of all Subdur Natitia, Protector of the Sacred Waters, Fire Maker; Lar Camissa, the Undefeated. Lar Camissa, the Mighty. Lar Camissa, Mother of Multitudes. Lar Camissa . . ."

The titles and praise continued for a long time, and it seemed a lot for a creature riding a slug around the shore of a subterranean lake. But Khara waited patiently until the recitation was done before speaking. "I am Kharassande Donati, a simple girl fleeing danger and looking only for peace. These are my companions: Gambler, Renzo, Tobble, and Byx."

Finally, Lar Camissa of the many honorifics spoke. "Leave my domain immediately or die."

It was a threat, but my first reaction was not fear, but admiration. She had the most musical voice, layered with sounds, so that her words seemed to come from a dozen instruments playing together.

"Our fondest wish is to leave by—" Khara began.

"Do you insult us?" Lar Camissa demanded.

I noticed, with some shock, that unlike the regular natites with their unusual glowing extra eyes, Lar Camissa had at least four more, two glowing from her lower neck and two rising from tentacles near her shoulders.

"No, Your Majesty," Khara said. "I merely mean—"

"Is my realm so poor, so worthless, that you come here to demean us?" I could call what she made "speech," but it was closer to singing, and closer still to lutes and harps playing in unison.

"Your Majesty, we are no threat, nor do we—"

"Threat?" Lar Camissa trilled. Her minions glared hard and fingered their weapons. "You presume that you have power to threaten me?" The music took on a discordant tone.

"No threat," said Khara, clearly swallowing her impatience, "was made or suggested."

This went on for many more rounds. Whatever Khara said, Lar Camissa turned it into an insult or a threat. Again and again.

Khara's face was growing stormy.

"Great Queen," I said, speaking up despite Khara's furious look, "I am Byx, a dairne. My people are known for an ability to unfailingly separate truth from lies. I can confirm that my friend Khara speaks truth."

"A dairne?" Lar Camissa seemed impressed. "I have heard stories about your kind. Hmm." She cocked her strange head and wiggled her tentacles, considering. "We are intrigued. Come. Join us for a royal meal."

We exchanged wary glances, unsure whether to be relieved or terrified by her sudden change of heart.

Within moments, the natite guards formed themselves into an escort, and Lar Camissa urged on her vile steed. In her lovely vibrato voice, she invited Khara to walk beside her.

The rest of us followed behind, taking in the odd sights. The natite village was deceptive. We'd assumed we were seeing simple stone huts resting on shale. But as we passed them, we realized we were seeing only the most outwardly visible part of the village. Most of the village was underwater.

At the center of each hut was a pool that led down through the shale and out into the lake. The "huts" were a great deal more like wells than houses.

They weren't empty, though. Each hut contained a dry space where a natite could sit or lounge. And it seemed to my inexperienced eye that the stone walls were adorned with objects of art, small tapestries of woven lichen and moss.

Lar Camissa's stone hut was twice the size of most. We entered by ascending a ladder and then climbing down slippery steps set into the interior wall. A large pool of black water filled the central room. Still, the dry space around it was capacious enough for all of us to find a place to sit.

Lar Camissa sat on a rock seat, while we settled on the shale floor. A natite rose up from the water, holding two large blue shells that each contained a pint of water.

"Drink with us and be welcome," Lar Camissa said, with a pleasant smile.

My friends and I nodded uncertainly. The Queen's earlier threats still rang in our ears.

She took one shell goblet. The rest of us passed the second one around, each taking a tentative sip. The water was delicious and strange, as cold as ice, as clear as air, like winter's first snowflake on the tip of your tongue.

With the water drinking done—though I'd have loved more—we listened to Lar Camissa share the tale of a furious split between her people, Subdur natites, and another group of natites. The Subdur natites had gone into exile, fleeing for their lives, and had found this miraculous place of life-giving water.

While she spoke, servants rose from the water to bring us colorless raw fish and boiled seaweed. Khara recoiled from both but managed to get some down and show a shaky smile.

Tobble ate the seaweed contentedly. Renzo devoured his food with relish, as if he'd been served his favorite dishes.

I didn't have a strong feeling about raw fish one way or the other. My small band of dairnes had often been hungry. We'd learned to eat whatever we could, whenever we could.

"Now, tell me why you have come and what you wish of us," Lar Camissa said as she chomped away. Evidently, talking while eating was normal for natites. She glanced at me and added, "The dairne will tell us whether you speak true."

"We were trying to climb the mountain pass when we were attacked by razorgulls," Khara explained. "We escaped into a cave and finally came to Your Majesty's realm."

"It's true," I chimed in. "You can see the cuts from—"

I gasped. I'd held out my arm to show one of my own stinging cuts, but it was no longer there. Had it been on the other arm?

I touched the other wounds I recalled. All were gone.

The Subdur Queen laughed, and it was like hearing a chorus of flutes. "You have drunk of the waters. They speed healing." She looked sly. "Why do you think we stay hidden? If the secret of the waters were known, all the world would come against us and take what is ours."

Instantly, the mood went tense. Gambler's tail flicked. Renzo stiffened.

"Which brings me to our problem. How can we be sure

that you will not tell the world our secret?" Lar Camissa demanded. "And lead them to us?"

Khara seemed caught off guard, and for several seconds, we sat in silence.

It was Renzo who spoke up. "We've seen only one way into this place, Great Queen. If you sealed up that opening, we would know of no way in. And when we leave, you can cover our eyes and guide us out."

It was the sort of solution a clever thief might come up with.

The translucent Queen looked thoughtfully at him, then searched our faces one by one. "That is agreeable," she said at last. "But first you must perform a task for us, a task we cannot do ourselves."

"How bad could that be?" Tobble whispered to me.

Then she told us, and we had our answer.

7
The Queen's Demand

I've ridden horses. I've even ridden—for a short time—a stampeding garilan, a six-legged herd animal with a crimson body, a golden tail, and an inexcusably long neck.

Neither came easily to me. We dairnes trust our feet (or, in an emergency, our glissaires).

So it was with more than mere trepidation that I climbed atop a slimy white slug pony, with a boost from a helpful natite. The pony was taller than a horse, though his head—if a tube ending in a squeezing-and-releasing sphincter can be called a head—was held low to the ground.

In order to get astride the creature, I had to climb, even with the natite's help. I dug my fingers and toes into what felt like cold jelly and scampered up, coating my front with slime in the process.

He was not my favorite steed. Without a saddle, being

astride was like sitting in a puddle of goo. He moved in a rhythmic pulsation that made me nauseous.

On the other hand, he and the other ponies seemed unshakably calm. They did not stray or take alarm, but oozed along steadily.

Lar Camissa, who did not join us, gave us three guides, one of whom, Daf Hantch, seemed to be of high rank. He was dour and quiet, and his voice had none of Lar Camissa's music in it.

We rode around the lake, then veered off into a side tunnel that went steadily downhill. The air temperature rose as we advanced. Our escorts looked weary on their mounts, as if we were marching through a desert under a pitiless sun.

Near the lake, the phosphorescence lit our way, but in the depths of the tunnel, the only light came from the glowing eyes of our natite guides.

"I wonder if we can trust them," Gambler murmured as he trotted alongside us. "They could be taking us somewhere to abandon us in total darkness."

After a while I detected a new light ahead of us, a soft orange glow that seemed to brighten as the temperature rose. Our guides gasped for breath and the slug ponies oozed along ever more slowly. It was warm, but only about as warm as a mild spring day. Nonetheless, the temperature was obviously putting a great strain on the natites and our rides.

We took a sharp turn. The stone walls, which had been rough and dripping with moisture, had grown dry and smooth.

Daf Hantch called a halt. "We can go no farther," he said, wheezing.

Khara climbed down from her slimy mount, and I happily did the same. "Then you'd better explain your Queen's demand," she said. "What exactly are these objects she wants us to retrieve?"

Daf Hantch took a long breath. "When we fled persecution and came to live beneath the ground, we took with us our most sacred objects: the Crown, the Shield, and the Eye. The first among them, the Crown of Beleeka, was a symbol of Lar Camissa's noble birth. Second was a less important but still venerated object, the Ganglid Shield. Finally, there was the Eye, a toy of no great importance, except that it was a childhood gift given to the Queen by her mother."

Khara crossed her arms over her chest. "And?" she asked.

"A traitorous band of the Queen's soldiers tried to abscond with the objects soon after our arrival here. As they escaped, there was a violent volcanic eruption. The gods, no doubt, were angered at their betrayal."

"No doubt," said Khara, and Renzo hid a smile.

"The soldiers were buried in magma, and the treasured items lost to us."

"And you want us to get them back?" Khara asked.

Def Hantch nodded. "If you continue on, you will find a stream amid streams, pools within pools, peril and promise. Within the inner pool at the bottom of the unscalable height lie those three sacred objects."

Khara glanced at me, and I gave a subtle shake of my head. He was lying by omission, leaving out details to outwit me, to fool my senses.

"If we bring you these objects, you will let us go freely?" Khara asked.

"The Queen has said so."

No, she had not, actually. She'd made no promise, just a request. Once again, Daf Hantch was being evasive.

Khara didn't need me to tell her that. Still, she nodded along, as though she believed the old fraud.

"We shall wait here," Daf Hantch said, still struggling for breath. "There is no other way in or out." He flinched as he said it and shot me a look that I pretended not to see, just as I pretended not to have heard this new lie.

Let him think we believed him.

We left the natites and our slug ponies and advanced on foot. It was hot even for us, midday-summer hot—not unbearable, but not pleasant, either. The light continued to intensify, and soon we saw the source.

Before us lay a large cavern crisscrossed by streams of magma. But that wasn't the worst of it. The magma also trickled from the cave roof, a slow rainfall of drops so hot they could burn through clothing and flesh. Our goal was at the far end of a hundred yards of falling death. There the cavern wall went up and up, a stone cliff disappearing into gloom.

At the base of the cliff was a rectangular pool encircled with stone. A small stream of water followed a channel cut into the stone face, refilling the pool and sending up a column of steam. The overflow from the pool drained away in a serpentine path, weaving its way between streams of magma, boiling in places where it came too close and steaming along its entire length.

Between us and the pool we hoped to reach were great plopping drops of molten rock, a network of magma rivulets, a stream of steam, and beneath it all, a crusted black floor.

I gulped. I suspect everyone did.

"Do these natites think we're invulnerable to falling lava?" Khara demanded, laughing in disbelief. "We can't cross that!"

Renzo, however, was studying the situation. I watched him, the way he searched carefully, left to right, up and down, taking in every detail. He took his time about it, nodding to himself as he considered and ignoring our expressions of irritation and disbelief.

Finally he said, "I can do it."

"You can do *what?*" Khara asked.

"I can get to the pool and grab whatever's there."

"You're daft," Khara said.

"That may be," he answered with a wide grin. "But I am also a very good thief. I've made my way in and out of the homes of wealthy people with high walls, furious dogs, and hard men-at-arms. I can do this."

Khara frowned. "All right, Renzo the very good thief, what do you see that I do not?"

"Some theurgy beyond anything I know is at work here. The floor is sloped up, causing the magma drops to run down the channels before they can cool and stick, but even so, the fashioning of those channels was not done without theurgy. No degree of slope could keep those channels free of accumulated magma. No, there is magic at work here, ancient and very deep magic." He gave a rather smug smile. "But in addition to theurgy, we have mathematics."

Gambler jerked his head up with un-felivet-like surprise. "You know of mathematics? It was one of my areas of study on the Isle of Scholars before I . . . well, before I irritated the wrong people and ended up in the dungeon where you found me."

"I pick things up here and there." Renzo pointed. "There are seventy-two distinct drips landing in seventy-two spots. At first, it seems random: there would be no way to avoid being burned. But I see a pattern, which could be explained more easily if I had a scrap of paper and a pen. . . ." He looked around, as if expecting someone to offer him these things, then noticed the exasperated impatience on Khara's face. "Or I could discuss the mathematics with Gambler at a later time."

"Probably best," I agreed.

"The point is, there's a rhythm, a mathematical pattern. It won't be easy, but I think I can do it in twelve jumps. The fourth and ninth jumps will be the hardest."

"If you survive to reach the pool, the water is billowing steam," Gambler said. "You'll boil your hand."

"Indeed. I would need something to fish out the objects. Something that could withstand the heat." He looked meaningfully at Khara's sword.

"No, no, no," Khara said. "This is the Light of Nedarra! This belongs to my family and always will. It's priceless."

"Yes. And I am a thief."

Khara pursed her lips, scowling. "Yes or no, Renzo," she said. "Right where Byx can hear you and judge your truth. Yes or no, will you steal my sword?"

Renzo made a small smile and tilted his head impishly. "I won't answer that, Khara. Either you trust me or you don't. You are the leader of our little ragtag band, and we trust your instincts. So what do your instincts tell you about me?"

Khara did not look pleased, not at all. A sound not unlike an animal growl rose from her throat. She took a threatening step forward, hand on the hilt of her sword. But Renzo never stopped smiling.

For a long time they stared at each other, Renzo amused, Khara furious and suspicious. Finally, she drew her sword. For a split second I was not at all sure she wasn't going to slice off his head.

"Take it," Khara said, thrusting the hilt toward Renzo.

"Thank you, Khara," Renzo said, with only a trace of mockery.

Khara's answer was something like "Grrrrrr."

8
A Masterpiece of Careful Planning and Flawless Execution

We dairnes aren't great dancers. Nor have I ever had the pleasure of watching professional dancers display their grace and skill. Still, Renzo, I suspect, would have put them to shame with his moves.

He waited, nodding his head to a rhythm I could not perceive. Then he leapt high and wide, landing astride a channel just as a big glop of burning stone rolled past.

Another leap, and he found himself in a narrow spot where two channels passed within inches of each other. He leaned back as a drop skimmed his chest by a hair, then forward as another drop came even closer to his posterior.

A pause, then leap number three. Renzo landed, surefooted, in a space where no drops were falling. Finally, he could catch his breath.

It was terrifying to watch. And yet we couldn't look away.

As Renzo had predicted, the fourth leap was one of the worst. He had to use Khara's sword, swung sideways, to bat away a drop of magma.

It took Renzo half an hour of leaping, twisting, and bending before he reached the pool, having suffered what must have been a painful burn down his left arm, a burn that left his shirtsleeve in tattered black ash and the flesh beneath an angry red.

I wanted to call out and ask if he was all right. But I was afraid I might startle him, with horrible consequences.

Finally, amazingly, Renzo was standing next to the steaming pool.

He waved with Khara's sword. She grumbled under her breath, but I saw her eyes light.

"Do you think he'll come back?" Tobble asked me in a low whisper. "He wouldn't really steal Khara's sword and leave us behind, would he?"

"Of course not," I said. But I wasn't completely sure. The last human male I'd trusted had been a scholar named Luca. And he'd betrayed us.

Still, I told myself, this was Renzo. We'd gone through so much together. He wasn't like Luca. He was part of our family.

Renzo, wreathed in clouds of steam, thrust Khara's sword into the boiling pool and used the sharp tip to feel around.

Then he removed the sword, waited until it had cooled, and reversed his grip, sticking the hilt end into the water. He withdrew it slowly, carefully, like a fisherman with a tentative bite.

We saw something slowly coming into view. Renzo hauled it up by sheer strength, bracing his feet against the walls of the pool for leverage. A heavy metal object clanged onto the ground.

A shield! Renzo had snagged it by its carrying strap.

Again, more fishing around. Renzo, drenched with sweat, seemed to be growing increasingly impatient.

Finally he returned to us, holding the shield over his head. Like the theurgically enhanced channels, the shield, too, shed drops of magma as if they were no more than raindrops.

"I can feel another object in there," Renzo reported, wiping his brow. "But there's no way to get a grip."

"Break the sides of the pool," Gambler suggested. "The hot water will drain out, revealing the prize beneath."

Renzo nodded. "Yes, that was my thought, too. But once the water is released, it'll flow into the falling magma. The entire chamber may become one great teapot of steam."

"You wouldn't be able to get back through the steam," Khara said.

Renzo nodded. "It would be utterly impossible . . . if we were to come back this way. But there may be another way out."

Khara looked at me. "Did Daf Hantch lie about this being the only path?"

"Yes," I confirmed. "But that doesn't mean we can find the other way."

"Where does the steam go?" Tobble wondered aloud. He craned his neck, gazing upward.

"The wobbyk asks a good question," Gambler said, sounding a bit surprised.

Gambler still sometimes had difficulty seeing Tobble as a fully equal creature, a peer. Felivets eat wobbyks. It required a major adjustment in felivet thinking.

Of course, dairnes have been known to eat wobbyks, too. I'd reminded Tobble of that fact when we'd first met, but he'd been unfazed. Fortunately.

"The air is too dry, even with so much heat," Gambler said. "This place should feel wet. The air should cling."

We all stared straight up. And that was when an amazing thing happened. A bright shard of light peeked into view far above us.

"It's the moon!" I blurted.

"We're at the bottom of a volcano," Khara said. "Of course. The steam escapes up the spout."

"Which is how we shall escape, if we are lucky," Renzo said.

As the moon—that lovely sliver of hope—moved into view, Renzo shuttled us beneath the shield to the pool, one at a time. It wasn't easy to see through the steam and the bubbles, but there definitely was something in that pool. Something square, something made by hand and not by nature.

"Will your sword shatter the stone sides of this cistern?" Renzo asked Khara.

"In your hands? No," Khara said. "In mine? Yes."

Tobble had wandered away and now came tumbling back, excited. "There are steps! A circular stairway cut into the rock."

Khara considered this new information. "All right," she said. "When I break the cistern, the water will flow out. The box will be hot, too hot to touch. But with my sword I can slide the box out and Renzo can carry it on the shield. The rest of you start up the stairs, and we will follow."

I didn't like the idea of missing this bit of madness, but as I preferred to avoid being parboiled, I went along with the plan. We'd climbed perhaps a hundred stairs when we heard a huge blow, a yelp, a clattering of footsteps, a banging of steel, and, most heartening, giddy laughter.

We waited on a landing until Khara and Renzo came stumbling in, tripping over each other, dropping a rectangular stone box and the shield, and laughing like crazy people.

"Well done, Khara!" Renzo said when he could speak.

"Well done me? Well done you, Renzo."

"A masterpiece of careful planning and flawless

execution," Renzo said, and I didn't need my gift to understand that this was humor, not literal truth.

"Yes, with a great deal of frantic running and general panic," Khara replied, wiping away a tear of laughter.

9
An Endless Stairway

Renzo opened the ornately carved box. It had been cunningly made, and perhaps protected by durable theurgic spells, for the objects inside the box were bone dry.

With a low whistle, Renzo drew out a crown of gold decorated with precious diamonds, rubies, otrastones, and trynnes.

"I suppose you're thinking of how much you could make by selling off the jewels and melting down the gold, Renzo," Khara said.

"Nonsense. It's a work of art. Quite beautiful, don't you think?" He reached over and placed it on Khara's head. "It's worth far more intact."

Khara snatched the crown off her head and flushed angrily.

"I hate to say it, but it suits you," Gambler said.

"My family is noble, or was, once upon a time," Khara said. "But I am not. I am just a girl who sometimes works as a trapper or a poacher. Crowns are not for me."

"Just a girl who wields the Light of Nedarra," Renzo said. "In any case, if I were going to steal anything, it'd be your sword, Khara. It's worth ten times this crown."

"We should start climbing," Khara said, clearly ready to change the subject. "It's a long, long way up."

"No!" Tobble yelped. "I want to see the other thing!"

The other thing, the second of the two objects, was a tube as long as Khara's forearm, but no wider than my wrist. Compared to the crown, it seemed an object of little value, a cylinder wrapped in worn leather and bound with corroded steel rings.

"Do you want to play with it, Tobble?" Khara asked.

Tobble greedily grabbed the tube and turned it around in his nimble paws. "Oh, look! There is glass on this end. And . . . and a smaller glass at this end."

"Do you suppose Daf Hantch is still waiting for us to deliver the objects?" I asked

"Waiting to kill us, you mean?" Gambler said with a snort. "No, by now he's guessed we're not returning."

"But—" Tobble hesitated, still playing with the worn cylinder. "I wonder if . . ."

"What's wrong, Tobble?" I asked.

Tobble shrugged. "Is it wrong for us to take these things that don't belong to us?"

"They lied to us, Tobble!" Renzo cried. "They were almost certainly going to kill us!"

Tobble stared through the cylinder. "Still and all, it doesn't feel quite right."

"There's a reason for that, Tobble." Khara patted his back. "It doesn't feel quite right because it isn't."

"Oh, please," Renzo said with a groan. "I just risked my life for these things. They're worth plenty, and the coin they bring could well save our lives down the road. They're not going to do any good to anyone, stuck in the heart of a volcano till the end of time."

"Byx?" Khara said. "What do you think?"

I scratched an ear, delaying my answer. It was moments like this that reminded me why I could never be a leader. I had a million answers, not just one. Leaders weren't allowed to be uncertain.

"I suppose," I finally said, "you could make the argument that we're doing a small wrong for a greater good."

Renzo groaned again, but Gambler nodded. "I agree with Byx," he said. "Finding more dairnes, helping a species revive, defying the Murdano—that is by far the greater good."

"So I can keep this thing?" Tobble asked hopefully.

"Yes," said Khara. "You may keep your silly toy."

"But be sure to feel guilty about it," Renzo added with an eye roll.

"We really must continue climbing," Gambler said. "I'm sorry, but I haven't had much to eat, and what I have eaten was not good."

"Agreed," said Khara. "Let's go."

We climbed the eternal staircase in silence. It did seem as if we were trying to make it all the way to that distant moon. The ascent wound for two hundred steps at a time, pausing at small landings before beginning again. And again.

As we passed the fifth such landing, I muttered, "Who *built* these, anyway?" I'd been hardened by our long travels and many pains, but climbing thousands of steps was still a struggle. And I knew if it was difficult for me, it was even harder for Tobble, although he hadn't complained at all, and refused all our offers of help.

"This staircase was created from the top down, by someone wishing to defend against anyone below," Khara said.

"How do you know that?" I asked.

She shrugged. "Most warriors use their right arm to wield their blade. As you climb, see how there's no room for your right arm to move? Anyone descending would have much more room."

"That's the kind of thing that an average, everyday girl

armed with a sword worth more than a palace would just happen to know," Renzo teased.

"My toes look small!" Tobble interjected. He was toying with the cylinder, but we were all too weary to respond.

Up and up and up. When we reached the fiftieth landing—ten thousand steps—we stopped and ate a glum snack of jerky and dried sunweed. Gambler tried a bit of the sweet herb and spat it out. (Dog promptly ate it.) "I shall wait," Gambler said. "I'm not that desperate."

We returned to our exhausting, relentless climb. The only sounds were our labored breaths and heavy footfalls. The muscles in my legs screamed in silent agony, and the air couldn't seem to feed my hungry lungs.

Finally, after hours of struggle, we dragged ourselves onto the final landing, a wide, flat space large enough to hold a dozen men. There we came face-to-face with a door of thick, ironbound oak.

But before we could even contemplate trying to open that door onto whatever horrors lay beyond, we desperately needed to sleep.

We decided to take turns keeping watch, and I offered to go first. Khara and Renzo stretched out on the ground, using Dog for a pillow, while Gambler curled up in a corner, head tucked beneath a paw. Tobble fell asleep instantly—it was a special skill of his—with his head resting on my shoulder. He was still clutching the leather-bound object we had found in the stone box.

Carefully, trying not to disturb my sleeping friend, I reached into my pouch and retrieved the worn map I had carried with me for so long. In the silver glaze of moonlight, I traced my index finger over the path we'd taken so far.

There was Tarok, the sentient island rumored to be carnivorous.

There was Dairneholme, the village on the island where a northern colony of dairnes had once existed, according to myth.

There were the treacherous mountains, there was the icy sea.

And here we were, sitting in a volcano because of me. Because of my desperate hope that I might have glimpsed a solitary dairne on Tarok.

"Byx?" Tobble whispered.

"I'm sorry, Tobble," I said, folding the map. "I didn't mean to wake you."

"I was dreaming. There was fire and lava, and I was trying to escape on a slug pony, but I couldn't."

"Why didn't you savrielle?" I asked.

Tobble tilted his head. "What's that?"

"Don't wobbyks savrielle? It's when you control what's happening during a dream."

"While you're asleep?"

"Of course," I said. "That's the whole point. Dairnes do it all the time."

"Oh, my." Tobble looked impressed. "How did they teach you that?"

I shrugged. "It takes a lot of practice."

"If I could savrielle, I would have flying dreams every night," Tobble said, adjusting the tie at the end of his braided tail. He pointed with his chin at the folded playa leaf in my hand. "You were looking at your map."

"Yes."

"Don't worry, Byx. We're going to find the island. And we're going to find more dairnes. I just know it."

I smiled. "You're a good friend, Tobble."

"And so are you."

"Rest," I said. "We have a long journey ahead of us."

"Long journeys are the best kind of journeys," Tobble murmured as his lids dropped and he drifted into slumber.

I patted Tobble's head. I felt hopeful and fearful, anxious and grateful, lonely and loved. In my old world, in my life with the dairne pack, had I ever felt so many things at once? Was I ever this overwhelmed? This confused?

I used to chafe at being the runt. My siblings teased me. My parents fretted over me. But now, looking back, I could see how easy I'd had it.

I had been responsible for no one.

And now I felt responsible for so many.

I gazed up with a sigh. The moon had slipped away on its own long journey, followed by a handful of luminous and steadfast stars.

10
The Far-Near

When dawn came, we prepared to open the door. We were hungry, and not especially well-rested, but at least we were in better shape to face whatever lay ahead.

Khara unsheathed her sword, and I drew my much smaller knife. Renzo clutched his knife in one hand and the shield in the other. Tobble, for some reason, seemed to think the cylinder from the box was a weapon, so he brandished it. Of course, as always, Gambler had his claws and cunning.

"All right, Byx," Khara said. "You pull the door. It probably won't open, but if it does, stand behind it until I say it's safe."

It was a humble duty, but the truth was that in a fight, I was the least useful member of our group. Even Tobble could startle an opponent with his wobbyk fury.

I gripped the door handle, a heavy iron ring, nodded to Khara, and pulled. To everyone's surprise, it swung open, albeit with a great deal of squeaking.

I couldn't see anything from my position behind the door, and waited impatiently until Khara said, "It's all right, Byx. You have to see this."

I stepped around the door and felt a blast of cold, clean air. Only then did I notice that my feet were in something cold and white. Snow!

It was breathtaking, after the dank recesses of the natite cavern. We were at the rim of a caldera, and the whole world seemed to spread before us like an endless map. To the north and east, dark mountains loomed. To the west, the land grew flatter and less imposing.

Renzo and Khara stood side by side, shielding their eyes against the brilliance of the sunrise.

"You see that smudge?" Khara asked, pointing. "Could that be a village?"

Renzo squinted. "Perhaps. It's hard to be sure."

"It is a village," Tobble said, with surprising certainty. "I see a large lodge at the center. And timber walls and earthen palisades around, oh"—he muttered to himself, counting— "maybe fifty buildings."

Khara, Renzo, Gambler, and I all did the exact same thing: we turned and stared at Tobble in disbelief.

Tobble was not returning our gaze. He was holding his silly cylinder up to his right eye. The other eye was closed.

"Um . . . what?" I asked Tobble.

He lowered the tube. "I call this my Theurgic Big and Small Maker. If you look through it one way, everything appears tiny and far away. If you look through it the other way, things appear large and close."

Khara took the tube from him and held it to her eye. Her expression began as a dismissive smirk, melted into blank astonishment, and grew into wonder. "Oh, well-found, friend Tobble," she said at last. "Well-found indeed."

Renzo was next to stare through the tube. His expression followed a similar path.

Finally it was my turn. Dairnes have excellent eyesight— though it's not nearly as impressive as our sense of smell—but suddenly I had the magnificent eyes of a raptidon.

"This is a theurgic miracle!" I exclaimed.

But Renzo shook his head. "I don't sense any theurgy."

"Nor do I," Khara said. "This is a made object, a result of learning and craft."

"It's a very useful thing," Renzo said. "Forget the crown and the shield. Any general of any army ever would give his right arm to have this nameless object."

"It's not nameless," Tobble objected. "It's my Theurgic Big and Small Maker. But I suppose if you say it is not theurgic, I should change the name." He tapped his fuzzy chin. "How about we call it a 'Far-Near'?"

The Far-Near had told true. There was indeed a village, a fortified human village, in the distance. However, it took most of the day to make it down the steep and rocky volcanic slope, and it was nearly night when we drew near. The temperature seemed to fall with each step downward. It was invigorating at first, but soon we found ourselves shivering and donning every last bit of clothing in our packs. Nonetheless, we decided to sleep rough, since strangers arriving in the middle of the night are rarely welcome.

In the morning, cold and hungry, we marched up to the closed gate of the village. As we approached, six archers rose from behind the points of the log-built palisade. Six arrows flew, and six arrows stuck hard in the ground, just inches from our toes.

I was immediately glad we'd waited till morning, for if this was how we were met in broad daylight, I could only imagine how much worse it might have been. The archers' accuracy was disturbing: they could quite clearly have killed us.

An armored knight, his face concealed behind a slitted visor, appeared atop the wall, and beside him a herald. It was the herald who challenged us.

"My lord Mirob the Mighty demands to know who you are and the nature of your business."

"We are simple travelers," Khara said.

The knight whispered in the herald's ear.

"My lord Mirob the Mighty says to move on in peace. But you may not enter."

We were obviously not ready to try to force our way in. But Khara wasn't done. "If we're given food and waterskins, we will happily move on."

The herald started to answer, but the knight held up a hand to stop him. "We will bring food and water," the knight said. "But in these perilous times we cannot allow strangers to enter."

"Why are these times perilous?" Khara asked.

"I see you're strangers to these lands, or else you would know. War is coming. Across the mountains, the forces of Nedarra gather. And on this side of the mountains, the Kazar Sg'drit prepares as well."

"Pardon me, good sir," Khara said. "But I thought Dreyland was ruled by King Marekyn."

"He is . . . no more." The knight shook his head, adding in a lower voice, "I will speak no further of the Kazar."

That was that, and the knight withdrew from view. It wasn't the first time we'd heard rumors of war brewing between Nedarra and Dreyland. But there was nothing we could do about it, in any case. We were a group of five, just five. It was not our problem.

My quest—our quest—was to find more dairnes. And that was our only concern.

At least, that was what I told myself as we waited.

Ten minutes later, two ancient women emerged from the fortified village by way of a small cheat door. They brought us loaves of fresh bread and dried meat, as well as waterskins, and then retreated without a word.

As we walked on, I noticed that Gambler was behaving strangely. His tail and head both hung low. He still moved with the powerful grace of his species, but I felt certain something was disturbing him.

"Gambler. Something troubles you."

"Yes."

"Do you wish to tell me?"

"Of course. I hesitated only because I've been working through what it all may mean." He sighed. "That title and name, Kazar Sg'drit? Those are, I'm afraid, felivet words. And dangerous ones at that. Very dangerous."

11

A Valtti Threatens

Khara stopped short. "What did you say?"

"Kazar is an ancient title, not a word we would use today," Gambler said. "Nothing we would be proud to claim. Long ago, a felivet rose to rule all our people, and Kazar was the title he took. It means 'absolute ruler.' And Sg'drit is a shortening of a much longer felivet word. It means 'one who is without compassion.' A killer."

"Well, that's not encouraging," Renzo remarked.

"We felivets have left those times, those beliefs, behind us. They were poisonous. Especially the notion that we are destined to rule all other species."

"That's just what the Murdano wants to do in Nedarra," Khara said. She glanced at me. "Even if it means exterminating entire species."

"If this is true, if Dreyland has fallen for the lies of a

valtti," said Gambler, his tail twitching, "it is a terrible humiliation for all felivets."

"Valtti?" I prompted.

"As you know, Byx, we are a solitary species. We hunt alone. We come together only to raise our young or to study. It is in our nature to be independent, to think for ourselves. But . . ." Gambler sighed. "There are times when a valtti rises—a felivet who provokes hatred of other species and convinces other felivets to join him. Those who will not join are silenced, either by fear or by imprisonment. It is a sort of madness, one that can seize hold of the weak-minded."

We marched on, considering the weight of what Gambler had revealed. If it was true that war threatened, what might come from a clash between the Murdano and a dangerous rogue felivet?

"Gambler, what should we expect from an army ruled by one of these valtti?" Renzo asked.

"Cunning. Deception. Subtlety. And absolute ruthlessness."

"Great," Renzo muttered. "Let's find Byx's island and get far away from this madhouse. Carnivorous or not, it will be an improvement."

It wasn't long before we saw signs of preparation for war. At the juncture of two small rivers, we came upon an army camp, a vast array of tents in neat rows.

"Tobble, may I borrow your Far-Near?" I asked.

I held the tube to my eye and once again saw the miraculous results. Beyond the tents were stables and paddocks containing hundreds of horses. I saw platoons of grooms hauling hay bales. A cooper and his assistant were fashioning barrels. Two blacksmiths hammered horseshoes, while others pumped bellows to keep the fires hot.

Near the edge of the camp sat a mountain of crates, presumably holding food and other supplies. On the nearest of the two rivers, three sets of docks had been built to receive boats: one for disembarking troops, one for mule-drawn sleds, and one to unload freshly cut logs. At this last dock, an army of humans and some smaller species was busy trimming logs with huge saws.

I made a quick count.

"I believe there are as many as a thousand tents, with perhaps four soldiers per tent."

"So four thousand soldiers, with more on the way," Renzo said. "And many of those astride the bridges we need to cross."

Khara put her hands on her hips. "You're the thief, so you tell me: Could you get through that camp and cross the bridges?"

"Of course," Renzo said. "If I were very, very lucky. And alone. With you five? Not a chance."

"How about passing beneath them?" I asked.

Renzo shook his head. "You'd still need to get through the sentries and their dogs. Give me that stupid tube," he said, and took the Far-Near. "I'm no geographer, but from what I know of Dreyland, if we go north, we should find a ford, a ferry, or an unguarded bridge eventually."

He sighed a bit too loudly for it to be encouraging.

"This is a land preparing for war." Gambler scanned the countryside. "We must remember that if we encounter anyone, no one is counted innocent until they prove themselves to be so."

"War," I grumbled. "Of all the stupid things humans do . . ."

Renzo laughed. "You are not wrong, Byx."

"It seems in this case it is not humans alone," Gambler said darkly.

"But what is the purpose?" I asked.

"Power," Renzo said. "Men—and, it seems, some felivets— want power. They want to dominate and control. They want to take the power of life and death into their own hands."

It was a more thoughtful answer than I'd expected from the young thief. But then, Renzo often surprised me.

Khara tapped a finger to her lips, considering. "We believe the living island is headed that way," she said, gesturing north. "For all we know, it may be at the place where the mountains run into the sea. Or it may have moved past that by now."

Gambler followed her gaze. "It is a slow-moving thing, that we know for certain. It seems unlikely that it would have gone much past the foot of the mountains."

"There's no other way," Renzo said. "We must get across the rivers or we cannot reach the sea."

"If we cross the rivers, we must still reach the sea, and then travel along the shore, searching for signs," Khara added. "And the terrain will be rough, as we know."

I gave a heavy sigh. Khara saw that I was glum and patted me on my shoulder. "Never become discouraged, Byx."

"I'm not discouraged," I said. "Just worried about all of you, risking this for me."

"No, Byx!" Tobble exclaimed. "This isn't just about you anymore. It began that way, yes. But now we know how important it is to find more dairnes."

I smiled and tousled his fur. "Perhaps we're playing some great role in the fate of the world," I said. I was teasing, but Tobble nodded seriously.

"Yes," he said. "I believe Hanadru, the great artist who lives in the clouds and paints the fate of all on her great easel—"

"Really, Tobble?" Khara asked. She wasn't mocking. But she clearly thought the idea was silly.

"You may not believe in Hanadru," Tobble said with quiet dignity. "But she is one of the Pure Spirits of my people."

"I don't believe in fate, whether it's some god named Hanadru or someone else," Renzo said. "Fate is for people afraid to take responsibility for their own lives."

Khara stared northward. She held out her hand, and I passed the Far-Near to her.

Carefully she scanned the horizon from left to right. She took her time, but no one spoke. At last Khara said, "This is my advice. We go north because no other direction is possible at this point." She gave Tobble a gentle smile. "And may your Hanadru paint our path with a generous brush."

PART TWO
STRANGE
ENCOUNTERS

12
Vallino

Hanadru was kind.

The land around the volcano's base was vast and open. Small farms and villages dotted the area, but we were able to make our way through the snowy fields without anyone seeming to take notice.

"How do wobbyks fare in the cold, Tobble?" I asked as we trudged along.

Tobble shrugged. "We're seafaring folk," he answered. "I've seen my share of ice floes in the North Tara Sea. Snow doesn't bother me much."

"How about you, Gambler?"

"Like all felivets, large or small, I prefer warmth," Gambler replied in his husky voice, which always struck me as half whisper, half growl.

I smiled. How often had I seen Gambler stretched out in

a shaft of sun, his eyes slitted so that only a hint of pale blue was visible, his long tail twitching like a black serpent?

"But we are adaptable creatures," Gambler continued. "Our coats are thick, our paw pads tough. I, too, shall be fine." He looked at me. "Of course, my fur is no match for Byx's."

It was true. Another thing that separated dairnes from dogs was our coveted silky fur: incredibly warm when the weather was cold, remarkably cool when the heat was intense.

"My toes are getting numb," Renzo complained good-naturedly. "I miss the horses." As soon as the words were out of his mouth, he slapped his forehead. "Khara," he said, "I'm sorry. I—"

She waved her hand, brushing away his apology as if it were a pesky gnat. "We all miss the horses. Especially Vallino. But we needed to sell them. There's no way they could have handled the terrain in Dreyland. No way at all."

I'd begun my relationship with Khara's horse, Vallino, unhappily, as a bound captive slung over his back. For a while I'd assumed horses were nothing more than "wagons with tails," as Gambler had once put it.

But when I'd found myself facing certain death, it was Vallino whose speed and cunning had helped me stay alive. I owed him my life. And I knew Khara felt the same way.

"Still," I said, "I wish you hadn't had to make that sacrifice."

"We're all making sacrifices," Khara said. "And we'll be making many more before this is over."

Khara had sold two of our horses to a hunting party near the border with Dreyland. We'd all agreed that the route ahead of us was not a place for even the most agile horse. But she'd held on to Vallino, maintaining that she would know when she found the right buyer.

It was rare to see a horse in those parts—mostly it was sturdy pack animals like mountain yariks—and rarer still to see one of Vallino's quality. But despite offer after offer, Khara had ignored them all. Privately, Renzo confided to me that he was afraid she wouldn't have the heart to part with her beloved steed.

That very afternoon, we'd passed a young girl, her face ruddy in the cold. I guessed by her size that she was a bit younger than Khara. But I hadn't spent much time among humans, so I couldn't be sure.

We were close to a small village, so I was trotting along on all fours, pretending to be a dog—not one of my favorite pastimes, but one I sometimes had to endure. If I were to be identified as a dairne, I might be captured or even killed.

"He's beautiful," the girl said, approaching Vallino. She pulled off a worn gray mitten with her teeth. "May I?"

Khara nodded. The girl scratched Vallino just behind his right ear, his favorite location. "He's a Ravenno trotter, yes?"

"You know horses."

"Wish I knowed more. I ain't seen one this grand since I saw a big herd roaming the Nedarran plains."

"How's the hunting in these parts?" Khara asked, nodding to the bow and arrows strapped to the girl's back. They resembled the ones I had seen Khara use to great effect.

On me, in fact.

"Been better." The girl gave Khara a shy smile. "Been worse, too, I reckon."

"And the snow pack?" Renzo asked. "Past the Noordham Ridge?"

"Higher than usual for this time o' year." The girl reached into a torn leather pouch. "He likes sugar, does he?"

"Renzo?" Khara asked, nodding at him. "He'll eat anything, and more than his share."

The girl laughed. "I was meanin' your horse."

"Vallino's his name," Khara said. "He loves anything sweet."

"I have but this one bit. I was saving it for somethin' special." The girl presented a small, misshapen lump of sugar on the palm of her hand. Vallino gobbled it down with evident delight.

"That's very kind of you," Khara said.

"Mailley's my name," said the girl, giving Vallino another ear rub.

"And I am Khara."

"I, as you may have gathered, am Renzo." Renzo gave a deep bow. "Along with Tobble, Gambler, and our two dogs, Dog and"—he gave me a little smirk—"Byx."

Mailley patted Dog's head, then turned her attention to me and stroked my back.

It was rather nice, I hated to admit. I wagged politely.

Mailley shrugged. "Well, I should be on my way. Safe travels to ye."

"And to you," said Khara.

We watched as the girl trudged away. "Mailley reminded me a bit of you, back when we first met," Renzo said. "Only she's far less grumpy."

I waited for Khara to react to Renzo's teasing. But she merely took Vallino's reins and headed on with a sigh.

Renzo patted my head. "Come, doggie," he said, just to annoy me.

I looked up at him, considering my options. Then I raised my rear leg and relieved myself on the toe of his leather boot.

Sometimes there are advantages to playing dog.

We walked perhaps a quarter league more before Khara stopped in her tracks and spun around without explanation.

Quickly we backtracked, and moving at speed, we were

able to catch up with Mailley.

"I thought you were heading north," Mailley exclaimed when we reached her side, all but Gambler panting a bit.

"And we are," said Khara. "But Vallino"—she took a deep breath—"is heading south."

Khara whispered something in Vallino's ear. Then she handed the reins to Mailley. "He likes meadow oats," Khara said softly.

"But I don't understand—" Mailley stared at the worn leather looped over her mitten.

"And apple slices," Renzo added.

"He's stubborn when it's cold in the morning," said Tobble.

"And fast as the wind when he's happy," added Gambler.

I couldn't say what I wanted to add: that Vallino had saved my life. That he was a good and decent friend. That I would forever owe him.

Instead I whimpered softly. He nickered in response.

"But . . . ," Mailley began again, her eyes glistening.

"Don't let him eat too many sweets. And watch for burrs in his tail. He hates that."

Turning on her heel, Khara paused. "And he loves ear scratches. Especially just behind his right ear."

After that, she never glanced backward, but I did. I saw Mailley, her face buried in Vallino's mane, sobbing.

"Why is Mailley crying?" I asked Gambler under my breath. Dairnes cry, but only in profound moments of grief.

"Those are, I believe," said Gambler, "tears of joy. Humans cry for many reasons."

I glanced at Khara. I saw no tears. But I felt certain the pain was there.

I knew all about grief.

13
Dreaming of Dairnes

We were lucky enough to find not only food, but lodging with actual human beds. They were far too large for me or Tobble, so we shared one. Khara and Gambler took one room, while Renzo, Dog, Tobble, and I slept in the other.

Down in the tavern, we ate wonderful bread and cut up a roast of some unfamiliar but delicious animal, piling our plates high. We drank cider and even shared a suet pudding that Gambler disdained as "too sweet" for any self-respecting felivet to eat.

Afterward, we took a pitcher of cider up to our room, and I began to ply Renzo with questions. Where had he been born? (He wasn't entirely sure.) Who were his parents? (No known father, and his mother had died of Rasp Fever.) And how had he become a thief?

This last question elicited a more complete answer: "Once my mother died, I was alone."

"That must have been frightening," I said, knowing all too well how he must have felt.

Renzo shrugged. "I didn't have time to be afraid. I was hungry. I was ten years old and alone. No one was going to be offering me work, so I started stealing food from stalls. Sometimes I got away clean. Other times I had to leg it." He laughed at a memory. "Once I had to leap from a twenty-foot wall into a moat. I could have been killed. Instead, I ended up in mud up to my waist. They caught me, naturally."

Tobble's eyes went wide. "Did they put you in the dungeon?"

"Oh, of course." A laugh. "But they let me go once they'd given me the lashes."

"The . . . the what?" Tobble asked, paws clasped.

Renzo stood up and pulled his shirt over his head. "Twenty lashes."

His back was covered in faint pink stripes. Some were raised and wider than the others.

"Did it . . . ," Tobble began, before wincing and falling silent.

"Did it hurt?" Renzo asked, dropping his shirt. "Absolutely. I yelled and cried like a baby. Afterward, I could barely crawl, I was so weak. An old man took pity on me . . . well, I thought it was pity, but old Draskull was not overly supplied with kindness. Draskull ran a gang of thieves, and he put it to me simply: steal for the gang and I would have people looking out for me. Steal on my own and, well, Draskull would make sure I got caught."

"So . . . ," I prompted, when Renzo seemed to sink into his memories.

"So I stole for Draskull and he made sure I had clothing and food. He didn't beat me, much. Just when I made a mistake. He was a great thief, Draskull, and I learned well from him."

"You sound almost grateful," Tobble said, confused.

Renzo nodded. "The poor have few choices in this world. There are good masters and bad ones. Draskull was not good, and he could be brutal, but I picked up my craft from him. And by the time I arranged for him to be caught by the militia, I had learned a great deal."

"Wait, what was that about arranging for him to be caught?" I inquired.

I saw a glint in Renzo's eyes, a look at odds with his usual glib, easygoing ways. "You see the heavier scars on my back? Those were left by Draskull. He liked to use a bamboo stick. Fewer beatings, but worse."

"So you got revenge?"

Renzo smiled. "Don't let anyone ever tell you that revenge is empty." His smile broadened. "The day that old creep was arrested was a happy, happy day for me."

Tobble's eyelids were growing heavy. Within seconds,

he was sound asleep. But I had more questions for Renzo. I hoped he didn't mind. My siblings had often teased me about my endless curiosity.

"Renzo," I said, lowering my voice so I wouldn't wake Tobble, "may I ask you something else?"

He shrugged. "Of course."

"Why do you stay with us?"

He tapped the shield we'd taken from the Subdur natites. "See that? It's worth more than everything I've ever stolen, put together and tripled."

"And that's all there is to it? An opportunity for riches?"

"Yes," he said simply.

I smiled. "You forget to whom you're speaking."

"Dairnes," Renzo said with mock anger. "I can see why no one wants your kind around."

We both laughed, and soon Renzo, too, was asleep. He snored, but not with Khara's toadlike volume.

I lay awake for some time, as Tobble wheezed softly and Renzo snored intermittently. When at last I slept, I dreamed of a clear lake, mirror smooth. Sitting atop Gambler's shoulders at the edge of the water, I gazed down and saw a perfect reflection of my face: the golden fur, the droopy ears, the eyes full of questions.

A wind whipped up, rippling my image. Suddenly Gambler vanished, and I dropped into the icy water. Gasping for air, I surfaced to see myself standing there.

But no: It wasn't me, was it? It was another dairne.

Real and breathing and alive.

"Diy alwoo m'rrk reh wyrtanni," he whispered.

Dairnish. How long it had been since I'd heard my own language! It took me a moment to understand his words.

You are not alone.

A tiny corner of my mind, the one trained to savrielle, worked to respond, to take hold of the dream. "How do you know?" I tried to ask, but my voice came out as a wordless whimper.

I repeated the savrielle chant, just the way I'd been taught. *You are the dream and the dream is you*, I told myself. *You are the dream and the dream is you.*

I grasped at the lingering wisps I could recall. The lake bottom; the sand between my pads; the dairne's wistful smile; the sweet, familiar smell of his fur. Like morning mist, like tendrils of smoke, like echoes of a song: it was all there, and yet not.

I woke up shivering. I could still feel his warm breath, still see the look of recognition in his eyes.

And I could still hear his words.

You are not alone.

14
An Old Enemy Returns

In the morning we breakfasted on strong tea, scones, and rashers of bacon. Khara pried one of the smallest stones from the crown Tobble still carried in his pack and found it was worth enough to pay for the food, lodging, and some fresh blankets.

We headed northeast. The snow was lightly packed, the air cold but refreshing. From time to time we consulted the Far-Near to see whether we had passed the last of the army's encampment.

"There's a large body of people ahead, moving slowly," Khara reported after checking our intended path. "Sorry, Byx."

I switched to all fours to appear doglike. As we approached the party ahead, I scented something unpleasant: human filth. The smell of a clean human is tolerable, if not particularly pleasant. But a dirty human is quite hard to ignore.

As we advanced, I saw why. The people ahead of us weren't farmers heading to market, or even soldiers moving to a new position. We were approaching men in chains, led by a big human on a horse. A burly gray felivet was bringing up the rear.

It was a horrible, stomach-lurching sight. And then I saw something even more terrible.

I recognized one of the chained and filthy humans.

Luca.

Luca, who had saved my life.

Luca, who had tried to end my life.

For a while, Luca had been part of our little group. We'd trusted him. He was a scholar and, in fact, had studied dairnes extensively.

Luca, however, was more than just a scholar.

He was also a scion of the traitorous Corpli family, ancient foe of Khara's clan. Luca eventually betrayed us to the Murdano, in the hope of gaining influence and using it to restore his family's fortune.

But we had outwitted Luca—and the Murdano as well.

I looked up at Khara to see whether she had recognized our old foe. She had.

Luca's hair was filthy and matted. His fashionable clothing had been traded for a canvas shift. I could see his feet through his torn boots.

We reached the tail of the column of a dozen chained men. The gray felivet turned and scowled a warning at us but did nothing to stop us as we walked past, and when he caught sight of Gambler, he slunk to the side.

As we passed, Luca did not even notice us, but kept his head down, his eyes focused on his next weary, stumbling step.

We moved on. Khara's face was set in an expression of unhappiness and uncertainty. After about a hundred yards, she paused.

"Byx," she said. "I . . ."

I nodded. "If you're asking what I think you're asking," I said, careful not to be observed speaking by strangers, "the answer is yes."

"Renzo?"

Renzo's eyes narrowed. "Once a traitor, always a traitor."

"Gambler?" Khara said. "Tobble?"

Gambler said, "I would see no creature in chains."

Tobble considered. "Nor would I," he said. "Although I agree with Renzo that Luca is not a human to be trusted. Ever."

"Why are they in chains, do you think?" I asked. "Are they criminals?"

"Possibly," said Khara.

"Likely," said Renzo. "Given that it's Luca."

"They could be thralls," Gambler said. "In which case we should free them all."

"I'm not sure we can take that risk." Khara shook her head. "The whole countryside would be alerted."

"I say it's a risk worth taking," Gambler said.

Khara pursed her lips. "All right, then."

"Tobble," Renzo said, "hand me the crown, please."

Renzo pried out three large stones and passed them to Khara without commentary, aside from a slight shaking of his head.

We watched as she spent ten minutes haggling with the man in charge. At last, he unlocked all the men's shackles. They scattered quickly, clearly stunned at their good fortune.

Khara strode back to us, with Luca following behind, stumbling a bit.

"Friend dairne, I am relieved to see you well," he said when he reached me, his voice hoarse and weak.

"'Friend?'" I demanded.

Luca winced and looked down. Tobble dug food from his pack and handed bread to Luca, who ate with the grace of a famished pig. He drank some of the cider we'd bought at the tavern.

"We have no spare clothing," Khara said. There was no pity in her voice.

"I have worn this garment for many days," Luca said. "I will survive."

"Your kind always does," Gambler said with a sneer. He would see no creature chained, but that did not mean he had warmed to Luca. "The slightest wrong move and I will taste your blood."

"Only if you are able to kill him before I do," Khara said.

Luca nodded. I saw raw flesh on his ankles, wrists, and neck where the shackles had been.

We walked in silence after that. Luca seemed to sense that we were in no mood to engage with him.

He broke the quiet about an hour later. "Are you making for Beragaz Ford?" he asked.

"Beragaz Ford?" Khara said. "Why would you think that?"

Luca shrugged. "I assume you're hoping to reach the sea. If your goal is still to reach the sentient isle you came so close to in Nedarra."

"You were following us?" I demanded.

Luca shot a look at me and said, "Yes. From a distance. And you were away before I could catch up to you."

"What were you planning to do if you caught us?" I asked.

Luca hesitated, no doubt caught between fear of my truth-telling power and a desire to lie. He rubbed the red ring circling his neck. "I would have seized you, Byx, and sent you to the Murdano with my compliments." He almost smiled. "And, of course, I would have taken Khara's sword."

"And what would you have done with the Light of Nedarra?" Khara demanded.

"I would have delivered it to my father, and together, with the sword to inspire our people, we would have raised an army to defend the Murdano in the coming war."

"I don't need Byx to tell me that is an incomplete response," Khara said. "Would you then have surrendered the sword to the Murdano?"

Luca's silence was the answer.

"I see," Khara said. "You would have waited until the time was right and turned against the Murdano, placing your father on the throne."

Luca managed a derisive laugh. "Well, we all have dreams, do we not? Even, perhaps, you, Kharassande of the Donatis?"

I expected an angry retort. But Luca's suggestion that she had plans of her own left Khara unable to speak.

At least, unable to speak in the presence of a dairne.

15
A Means to an End

We spent the night in an ice-glazed field thick with snow-blossoms. The smell was wonderfully clean and earthy, the cold not so wonderful. But we had food and water and a little cider, and earlier we'd bought some clothing from a farmer, leaving Luca looking decent, if not stylish. I wondered how long it would take him to recover his old arrogance.

After we'd finished eating and our small fire was going strong, Luca said, "I suppose, as I was saying before . . . and I'm not asking you to tell me . . . that you are hoping to go east to the sea."

No one answered.

"It's just that I wonder if you know much about the geography of Dreyland," Luca asked.

Again, no answer. Just suspicious looks traveling from Khara to me to Renzo, a felivet eye roll from Gambler, and a snort from Tobble.

"I know something of the area," Luca added. "I studied maps of Dreyland back on the isle."

"I've been here a time or two," Renzo said. "We don't need your help."

"I know of a bridge over the nearest river," Luca persisted.

"You want to guide us?" Khara inquired, and her tone was not friendly. "Into another trap?"

Luca bowed his head. "Khara, I am loyal to my family. But my family is in Nedarra. Here I am friendless."

"How did you end up here, then?" She was challenging Luca to speak the truth.

"It's true that I followed you, hoping to take your sword. I came up the coast. I was able to get past Nedarran guards because I carried a letter from my father, who still has many friends."

"He's telling the truth," I confirmed.

"I sneaked past the Dreyland border by climbing a cliff face. I believed you had come the same way. I was certain I was right behind you. And then I ran out of food and money and was arrested for stealing fruit from a vendor's stall."

Still the truth.

"The guards sold me to the bondseller. And I was doomed to work in the slag mines until I died. Until you rescued me."

"We took pity," Khara said. "That doesn't mean I believe you."

That was untrue: she did believe him. But I stayed silent.

"And I certainly don't trust you," Khara added. She crossed her arms over her chest. "Tell us this, Luca. We left behind us a Knight of the Fire and six members of the Murdano's Pale Guard, all dead."

"Impressive."

"Do you know if the Murdano has sent more soldiers to track us down?"

"I don't," Luca answered.

I nodded at Khara. Truth again.

"But I doubt," Luca continued, "that the Murdano would risk sending new soldiers past the Nedarran border into Dreyland. Especially not with war looming."

Gambler licked a paw. "On that, I must agree with the traitor. The Murdano has bigger worries than us at the moment."

"Still," Renzo said, "it can't hurt to cover our tracks as we move. The Murdano would very much like to have a dairne in his arsenal."

For a few moments we all stared at the fire as it spun sparks into the darkness.

"Look," Luca said, turning his eyes on me, "I ask Byx to confirm whether I speak the truth. I can lead you to the Beragaz Ford. I don't know for sure whether it is guarded. But it is the quickest path to the east. And I have neither friend nor ally in this land."

"True or not," Renzo said, "I'm not interested in listening to this character."

Luca sighed. "So be it." Slowly he stood and walked into the darkness a few feet outside the circle of firelight. I heard the crunching sound as he sat down out of our sight on the cushion of snowblossoms.

"I think we should know whatever he knows," I said to Khara.

She nodded and tilted her head in his direction.

I stood. Gambler rose soundlessly and padded beside me.

Luca did not look up when we approached him.

"What can you tell us?" I asked.

"If you lie, you will find out just how quickly I can gut you," Gambler said.

Luca nodded, his face barely visible in the faint starlight. "You know that a rogue felivet has taken over Dreyland?"

Gambler looked uneasy. The situation wasn't his fault, of course, but I sensed that he took it personally, as a felivet.

"Well, the Kazar Sg'drit is a piece of work," Luca went on. "As corrupt and vile as the Murdano and his court are, Sg'drit is worse. He's diverted entire rivers in order to turn low-lying marshlands into harbors for his fleet. He's forced tens of thousands under his thumb and imprisoned as many more. His dungeons are so full that he houses prisoners in outdoor camps patrolled by terramants."

"Terramants?" Gambler was surprised. "I thought the terramants served no one."

"They do when they're starving," Luca said. "Sg'drit destroys fields where the terramant food supply is located. His poisons sink deep in the ground and kill the subterranean creatures terramants feed on. Not all serve Sg'drit, but many have turned to him in order to survive. He's systematically crushing one species after another, or cowing them into obedience."

Gambler cocked his head. "And how exactly would you know all this?"

"I keep my ears open," Luca replied, with a flash of irritation. "No one cares what a thrall overhears." He plucked a white snowblossom and pulled off its petals, one by one. "Beautiful, aren't they?" he asked. "Did you know they only bloom in moonlight?" He had a strange, wistful look on his face. "I had a professor back at the Academy. Tough old stick, that one. I was the only student in his verden flora class that year to score with honors." He tossed the flower aside. "That was before I decided to study dessag fauna—near-extinct species like your own, Byx."

I remembered the first time Luca had seen me at the Academy. He'd circled me, transfixed, noting my glissaires, my opposable thumbs, every detail that made me *me*. He'd studied dairnes before but had never actually seen one.

I'd felt like a freak of nature that day. And in a way, I was.

"Interesting thing about snowblossoms," Luca continued. "They're basically weeds. Invasive. Farmers hate them. They grow like crazy, take over, make it hard for anything in their path to survive." He gave us a cold smile. "Rather like humans. And felivets."

"Not all of them," Gambler said.

"I don't understand the desire for war," I muttered. "Or the need to control—or even destroy—entire species."

"Poor Byx," Luca said, with the hint of a sneer, "you still understand so little. War isn't the end—war is a *means* to an end."

My heart felt tight as a fist. "But what end justifies war that will kill multitudes?"

"Power," Luca said, his tone flat. "They do everything for power."

The terrible thing was that he believed it.

Worse still was that I believed it, too.

"Soon enough, scholars at the Academy won't just be studying the end of your species, Byx." Luca gave a short laugh. "They'll have lots of extinct species to learn about. Think of all the eumonies! Oh, the revelry!"

"That's enough," Gambler snapped. "Or we'll be staging a funeral for you."

"Species come, species go," said Luca. "No need to take

offense. New ones replace the old. It's the way of the world."

"But when humans are responsible, or someone else—" I began.

"They're just more efficient than nature," Luca said.

We fell silent. A cold wind rustled the snowblossoms. The sound should have been lovely. Instead, it was vaguely sinister.

"Say, do you still carry that notebook I gave you?" Luca asked.

I withdrew it from my pouch. I'd kept notes about my feelings and experiences in it, when time permitted and I could make ink from local plants.

"You should write down everything you know about dairnes," Luca said. "Culture. Lore. Music. Stories. All of it."

"Why?" I asked, already sure I knew what his answer would be.

"For scholars." Luca pointed an index finger at his chest. "People like me. Like I used to be. When you dairnes are finally extinct, there will be a record."

Gambler nudged me with his head. "Come on, Byx. Before I do something I won't regret."

We left Luca there, sitting alone in that field of lovely, dangerous blossoms.

16
The Crimson Forest

We reluctantly agreed to accept advice from Luca, and the Beragaz Ford turned out to be right where he'd said it would be. We reached it after two long days of walking. It was not a bridge, just a place where the water was shallow enough to cross.

Renzo and Gambler searched the area for signs of soldiers but found only footprints. Many footprints, in fact, which made us think an army had crossed the area recently.

The river, calm but frigid, came up to my neck at the deepest point. Khara went first, and Tobble rode Renzo's shoulders. Gambler took some time to work up his nerve, then raced across in a comical way, as if he were trying to run on the surface of the river.

The worst part was fighting the chill after we had become wet to the skin. Snow had begun to fall again, though thankfully there was no wind.

"From here I estimate we're only sixty or seventy leagues to the coast," Luca said, wrapping a blanket around his shoulders. "Some of the terrain is pretty rugged, though."

"Yes," Renzo grumbled. "They already know. I told them so."

As we trudged on, we were cheered to see a brilliant crimson-leaved forest ahead. We hoped we might find some game to hunt and eat, along with grubs or herbs for Tobble. Bone-tired and chilled as we all were, a warm meal around a cheery, crackling fire was just what we needed. That, and a good night's sleep, we felt certain, would get us back on track.

"Once we're under the trees, we will need to cover our tracks," Khara said, nodding back at our footprints in the snow.

"But surely new snow will cover old tracks," I said.

Renzo shook his head. "Not from an experienced tracker like, say, Khara."

Khara smiled slightly at his compliment. "New snow will fall evenly, and unless it is very deep indeed, it will merely make our tracks a bit less distinct."

Tobble glanced behind, swiveling his giant ears. "Why are we worried about tracks? Who's following us?" he asked nervously.

"No one, so far as I know," Khara answered. She shot a meaningful look at Luca. "But you can't be too careful."

I understood Khara's feelings about Luca. She had made

the decision to rescue him. She knew he was speaking the truth now. But she did not like him or trust him. I was certain she did not forgive him, and, for that matter, neither did I.

It was hard, harboring so many different feelings about someone. Was this what growing up was going to be like? Would everything be this complicated and perplexing? Gray, instead of black and white? Would happiness always be tinged with sorrow? Anger with pity?

I remembered the last time I'd seen Maia, my mother. We'd been watching butterbats float on the breeze. "I'm bored," I'd complained. I wanted to have adventures, to see the world, to be brave.

I'd been in such a hurry to grow up! My mother had looked at me and whispered, "No need to rush toward bravery. No rush at all."

I was finally beginning to see what she'd meant.

We reached the edge of the forest after a long downhill march over broken ground. A narrow but fast-running stream cut straight along the forest wall, like an ineffectual barrier. We found a spot where both banks were high, and we leapt across easily (although Tobble held Renzo's hand, just in case).

I paused on the other side, testing the air with my nose. Gambler did the same, and we exchanged a worried glance.

The scents were all wrong. Forests smell of green things growing and green things rotting. But this forest reeked of a different decay, at once cloyingly sweet and mixed with a sharp edge of ammonia.

I looked up and saw a tracery of branches that was less angular than usual, more sinuous. The effect should have been graceful, a twining of arcs and bows and spirals. But there was no reassurance to be found in those branches. It was like looking at shoddy weaving, as if all the trees were part of some vast, neglected carpet.

Renzo approached a smooth gray tree trunk and placed his hand on it. He drew back sharply. "It vibrates! Come feel."

I didn't want to appear cowardly, so I stood beside him and laid my hand on what felt more like a garilan's hide than actual bark. It was cold to the touch. But I sensed a slow, deep pulse, a beat like a giant's heart.

"Let's keep moving," Khara said. "Night is coming and we must either be through this forest or spend the night in it."

Her words definitely put some spring in my step: I did not wish to spend the night here. None of us did.

"I keep looking for a fallen branch," Renzo said. "I could use it to confuse our tracks. But I haven't seen a single one."

"No ground cover, either," Tobble agreed. "Though surely enough light reaches the ground here to grow a bush, or a thicket or two."

He was right. The earth was bare, just dirt and rock. The snow filtered down but melted on contact with the ground.

Khara increased her pace, not in an alarming way, but subtly, as if hoping it would not be noticed. But the stink, the eeriness, and the pulsation—which now seemed to come from the ground itself—had lit outright fear in me. I felt the cold dread growing with each step, and I knew I was not alone: this was perhaps the longest Tobble had ever gone without speaking, and when I looked at him, I saw a frowning brow over eyes that darted in every direction.

"Did you know this was here?" I asked Luca.

He shook his head violently. "No. And if it were my decision, I'd turn around and leave."

I started to respond but stopped cold when I saw Gambler stiffen, ears on alert.

"I hear something," he said in a hushed voice, and then I heard it, too.

17
The Fall

We all stopped and listened. My hearing is probably the most acute after Gambler's, although Tobble has remarkable ears as well.

"A soft sound?" I asked.

"A slithery sound?" Tobble whispered.

Gambler didn't answer. He didn't have to. The sound was nearer and louder. He and I both yelled, "Run!"

Darkness deepened until we could scarcely find a path. We ran, but not as fast as we would have liked. The trees were too close together, the light too pale. The slithery sound increased in volume until even Khara and Renzo could hear it. It was as if someone were right behind us, dragging a bag of wet stones over mud.

The trees grew almost impenetrable. "We have to stand and fight!" Khara cried, unsheathing her sword.

Renzo drew his knife and I did likewise. We stood, back to back, the six of us. Luca had no weapon, but his fists were balled and ready. Tobble, armed with only his Far-Near and his unpredictable temper, stood beside me.

The sounds stopped.

We stood there, listening, breathing in the acrid ammonia smell, surrounded by the eerie, bloodred canopy that felt less and less like a leafy arbor. But nothing came.

Khara exhaled slowly. "Let's move on," she said at last.

We did, clawing our way through the tightly knit branches. But immediately the unearthly slithering sounds returned.

Stumble, claw, pant. Stumble, claw, pant.

Fear is different when you are running. To flee is to acknowledge your own inability to fight back and win. It's an admission of weakness, and weakness feeds fear like dry straw on a fire.

Out of the corner of my eye, I caught a sudden movement: something dark, with short wings and a long body. It flew directly at us, and Renzo reacted with incredible speed, slinging our purloined shield from his back and holding it up seconds before the creature would have struck him.

The impact knocked him to the ground, but whatever the dark foe was, it flew past.

"Keep moving, keep moving," Khara urged, sword at the ready, searching the darkness for our unseen enemy.

I took a step, stumbled, recovered, and took another step—into nothing.

My left foot was on solid ground. My right foot was in air.

I felt, more than saw, a wide, deep hole before me. It was easily one hundred feet across, a vast, yawning emptiness.

"Aaah!" I cried, as I toppled forward helplessly.

Renzo grabbed for me, but his hand slipped from my fur and I fell. I tumbled perhaps fifty feet before I remembered my glissaires. Spreading them wide, I caught the air and turned my fall into a swoop.

But a dairne's glissaires are not true wings. We cannot fly, only glide. And except in rare cases of very strong updrafts, we can only glide downward.

On I plummeted, swooping, terrified my own speed would slam me into the walls and knock me unconscious, at which point I would presumably fall to my death.

I arced in a tight curve, as above me the frantic cries of my friends grew fainter. I could keep spiraling down, or take a gamble and deliberately straighten out until I hit something.

I chose the second path.

I was rewarded with a crash into a dirt wall that buckled my elbows and collapsed my glissaires.

I cried out again, or tried to, but I was choking on falling dirt. I scrabbled frantically, hands grabbing nothing but damp earth. Down I tumbled, battered by the wall, screaming and clutching at anything and everything.

I landed hard, shockingly hard, all breath pounded out of me.

My lungs straining, my mouth half-filled with soil, my heart lurching, I realized with a start that my left hand had hold of a protruding root. My right foot had, by some miracle, found a ledge.

I looked up: starlight and an edge of moon.

"Byx!" It was Tobble.

I couldn't see anyone. The lip of the hole had to be two hundred feet above me. What I could see, crowding the rim of the hole, were the outlines of those eerie trees.

I heard Khara's furious cry, followed by Renzo's shouts and Gambler's roar, and knew that battle had been joined above me.

I had no wind to spare for shouting, and they had no time to spare for listening. My heart hammered, my blood raced, my brain was a screaming sound beyond reason. I could not hang on, not for long. And my friends were under attack.

I had no choice but to trust to my glissaires and try to glide to the bottom, wherever that might be.

I looked down and, for the first time, saw the hint of a floor. A faint reddish glow revealed the circular bottom, a perfect counterpart to the opening above. This hole I'd fallen into was too symmetrical, too neat, to be some random feature of geography, I realized.

I glanced down again, as desperate grunts and cries from the battle above escalated.

The red glow was brightening. I felt the first wave of warmth rise up, and for a giddy moment, I wondered if the updraft might be enough to carry me upward and out.

That thought died the instant I looked up to judge my chances, for things were changing with dramatic speed. The trees that ringed the hole were moving. I saw swirling branches against the moon, branches that looked more and more like something horrifying.

I blinked. Blinked again.

The branches were turning into giant worms.

Something dropped past me. I couldn't see what it was, but it was followed by another. Then another.

I heard Renzo shouting from above, "Look out!" But his cry was not for me.

Suddenly, like a torrent released from a burst dam, there came a deluge of writhing worms. They fell inches from me as I pressed into the dirt wall, some as short as my arm, some as long as a spear and as thick as a sapling's trunk.

It was like standing behind a waterfall. A writhing, ammonia-stinking waterfall of worms.

Cries of fear met my ears, and through gaps in the

horrible rain, I saw Gambler carried over the edge by the flow. He fell, snarling and slashing.

"Gambler!" I screamed.

A moment later Khara, Renzo, and Dog fell together, helpless, covered in falling worms.

"Noooo! Noooo!" I cried.

I heard, rather than saw, Tobble. Somehow he'd held on against the tide, but now he, too, was falling, following the thinning cascade.

Deep in the dairne mind there must be a department for calculating angles and odds, and that part of the brain seems to function all on its own. Instantly I pushed away from the wall faceup, twisted as Tobble fell past, and snatched at his braided tails.

This required folding one glissaire, which of course sent me plunging and spinning, but I drew Tobble close. He had the good sense to grab hold so that I could spread both glissaires, lessening the speed of our fall.

As best I could, I converted falling into a more horizontal movement, spiraling down and down as the last of the worms fell around us.

Then, outlined against a rising moon, I saw Luca, still atop the edge of the hole.

He had betrayed us.

Again.

A moment later, I knew that I would forever regret that ungenerous thought. For as Luca called down to us—"Byx! Khara!"—something hit him from behind.

I had an impression of something in flight. Luca screamed. Tentacles whipped around him with inhuman speed.

He cried out again. I heard the horrifying sound of bones crushing.

And then I, too, screamed in horror, as Luca's bloodied body dropped into the pit.

18
The Search Begins

Hitting bottom was like landing in an endless pile of fish: disgusting, but—thankfully—cushioning. Worms flew as we plowed into them, and we came to a stop covered in the things. Some even split in two, apparently none the worse for wear.

Though hideous, they did not seem to be venomous, like snakes, or even particularly interested in us. They writhed madly, as if intent on reaching the bottom of the worm layer to get at the glowing ground beneath.

"Khara!" I cried. Standing on the shifting, slimy mass beneath my feet was difficult, but I struggled to stay erect long enough to be able to see my friends.

Tobble wailed, "What is happening?"

"Khara! Renzo! Gambler! Dog!" I yelled. Then, even more hopelessly: "Luca!"

I saw something lying in a heap and moved toward it.

Tobble grabbed my arm, holding me back. "No, Byx. You don't want to see."

I had never heard Tobble sound so grim. And when I looked into his face, I knew that he had seen what he now wished to spare me.

"Is he—"

Tobble began to speak, but could not. He bent over and vomited onto a knot of worms beneath him.

"Byx," he finally managed to say, "I can't breathe. I can't . . . the worms! Byx, I'm so afraid!"

"They don't seem to want to hurt us," I said, trying to reassure Tobble.

He looked past me and froze. Moving his mouth as if to speak, he instead let out a strangled cry.

I felt it before I turned to see it: a terramant. An insect so massive, so alien, that the carpet of worms seemed quaint by comparison.

I tensed, preparing for the death that was about to come, trying as best I could to shield Tobble from the horrific insect.

But the terramant seemed indifferent to Tobble and me. It walked past us on its six jointed legs, ignoring the squirming mass beneath, and headed to the lump Tobble wished me not to see.

It lifted what was left of Luca and trotted away.

"Look!" Tobble yelled, pointing.

The terramant was heading briskly down a tunnel, the same way the millions of worms now seemed to be going.

Beneath our feet, the worms raced to follow their brothers and sisters, and all at once I felt the lovely solidity of actual, worm-free ground.

As suddenly as they'd appeared, all the worms were gone. "Khara!" I called. "Gambler! Renzo!"

There was no sound but the dwindling, wet noise of the departing worms.

"We have to follow," I said.

"But—" Tobble began. "But we're small. And the worms, Byx. I can't."

"Yes," I said. "We are small. But we'd be smaller still if we didn't go after our friends."

Tobble straightened his shoulders. He shook his head once, as if tossing off unpleasant thoughts. "I'm sorry. When we're not at sea, wobbyks spend parts of our lives underground. We know what lurks here."

"No need to apologize, Tobble."

Tobble put his paws on his hips. "Lead on, my friend."

Lead? The word startled me. I'd never wanted to lead anyone or anything.

It was one thing to make a brave noise about following our friends, and a very different thing to figure out how, exactly, we were going to do that.

I tried my best to look resolute and confident, but of course, Tobble knew me too well.

"It's all right," he said. "I know you're as scared as I am."

"Maybe more scared." It was a relief to admit it.

We set off at a quick walk, hoping it was the right direction, and hastened by the fact that we were going downhill. But this was nothing like the caves and tunnels we'd encountered in the Subdur natite world.

There was nothing natural about this long slide. The walls were slick, the floor was smooth, and the tunnel was as straight as one of Khara's arrows. We weren't in the recesses of nature. We were within a creation of sentient creatures. And there could only be one species responsible: the terramants.

As a young dairne, I'd been taught from an early age to fear felivets, though in truth the huge felines had ceased hunting dairnes as soon as they'd discovered the Murdano's plans to exterminate us.

Natites, we'd learned, ruled the seas and bays, which made them as distant from our lives as the dull lyric poetry we'd been forced to memorize.

We knew to fear some of the raptidons. Hawks, rock ospreys, and kestriddi considered dairne pups a delicacy. (It was harder to carry us off for dinner once we weighed a stone or two.)

And of course, we knew plenty about humans from

distant glimpses, oft-told stories, and endless warnings.

But of all the governing species, the terramants had always seemed the strangest, the least like us. They were physically so odd, with triangular heads surmounted by two bulbous eyes and six spiderlike legs. Four additional appendages surrounded a gnashing mouth, and each of those shortened limbs ended in a wickedly curved claw. Terramants had nothing of the familiar or reassuring about them.

My parents often reminded me and my siblings never to judge a species on the basis of its appearance. And Dalyntor, the wise packelder who'd been our instructor, had spent many hours lecturing us on the immutable law of "pacequilibrio": the need for balance and variety in the natural world.

Every plant, every animal, every insect serves a purpose, Dalyntor said, no matter how annoying, how ugly, how frightening, or how unappetizing it might be.

Or, as my father liked to say: "Never doubt that nature has a sense of humor."

Still.

Terramants were hideous.

It was hard to imagine why the world needed insects the size of horses.

I feared that our descent might take hours, or lead into total darkness. (I'd had enough of that.) But as we trudged on, it became clear that illumination had been placed at regular intervals, in the form of a glowing green goo set into recessed pools a few feet across. It wasn't exactly blazing sunlight, but it was better than nothing.

Long before we reached an end to the slope, the stench of ammonia grew dizzying. But the sound was even worse: a relentless gnashing and clicking.

The sound of flesh being chewed.

And then Tobble yelped. "Ahh! Look!"

19
Conversation with a Terramant

It was a terramant. One glowing, multifaceted eye stared intently at us, while the other eye swiveled independently, like a bizarre gem.

We stood paralyzed with fear, and Tobble whispered shakily, "What do we do?"

The eye that had been focused on us curved downward, landing on a fat worm that seemed to have lost its way in the stampede. The terramant bent its front legs in a blindingly fast parody of a courtly bow. Two bladed shorter limbs snatched up the worm and nimbly shoved it into the terramant's mouth.

I cautiously raised a hand to see if the terramant would take note of us. It did not. I took a tentative step forward and he didn't react.

"Let's go," I said, not at all sure it was a good idea.

I walked straight toward the creature, then past him.

Tobble kept pace so closely he was practically stepping on my heels.

"Well," I said, breathing a sigh of relief, "that went better than it might have."

Once past the outlying terramant, we reached a place of branching tunnels. On closer observation we realized they were not true tunnels, but depressions only a few dozen feet deep. In each were three to five terramants, all gobbling worms. As we passed each nest, one or more of the creatures would cock an eye our way and then dismiss us.

"They're looking for something, but it isn't us," I said.

"Worms. They're looking for worms, the disgusting things. The smell!"

"Are these the mudworms in that song you taught us?" I asked.

"I've never exactly seen an actual mudworm. And since these don't seem interested in eating us, at least not yet, maybe they're a different kind of worm." Tobble gulped. "Still. They're horrible. Disgusting. Awful."

"I wonder what the terramants will do if I call out to Khara," I said.

Tobble shivered. "I just hope they kill me quickly."

I hesitated, well aware that I was not up to the task of making life-or-death decisions.

"Khara!" I cried.

The terramants seemed unmoved.

"Khara!" I raised my voice to a louder pitch. "Khara! Renzo! Gambler! Dog!"

Nothing.

"They must have come this way, carried by the rush of worms," I said. "If the terramants have no interest in us, maybe they let our friends pass unharmed."

"What is all this?" Tobble asked as we walked on past dozens and dozens of nests, each filled with clacking, chomping terramants. "This can't be how terramants live normally."

"Why not?"

Tobble shrugged. "It just feels wrong."

It did indeed feel wrong, but I knew too little about the subterranean species to be certain. Surely, if terramants made a habit of planting worm-tree forests around giant pits, I would have heard of such a thing. And if not me, then no doubt Khara or Renzo or Gambler, all well-traveled folks, would have known.

"Do they speak?" Tobble wondered.

"I believe that clicking sound is their speech. But they must be able to understand the Common Tongue. After all, there were terramant scholars at the Academy. They had to communicate with other species all the time."

"Hello?" Tobble said to the nearest terramant, who was munching a slithering worm.

No response.

"Or maybe not," I said.

"Some of us speak the Common Tongue."

Tobble and I both leapt about three feet straight in the air. We spun in what must have seemed a comical way and came face-to-face—well, face-to-knee—with a terramant.

"You—you—" I said. I collected my wits and managed a complete sentence. "You speak the Common Tongue?"

"The question answers itself, no?"

"Um, yes . . . sir?" I replied with a gulp.

"What form of creature are you?" he asked.

I could not make out how the terramant formed his words, for I saw no movement of his mouthparts. How vowels and consonants could be so precisely created with that horrifying, worm-eating maw was beyond me.

"I am a dairne. My name is Byx. This is Tobble, a wobbyk."

The terramant cocked his triangular head to one side. "We have no instruction regarding dairnes or wobbyks."

"Does that mean—wait, friend terramant, does that mean you do have instructions regarding other species?"

"Humans, natites, and felivets are to be taken to the Two and the Three."

"Pardon me, but do you have a name?" Tobble asked, ever polite.

"I am Seventy-Eight of Eighteen Hive of the Group of Thirteen."

"Do you have a . . . a nickname?" I asked.

"No."

"Ah," I said. "May I ask who the Two and the Three are?"

"They are the ones who decide."

I was beginning to get the measure of the monster. This particular terramant seemed perfectly willing to answer questions. And not, it appeared, interested in consuming us.

"You've seen no humans or felivets recently?" I asked.

"No."

"Is it possible that they passed by unseen?"

"No. They were seen."

I felt my heart lurch. "Seen, but not by you? By some other terramant?"

"Yes."

"And do you know where they are?" I asked, trying to keep the urgency out of my voice.

"Yes."

"And . . . and was one dead human also found?"

"Killed by a defender of the forest."

"What was it?" I asked. "This defender?"

"I know no other name for the species. They are creatures of the Kazar Sg'drit."

I swallowed my impatience. "Can you show us where the others are, the living ones?"

"They are with the Two and the Three."

"I see. And may I ask, what are the Two and the Three doing with them?"

The terramant shifted ever so slightly. "They hold them for presentation to the Foreman."

Terramant speech is not expressive, nor are their eyes, but still I felt a slight hesitation on the word "Foreman."

"And who is the Foreman?" I asked.

"The one who feeds us. The one who uses us."

This time I was sure I heard something in his inflection. Dislike? Disapproval? Resentment? What did I know about terramants? How was I to judge his tone?

The conversation between Gambler and Luca came back to me:

I thought the terramants served no one.

They do when they're starving.

"And what will this Foreman do with them?" I asked, watching the terramant carefully.

"If they are useful, he will make thralls of them."

"And if they are not useful?" I asked, fighting the quaver in my voice.

"If they are not useful," the terramant replied, "he will kill them."

20
Our Not-Very-Good Plan

The terramant had answered all the questions we could think of. When we asked how to find the Two and the Three, he used a claw to sketch a map in the dirt.

We thanked him and moved on, once more ignored by the other terramants we passed. In fact, we were more ignored than before, for now they did not even glance at us.

"I think they're expecting us," I said to Tobble. "Earlier they looked when we passed. Now it's like we don't exist." I had a theory. "I think they can communicate among themselves in ways we do not understand. Ways that seem almost like theurgy."

"Like bees?" Tobble asked. "It's well-known that one bee knows all that is known by other bees."

"That seems unlikely," I said, but Tobble was probably close to the truth. The terramants had been told to look for humans, natites, and felivets, not wobbyks and dairnes. But our "friend," Seventy-Eight of Eighteen Hive of the Group of Thirteen, might well have been sent to discover just what sort of creatures we were. And now that information had passed to all the other terramants.

It was good to be ignored. But if we were right, this also meant that every terramant could be given new instructions at any moment. New instructions like "Eat any dairne or wobbyk you encounter." And that was an alarming thought.

I had memorized the map we'd been shown, and we walked on, hovering somewhere between nervous curiosity and paralyzing terror.

At last, just as Seventy-Eight of Eighteen Hive of the Group of Thirteen had said, we reached a tunnel crowded at one end with a mass of terramants all doing what they did best: excavating.

It was fascinating, if horrifying, to watch. They worked in teams with perfect coordination. At the front of the heaving mass must have been the diggers, cutting energetically. The dirt they dislodged was hauled away by terramants harnessed to narrow, deep wagons. These came rushing past us and off into a side tunnel, where, presumably, they dumped the soil.

A third group smeared the walls of the tunnel with a slurry made from their own vomit. Finally, much smaller terramants, perhaps juveniles, smoothed and slurried the roof. They were no larger than I, and managed to cling upside down with apparent ease as they worked.

From our left came a deep bass sound, a single, resonant gong. Instantly, the terramants ceased working and came rushing straight at us.

"Down!" I cried, shoving Tobble beneath me.

How many insect legs rushed past us, around us, over us, I will never be able to count. But each leg somehow missed us, though sometimes by the tiniest margin.

When they'd passed, I leaned down. "Are you all right, Tobble?"

"Aaah! They're coming back!"

And they were, though not the same terramants. Obviously, they were changing shifts, sending some workers to eat while bringing in a new crew to continue the work without interruption. But once again, the terramants avoided crushing us in their insect stampede.

We stood up shakily, knocked some of the dirt from our clothing, and continued on our search.

"Khara! Gambler! Renzo!" I called, but there was no response.

"What do you suppose that tunnel they're digging is for?" Tobble wondered.

I shrugged. "Who knows why terramants do anything?

Maybe this Foreman will tell us. I imagine he's some sort of terramant king."

"We're just going to walk right up to a terramant king and demand to know what's happened to our friends?"

"It does sound ridiculous when you put it that way," I admitted, feeling a bit defensive. "But what other choice do we have? Do you want to just abandon them?"

Tobble grabbed my elbow with sudden fervor. I stopped and found myself staring down at an uncharacteristically serious wobbyk face.

"Never," Tobble said with force. "Never, Byx."

"Tobble," I said with an apologetic smile, "I know that. Of course I do. I was just—"

"Good," he snapped, and with that he took the lead, striding purposefully forward.

I followed, feeling terrible that I'd annoyed him. Tobble was as brave as I. Braver, even. He was as loyal as I. He was clever and kind.

And he was right that I had no plan.

"I don't know what to do," I admitted, although I wasn't sure Tobble heard me, since he was several paces ahead.

"We need a story," I continued. "But nothing comes to mind."

More silence.

"Tobble?"

Tobble turned. To my relief, his expression had softened. "Hmm." He pursed his lips. "Perhaps we are here to inspect the tunnel. We've been sent by the . . . what's his name? The rogue felivet?"

I searched my memory, summoning up Gambler's voice. "The Kazar Sg'drit."

"There you go," Tobble said. "We've been sent here to assess their progress."

"It's better than nothing," I said.

Tobble held up his paws. "Not much better than nothing."

"Onward, then," I said, "with our not-very-good plan."

We walked on along a tunnel glowing faintly green. The sounds of the ceaseless excavation grew fainter behind us, while ahead of us, two lines of terramants appeared, seemingly out of nowhere.

An honor guard? Or actual guards?

"Stand where you are," said a terramant voice.

We stood perfectly still.

"State your names, species, and business," the first terramant on our right demanded.

"I am Byx, a dairne, and I am here on a mission from the mighty Kazar Sg'drit the Merciless." I added the "mighty" and "merciless." I doubted anyone would object.

"I am Tobble, a wobbyk, and I am here on that same business."

The terramant let us stand there for a while. I had the distinct impression that he was communicating silently with other terramants.

"The Foreman doubts your story," the terramant said at last. "But he will receive you. Proceed."

We proceeded, filled with trepidation. My throat was tight, my hands trembling, my stomach tightly knotted. Fear: there it was again.

We walked another two or three hundred yards between rows of silent, unmoving terramants.

And then we saw our friends.

21
King Tobble

It was Khara I recognized first.

Or rather, Khara's head.

It was mounted on the side of the tunnel.

Just her head.

Sticking out from the dirt wall as if it had grown there naturally.

Renzo's head was just a few feet farther on. Just beyond was Gambler's great head, his ebony fur dusted with dirt. Dog's head was inches from Gambler's.

"Tobble," I managed, hoping to protect him the way he'd done with me. "Don't look."

But it was too late. Tears were already streaming down Tobble's cheeks.

I reached for him and we embraced, slowly sinking to our knees, gulping down huge sobs. Even as we held each other, I felt my shredded heart begin to turn into something familiar and frightening.

I'd known this feeling before, when my family, my pack, my world had been destroyed.

"I will kill them," I muttered, my face buried in Tobble's fur. "I will kill them, Tobble." The words poured out of my mouth like lava. "I will make them feel the same pain. I will—"

"Byx." Tobble's warm, round paw squeezed my hand. "Byx. Look."

I lifted my head and followed Tobble's gaze.

Khara was blinking.

Blinking!

She lived.

Khara lived!

"Khara!" I cried.

"Run away, you two! Run!" she whispered.

I ran over with Tobble. "You are alive," I whispered. "Khara, you're alive."

"Leave. Now."

I ignored her words, instead reaching out to touch her hair.

Tobble moved on to check Renzo and Gambler.

Each still lived, though they were quiet and cowed. Each, in turn, told us to run away.

I simply shook my head, and so did Tobble.

No, we would not run away.

Beyond my friends were other heads sprouting from the packed earth. Some were human, some were felivet, though it appeared that no one else was alive. I could not bear to think of the suffering they had endured in this living entombment.

"Tobble," I whispered. "You have the crown? And the Far-Near?"

"Yes."

"Put on the crown. You are now King Tobble, ruler of all wobbyks, and a close ally of Sg'drit. I am your dairne truth teller."

"But I can't. I'm just . . . me."

"You remember how arrogant the Murdano was? Be like that."

We stopped so Tobble could take the crown from his pack and balance it on his head. Were it not for his prominent ears, the thing would have fallen down over his neck like a massive necklace.

Tobble passed the Far-Near to me. "You should hold this. You're my assistant, after all."

We moved on, past the horrifying spectacle on the walls, until we reached a line of terramants blocking our route.

"You will approach the Foreman on your knees," said the largest. "Or you will die."

"Nonsense," I said with far more confidence than I felt. "This is King Tobble of the Wobbyk Kingdom, a close ally of the Kazar Sg'drit. He grovels for no one!"

The terramant didn't seem to know what to make of my declaration. We strode past with all the regal bearing we could manage and came face-to-face with a creature unlike any I had ever seen.

The Foreman was not a terramant. He was more insect than anything else, but not entirely so. He was large, twice the size of any of the terramants I had seen. His lower body was a chitinous shell, with thick, insect-like armor behind, and an exposed and more vulnerable front with a multitude of what looked like small legs. His midsection was a mass of writhing tentacles of different lengths and thicknesses, some no longer than a snake, others perhaps twenty feet long.

His head was covered by a chitin armor hood that shadowed his face, a face that at first looked like that of a natite. And in fact he seemed to be an aquatic creature, in part, for he sat on a throne in a shallow pool. Two streams of water poured continuously over him, draining from tubes in the mud walls. A rope harness kept his upper body upright, affording him a sitting position from which he could look down at us from an impressive height.

"He looks part lobster!" Tobble said.

This told me nothing, as I'd never heard of a lobster

before. But I wasn't concerning myself with what he was. I was focused on what he could do to us.

"Why have you come here?" he demanded. His voice was hard to understand, a grinding noise interrupted by insect clicks.

I swallowed my fear as well as I could. Our survival, and that of our friends, relied on how I replied.

Oh, to have had Khara's courage, Renzo's bravado, Gambler's cunning at that moment!

I was the runt of my litter. Not a leader.

But at least I had King Tobble by my side.

22
A Gift for the Foreman

"Great Foreman," I said, straightening to my full height, "this is King Tobble of the Wobbyks, senior adviser to and trusted ally of the great Kazar Sg'drit."

I was just about to add "as you can see from the crown upon his head," but stopped myself at the last minute. It would be a mistake to overexplain. The Foreman had seen the crown, and crowns were not something any ordinary person would have.

Tobble stood with all the easy arrogance of a creature entitled to wear the crown, plus a hint of the disrespectful in his pose.

After all, Tobble was a king, however small.

The Foreman turned blank red eyes on us. Two antennae rose in graceful arcs from his hooded head, and they twitched slightly. "I have not been informed of any visit," he said. He clearly wasn't convinced.

"There wouldn't be much point in a surprise inspection, Foreman," said Tobble, "if you were warned ahead of time, now, would there?"

It was all I could do not to applaud his performance.

"Inspection?" The Foreman could not frown, but doubt was in his voice.

"Yes," Tobble said. "And courtesy compels me to reveal to you that this dairne of mine can instantly and unfailingly separate truth from lies."

"I had heard . . ." The Foreman trailed off. "I had been told that dairnekind was no more."

"Do you imagine that the Kazar Sg'drit reveals all his secrets to the likes of you?" Tobble's incredulity was a thing to behold. "But before we begin, my friend the Kazar has sent a rare gift to you."

Tobble snapped his fingers, and I hastily drew the Far-Near from my leather bag.

"Well?" Tobble snapped at me. "Present the Kazar's gift before I have you whipped!"

I advanced, holding out the Far-Near. The monstrous being whipped it from my hand with a tentacle bigger than any snake I'd ever seen.

"If I may—" I began, but Tobble gave a dismissive wave. "Great Foreman, the Far-Near must be held to your eye. If you look through one end, all you see will seem very small.

If you look through the other, it will make distant objects seem nearer."

The Foreman held it tentatively to his right eye. He emitted a wet sound, which was probably a gasp. Then he reversed the Far-Near, scanning around the chamber.

"This is truly magnificent," the Foreman said. "Please send the Kazar Sg'drit, all glory to him, my deep and endless gratitude."

"What I wish to do now is hear of your progress on the work here," Tobble said.

"Of course," the big bug said. "I can report to you that the tunnel is ahead of schedule. We have established a means of feeding my thralls and—"

"*Your* thralls?" Tobble asked with a raised eyebrow.

The Foreman quickly amended, "They are, of course, the Kazar's thralls, as I am his servant. His loyal servant."

"No one doubts your loyalty," Tobble said with a graceful wave of his paw.

The Foreman proceeded to fill us in on all the details, which took quite some time. I was exhausted and anxious, my knees trembling. I could only imagine how Tobble was feeling.

After the update, we were invited to a sit at an overloaded table and dine on a variety of dishes, all of which seemed to feature worm as the main ingredient. It was upon the arrival of the food that Tobble carried off his masterstroke.

"This is a glorious feast indeed, Foreman. But I dine almost exclusively on fresh human meat." He patted his round tummy. "I find it is one of the few things that do not upset my digestion."

An hour later, we were escorted to the surface by six terramants. And with us, shackled and bowed, were Khara, Renzo—our fresh meat—and Gambler. Poor Dog was attached to a heavy chain.

At first the Foreman had been suspicious when Tobble suggested sending them with us. But Tobble had quickly spun a convincing tale about our having pursued the two humans, along with a treasonous felivet the Kazar would dearly love to throw into his torture pit.

"Torture pit?" the Foreman had asked.

"Of course. Don't you have one?" Tobble shot back.

We emerged back into sunlight with our friends, still very much alive, along with Khara's sword and Renzo's shield, and bade farewell to our escorts.

"Tobble," I said as the Foreman's lair receded in the distance, "I am quite certain you could join any traveling troupe of actors and be granted a starring role."

Tobble's whiskers quivered as he attempted not to smile. "That's *King* Tobble, I'll remind you."

"I need no reminder," I said, bowing low. "And I never will."

23
Neither Doomed nor Pointless

We managed to use Khara's sword and Tobble's nimble paws to get rid of the chain tightly looped around Dog's neck. The shackles on Khara, Renzo, and Gambler took longer to remove. All three seemed shaken and unsteady—more so after we shared what had happened to Luca.

But it was Khara who seemed to take their brush with death the hardest. She refused to speak, and when asked what we should do next, she merely trudged ahead. We followed in her wake.

We were exhausted and desperate for sleep, but we kept going until the sun peeked over the horizon and the hideous Crimson Forest was far behind us.

The forest that had never been a forest at all.

Khara, Renzo, and Gambler had heard much while sealed in their prison of soil. The forest, it seemed, was nothing but a bizarre farm, created solely to generate food for the terramants. Somehow the Kazar Sg'drit had found a way to grow vast quantities of worms in treelike structures. Theurgy, Renzo suspected.

The terramants, desperately hungry after the Kazar's poisoning of their main food source, had been easy to force into tunnel building.

When we were far past the forest, I approached Renzo. "Are you well?" I asked gently.

"No," he said. His mouth was set in a tight line. After a moment, he added, "I thought I would die there, Byx."

"When you were nearly roasted by the Knight of the Fire," I said, "it barely seemed to faze you. I wonder why this was so much worse."

Renzo said nothing. He quickened his pace until he was ahead of me, and I realized my curiosity was ill-timed, to say the least.

Beside me, Gambler said, "We all have our own particular fears, Byx. One can be brave nine times and be a coward the tenth time. This is true of all living things capable of thought."

Fearless Gambler feared water. Renzo feared starvation. Tobble feared mudworms.

And what was I afraid of?

I feared dying as the last of my species, never to spend another hour with one of my own kind.

I feared . . . well, I feared being afraid. Lacking courage when I most needed it.

I feared, I supposed, myself.

What did Khara fear? I wondered, watching her walk along, deep in her own thoughts.

"I have not had occasion yet to thank you for rescuing us," Gambler said.

"Tobble did most of the talking," I admitted.

"I know. It was Tobble I was speaking to."

"Me?" Tobble squeaked.

"You walked up and bluffed that great lobster creature," Gambler said. "As heroic a performance as I can imagine. We all owe you our lives."

Renzo came out of his sulk long enough to say, "Yes, we do. As a thief who has spent far too much time trying to con his way out of trouble, I would doff my hat, if I had a hat."

Even Khara spoke, albeit in a tone so soft we could barely hear her. "Thank you, Tobble," she said. "And you as well, Byx."

Tobble seemed uncertain what to do with all the praise. He tried walking differently, with a wider stance and longer strides. He pulled back his shoulders and puffed out his chest.

But after a few minutes, he grew tired and went back to being regular old Tobble. "Don't tell the others," he whispered to me, "but I wasn't brave. I was scared to death of those worms. The terramants weren't too fun, either."

Gambler overheard and uttered his felivet laugh, which was closer to the sound of a human clearing their throat. "If you're not afraid, you're a fool. If you are afraid, even scared to death, and keep your head? That is called courage. Now, friend wobbyk, I shall never be able to eat you."

I was sure that last part was a felivet joke.

Pretty sure.

We took a brief, much-needed rest, then headed onward across rocky terrain. It seemed we were always either climbing or descending. At the crests we could look around, but most of the time our view was limited. It was a good thing we'd given Vallino up when we had. It would have been impossible for him to make it through.

Finally, we huffed and puffed our way up the tallest of the snowy ridges. When we looked to the east, we saw the vast grayness of a distant sea.

"Still a long way," Renzo said. "But at least we can see our goal."

Khara said nothing.

In the evening, cold and wet from a rain shower that turned to snow and covered our path with slush, we made camp in a small hollow in the side of a hill. We had nothing to burn for a fire, so we shivered beneath absurdly inadequate blankets, and felt the wet seep into our clothing.

I slept fitfully. At one point I woke and saw Khara

standing by herself, looking away. I went to her. She made no acknowledgment.

"What troubles you, Khara?" I asked.

She took her time answering. "I was unjust, Byx," she said at last, her voice muted. "I thought Luca had betrayed us. The last thing he heard was my voice calling him a traitor."

"But Khara," I said, "he had betrayed us before."

"Yes, but this time I had a dairne telling me he was speaking the truth." She looked past me, staring, it seemed, at nothing. "I didn't trust him. And I didn't trust you. And while we're at it, I still don't entirely trust Renzo."

She fell silent but didn't leave. I wasn't sure what to say to make her feel better, so I simply stood beside her, hoping that was enough.

And after a while Khara spoke again. "I am the leader of this . . . this . . . doomed and pointless enterprise. I led us into that forest. I got Luca killed. I nearly got us all killed. I lay there, buried, helpless, believing I would have to remain there for days, hearing Renzo and Gambler weaken, knowing their hunger, knowing their fear. Knowing that it would take us a long time to die. Knowing I had led them to that."

"Khara, you are only human. Human, felivet, dairne . . . we all make mistakes. We all fail at times."

She nodded slowly, but I could tell she wasn't convinced.

"When we were in the tunnel," I said, "there was a

moment when Tobble told me to take the lead." I looked Khara in the eyes. "I have never been so frightened by a simple word. *Lead*."

"The first time is the hardest." Khara smiled, just a little. "But you may have to lead again before all this is done, Byx. You'd better get used to it."

"Does it ever get easier?"

Khara gave a short laugh. "Well, it gets . . . different. More familiar. But easier? No."

"We were talking before about what scares us. It was different for everyone." I hesitated, recalling how my questioning had seemed to upset Renzo, then pressed on. "Are you ever afraid, Khara?"

She exhaled slowly, her breath clouding in the icy air. "I'm afraid of failing," she said. "Of letting all of you down."

"Listen, Khara," I said, doing my best to adopt a wise, parental tone. "You can be uncertain, you can be angry at yourself, but we still need you. Take some time, if you need it, to think of how you might do better in the future. And then get back to the job of leading this doomed and pointless enterprise. Even if that means taking the risk of trusting others. There is one thing I know, Khara. You may fail sometimes. But you'll never let us down."

I thought I had offended her. But after a moment I felt her hand on my shoulder. "This is neither doomed nor pointless,"

Khara said softly. "We will find your island. We will find your dairnes."

I nodded. "You're right," I said, my voice catching. "This expedition isn't pointless. And,with you leading us, it may not even be doomed."

She laughed and gave me a hug. "Come back to sleep?" I asked, suppressing a yawn.

"In a while. I promise."

I trudged back to my pitiful blanket and lay down on the freezing, damp ground as snowflakes settled on my face.

The last thing I heard before sleep took me was Renzo, lying nearby, in a whisper that may have been intended for his ears alone.

"I like that girl. I like that girl a lot."

24
At Sea

In the morning the clouds hung low, at times sprinkling us with rain, and at other times dusting us with snow. At last we topped a steep embankment and saw the sea again. No longer was it a distant gray smudge. It was right before us, less than half a league away.

We no longer had our Far-Near, having gifted it to the Foreman. But even our natural eyes could see a fishing village just up the coast to the northeast. Beyond that, we could make out the masts and piers of a larger port city. To our right loomed the great massif that ran straight into the sea, forming the dividing line between Dreyland and Nedarra.

Just knowing how close we might be to the island—and to more dairnes—sent my heart racing. I tasted the wind, hoping, even though I knew it was unlikely, I might catch a trace of one of my own.

But no. I smelled no dairnes, just salt and sea.

"I don't see Tarok," Khara said, "but it may be beyond that curved spit of land, out of view."

"Sentient islands move erratically," Renzo said. "Depending on the food supply in the waters."

"Do you think it's really carnivorous?" Tobble asked nervously.

"Could just be rumors," Khara said. "A story to keep others at bay."

"After all, the worms in that tunnel turned out to be harmless," I said. "Despite that wobbyk song of yours."

"Those worms weren't harmless," Tobble said. He shivered. "I'll be having nightmares about them forever."

A road ran between us and the sea, full of marching soldiers and heavily laden wagons.

"How many soldiers does this Kazar Sg'drit have?" Renzo asked.

"No doubt more than the Murdano can muster," Khara said darkly. "If the terramants succeed in digging a tunnel beneath the mountains, the Dreyland troops will flood into Nedarra. Our—" She stopped herself. "The Murdano's troops are concentrated in the east, expecting an invasion by water. The tunnel will mean doom for them. Dreyland will push them into the sea."

"Does the Murdano have so few soldiers?" Renzo asked.

Khara shrugged. "Many will not head into battle for him. They might fight to protect Nedarra—if they knew the danger—but they won't rally to the Murdano."

"What about the westerners, the once-great families in exile?" Renzo asked, turning to Khara. "Your own family, for example. Wouldn't they work to save Nedarra?"

"My father would cut off his own hand before raising it in defense of the Murdano," Khara replied. "And many others follow my father's lead."

Gambler, perched gracefully on a thin, flat rock, sighed. "The first through the tunnel will be the terramants," he said. "They will not just kill. They will devour."

"Enough speculation," Khara said firmly. "We have a direction, we have a goal. This coming war is not our concern."

"Yet," Renzo whispered.

We waited for the soldiers to pass, then headed on. It seemed to take us forever to reach the shoreline, and when at last we did, all we found was a beach of dark sand extending leagues in each direction. Gazing out to sea availed nothing. A few distant ships were visible, but there was no island to be seen, sentient or not.

And then Tobble spotted it.

The sun was sinking toward the horizon, and we'd begun to think about dinner. Tobble, having noticed a scraggly bush whose leaves he claimed would enhance the flavor of our meal, had scrambled to the top of a dune.

I heard his voice, tiny in the distance.

"There! There it is!"

We raced up the black sand to join him. Sure enough, beyond a curved spit of land sat a small island. It was covered in vividly colored trees: reds, greens, yellows, completely unlike the muted evergreens on the mainland.

I was sure it was the one I had glimpsed so briefly on the Nedarran side of the mountains. Tarok.

Tarok was a rooklet, I'd learned from Khara and Renzo, a huge and ancient water beast. Over thousands of years, the rare creatures accumulated layers of dirt and vegetation until they became, in essence, living islands.

"That's it," I said, my voice just a whisper.

I strained with all my senses, trying to discern a hint of something that could confirm the presence of dairnes. The sound of our lilting language, the scent of our silky fur, the sight of a dairne-made tree nest.

Nothing.

Khara, head tilted, said, "There's something off about that village on the shoreline. Look at the paddock. I count eight . . . no, nine fine-looking horses. What tiny fishing village has ever been prosperous enough to stable nine horses?"

"Any extra coin a fisherman has will go straight back into his boat," Renzo agreed. "And I see only two craft drawn up on the mud."

"Down!" Gambler commanded. "Now."

We all ducked out of sight behind the dune. "What did

you see, Gambler?" I asked.

"A uniform. Green and tan," Gambler answered. "Just one, but where's there's one soldier, there are always more. When darkness falls, I will scout ahead."

Later that evening, we were huddled on the sand together when Gambler appeared soundlessly out of the darkness.

"It is no fishing village," Gambler confirmed. "I saw a platoon of soldiers, and more officers than is typical for a small detachment. Those were officers' horses."

"A surplus of officers," Khara mused. "Could be they're following the island's movements."

"Or they could be heading south to join forces with more troops," Renzo suggested.

"In any case, we cannot reach Tarok," said Gambler, "without passing through the village, right past fifty or more armed men."

"We could steal a boat," Renzo suggested.

Khara scanned the group. "Do any of you know how to sail?"

Tobble raised a hesitant hand. "I've sailed boats. Wobbyks are seafaring folk."

"What do you think our chances of taking a boat would be?" Khara asked.

"The tides turn every twelve hours," Tobble said. He rubbed his chin. "It looks—oh, I miss my Far-Near!—it looks as if the tide is coming in. It will be hours before the boats are floating."

"What about the owners?" Renzo asked.

"They probably won't show up till first light. We might make it out before anyone notices us."

"The natites patrol all waters," Khara said. "But they tend to be farther out to sea, not hugging the coastline. With luck, they won't notice us."

Then and there, we decided to steal one of the boats. We planned to wait until the tide floated it, then sail the half league or so to the island.

When Khara determined it was time, we walked out onto the mud, our feet sinking into the sucking goo with each step. We crouched and remained completely silent, although it seemed unlikely anyone could hear us. A loud and boisterous party was underway, including many drunk-sounding voices, and music was being played on a lute and drums.

We came to the nearest and smallest of the two craft. Gambler, who walked much more easily on the mud and was all but invisible at night, crept ahead and reported back that the boat was unoccupied.

We had some difficulty getting aboard, as the boat was still canted over in the mud, its single mast pointing at a forty-five-degree angle. The entire boat was no more than twenty feet long.

I searched the cabin and found a small amount of food—a

sausage and some crackers. It would be stealing to take the food, but then again, we were planning to steal the entire boat. My conscience was bothered, though. The boat, which was called *Gramis Rose*, according to the faded lettering on its bow, was someone's livelihood.

Khara seemed to be thinking the same thing. "Tobble," she said, pointing to his pouch, where he'd stashed the crown.

Tobble handed the gleaming gold circle to Renzo, who pried out another small gem. Renzo rolled his eyes and tossed the green stone to Khara.

"We can leave it in this," I suggested, yanking a chest from the floor of the boat. "It has the boat's name on it. Hopefully, the owner will find it before anyone else does."

"It's the best we can do," Khara said, and she placed the green gem into the chest.

"You two are getting soft," Renzo grumbled, but he helped Khara slog through the mud to place the chest on dry sand.

The boat reeked of fish, but we'd spent time in worse places. Soon we began to feel the hull move as the tide came in. At first, we rocked back and forth in the gentle swell. Then, all at once, the decks were level and we had water beneath us.

"We can set sail at any time, if the breeze holds true out of the northwest," Tobble said. "And sunrise is still an hour away."

"Good," Khara said. "Make sail, Captain Tobble."

"Aye, aye, Admiral," Tobble said.

Wobbyks are renowned fishermen in Nedarra, but their boats, while sturdy, are much simpler. I had to admire Tobble's brisk efficiency as he leapt to the stern, grabbed the tiller, and ordered Renzo to pull the rope that would raise the sail.

We skimmed across the water with grace and ease. Tobble held the tiller hard to one side as wind billowed the sail. The whole boat tilted at a sharp angle, and within minutes we were closing in on the sentient island that had filled my dreams since the moment I'd first set eyes upon it.

Like Tobble, how I wished for our lost Far-Near! All I could see was a lush expanse of dense trees, a dark mass against the cobalt predawn sky. My heart beat unsteadily, and my breath came quickly in the wet, tangy air. I might, just might, be about to see another dairne—perhaps even many—for the first time since my pack had been destroyed.

To smell our comforting, familiar scent.

To hear the sweet melody of our language.

To be with my own.

How many times had I played out this scene? Late at night while my friends slept, with only the vigilant moon to keep me company, I had imagined this moment. Would I strive to say something profound? Take my cue from the other dairnes?

Would I weep? Or laugh? Or both?

Would I look into their eyes and feel my old self return? Or had I changed so profoundly that I was no longer the old Byx, the runt of her litter, the least important member of her pack?

"Nervous?" Khara asked me as she joined me in the bow, risking the icy shower that came each time we sliced through a wave.

"Yes," I admitted.

"Well, I wish you joy and satisfaction, Byx."

Tears filled my eyes. "Thank you, Khara. It would never have been possible without you."

Khara touched my shoulder, and silently we watched the island grow ever closer.

I thought I glimpsed tears in Khara's eyes as well, but it was probably just the salty spray.

25
The Island, at Last

"Strike the sail! Out sweeps!" Tobble shouted.

Renzo lowered the sail and Khara and I slotted the two long oars. Khara took one and I took the other. Soon Renzo joined me, since I could not hope to match the strength of Khara's stroke.

We skimmed near, inch by inch, and for half an hour we rowed along, easily keeping pace with the slow-moving island until we came around to its seaward side. So far there had been no pursuit, but surely someone ashore would notice the missing boat before long.

Hopefully, the gem we'd left behind would placate the owner. And in any case, if we were behind the island, hidden from view, there was a chance, at least, that we could escape unscathed.

As dawn unfurled, the colors of the trees and other

vegetation grew brighter. "It's so beautiful," I said. "Do you really think it might be . . . dangerous?"

"Dangerous" sounded much better to my ears than "carnivorous."

"You're asking if it will eat us?" Khara asked. "I suppose there's only one way to find out."

"This place is layered with theurgic spells," Renzo said in a low voice. "I can feel them."

"What kind of spells?" I asked.

"Bits of ancient theurgy guarding against sea serpents and dragons."

"It all feels very, very old," Khara agreed. "No doubt centuries of wizardry have guarded and protected this place, but those spells feel weak now. The magic of the island has faded." She glanced at me. "Byx, do you sense anything?"

I shook my head. "Nothing."

"Well," Khara said, "I think it's time to land, Captain Tobble. Let's see what we can find."

"And let's hope this island has had its breakfast," Renzo added with a grim smile.

Tobble guided the boat onto a thin strip of beach. Onyx sand glittered like a night crowded with stars, crunching beneath the bow as we came to a stop.

Renzo leapt ashore to tie us off to a tree trunk. With each step he took, his boots left an imprint, the black sand turning to purple, as if momentarily bruised.

I was the next to climb off the boat, and instantly I felt a strangeness in the air: the echoes of theurgy, perhaps? Or maybe it was the utter lack of sound. No birds, no snapping twigs as curious creatures crept close to spy upon us. Leaves danced on the breeze without a whisper. Even the lapping waves had hushed.

Khara, Tobble, and Gambler joined me, each of us leaving the purple bloom of our footsteps as we trudged across the sand. When Gambler's huge paws touched the beach, he was so light on his feet that he barely left a mark, just a momentary lavender glow, like the last breath of a sunset.

"The sand is hot!" Tobble said, bouncing from foot to foot.

"My pads are burning," I agreed.

"It is a bit warm," Gambler agreed.

Khara touched the sand, then recoiled, leaving a wine-colored handprint behind. "I see what you mean."

"Even my boots are warm," Renzo said.

"Byx and Tobble," Gambler said, "climb on my back. My pads are thick. I'll barely feel anything, as long as we keep moving."

I climbed onto Gambler, and Tobble joined me. "I don't see anyone," I murmured, scanning ahead as Gambler trotted across the sand. "Hello!" I called. "Hello, hello! We are peaceful. We mean you no harm!"

Silence.

When we'd glimpsed it from the shore, the island had not appeared large, perhaps no more than a quarter of a league wide and twice as long. Khara stared at the lush curtain of green and yellow vines and interlaced trees before us, hoping to find a promising gap. When nothing appeared, she took her sword and began hacking through the foliage, gently at first, and then with more energy.

Renzo followed suit, and for the next few minutes the only sounds were their labored breaths and the dull clang of metal on branch. Still every footstep revealed itself in the sandy floor, then vanished. Gambler paced back and forth to keep the heat from getting too intense.

Every so often I'd call out, and listen for a response. Even a chittering wrenlet would have been a relief to hear. But we heard nothing, nothing at all but our panting, anxious selves.

"Perhaps," Tobble suggested, "your own language will work, Byx."

Of course! I tried again, this time in Dairnish. "Palouy rohnoom a rooex?" The words—Is anyone there?—sounded strange to my own ears.

Again, no response. No sound.

Khara and Renzo labored on, making slow headway, inch by inch. Ten minutes later, Renzo thrashed hard at an unyielding branch and gasped when it gave way to emptiness.

Cautiously, we peered through the hole they'd created.

"It's a clearing!" I said. "There are . . . waterfalls!"

We soon found ourselves standing in a large, open space. The sand vanished, and in its place was a thick carpet of red moss. "It's safe to walk on," Gambler reported, and Tobble and I leapt off his back.

The silence of the dense vegetation gave way to the sound of rushing water, mingled with an odd but lovely music. After the crushing quiet, it took a moment for my ears to adjust.

Before us lay a pool of water, perfectly circular, backed by a wall of glittering black stone. Small, thin waterfalls, perhaps a dozen, spouted from crevices in the rocks.

"Is that water?" asked Tobble. "The colors are so odd."

"It's beautiful, whatever it is," I said.

"Not sure I'd drink it, though," said Renzo.

The cascades varied in color: shades of amber, silver, and red. But as soon as they hit the waiting pool, the streams of water instantly turned black.

"That music," said Tobble. "It's coming from the water."

Indeed, Tobble was right. Each waterfall seemed to carry a separate tone with it. They mingled to make a sort of tuneless music, dreamy and haunting.

Sprouting from the pool were flowers on long, leafless stems. Each stem supported only one large golden blossom, spinning lazily, like a child's toy, and giving off a delicately sweet perfume.

The music, the perfume . . . It was familiar somehow.

Knowable.

Comforting.

I breathed in, trying to parse out the complicated smells. The scent from the flowers was overpowering. And yet something else, something familiar, I felt certain, was in the air.

A thought came to me, surprising as a shaft of sun through parted clouds, of the long-ago times when dairnes would celebrate belenmaas, nights when the moon was new and fresh and nothing but a sliver of silver. The whole pack would sing hopeful songs, sad ballads, boisterous tunes, always in perfect harmony, until the sun appeared.

I'd never experienced belenmaas, of course. By the time I was born, the few dairnes remaining in the world valued stealth over song. But my parents had taught us a bit of the old music, quietly humming us to sleep.

I closed my eyes, lulled by memory fragments of a song from my childhood. It was a simple tune, lilting. Silly.

Comforting.

I opened my eyes and breathed in again. Khara shot me a questioning look, but all I had to offer was a shrug. She loosened her sword in its scabbard. Renzo, too, had his knife at the ready.

Gambler broke the spell. "I smell human," he murmured. "Not long ago, either."

Human, yes. "I smell it, too," I said.

I motioned for my friends to stay put. Slowly I moved forward, not sure where I was going, but knowing I had to move.

Just beyond the waterfalls sat a long stone building with a thatched roof. No smoke rose from its chimney, and it had a deserted air about it. Still, the roof was in good repair, and someone had cut the grass back from the doorway to open a gravel-paved space around the building.

I moved closer.

The door creaked open.

The flowers spun. The waterfalls sang. The memories came.

Did I know before I saw, or see before I knew?

Did it matter?

No. All that mattered, all that mattered in the whole wide world, was that before me stood, at last, another dairne.

PART THREE
DESTINIES

26
Elexor

You are not alone.

The words from my dream came back to me.

It was true.

I was not alone, not anymore.

Before me stood another dairne. My blood. My own.

He was male and old, older than my father. His chin fur was gray, his tail white and thinning.

I moved toward him, forgetting caution, faster and faster until I was nearly running.

I came to a stop just inches away and said in the Common Tongue, my voice trembling, "Well met, father dairne. I am Byx."

He stared at me. Blinked. Cocked his head.

I was shaking, dizzy with expectation.

What would he say?

How would he greet me?

Would we embrace?

"Who are you?" the old dairne snapped. "This isn't what I expected."

I gulped, replaying the unexpected words in my head. They made no sense. Surely this dairne was happy to see me.

Surely he understood the importance of this moment.

"I—we are—" I stuttered. "I don't understand."

"Are you here to replace me?" the dairne said, his dim eyes brightening.

"Replace you?"

"But why else would you be here?" He peered at me, clearly disturbed. "It is strange that they would send one so young."

Khara came to my rescue. "My name is Khara," she said, running to my side. "This is Gambler, Renzo, and Tobble."

The dairne shook his head in irritation. "You are not at all what I was expecting. I was told to expect two spies, their men-at-arms, and a smuggler."

"May we know your name, old one?" Khara asked gently.

The dairne stiffened, as if it were an affront. "I am Elexor." His eyes narrowed in suspicion. "A name you should already know, if you have business here."

My mind galloped ahead, trying to understand what I was hearing, even as a cold hollow carved itself in my gut.

What was Elexor going on about? Didn't he know dairnes were thought to be extinct? Didn't he rejoice at seeing a young dairne?

"I think, Elexor," Khara said, "that you'd better tell us what is going on here."

"Who are you to demand explanations? Get off this island, all of you! You have no right to be here!"

Khara laid her hand on the hilt of her sword, but Gambler was more direct. He leapt the short distance between himself and Elexor and bared his gleaming incisors. "You can answer her questions," he said calmly, "or be my breakfast."

"Gambler! Be careful!" I cried automatically, even though I knew he wouldn't harm the old dairne.

After Gambler's show of strength, Elexor abandoned his objections. With much huffing and muttering, he led us into the stone building. It was clearly a dormitory or barracks, with four cots suitable for humans and a large straw mat that might make a bed for a felivet. A small kitchen space featured an open hearth, now cold, and a counter topped by pots and pans and crockery. Dog circled the room, sniffing with interest.

"What is this place?" Khara demanded. "And remember, we have a dairne of our own."

Elexor glanced at me and licked his lips. "It is as you see, a barracks."

"For whom?" Khara pressed.

No answer.

"All right, Gambler," Khara said, waving her hand in Elexor's direction. "Breakfast is served."

"No! No!" Elexor cried. "Would you leave my son an orphan?"

"Your son?" I blurted.

"He is innocent, a mere boy."

"I don't care if he's the crown prince," Khara snapped. "Tell us everything. Now!"

Elexor settled wearily onto a wooden chair. "The island is used to carry . . . certain individuals . . . between Nedarra and Dreyland."

"Certain individuals?" Khara asked.

Elexor shrugged and looked to the side. "Some in Nedarra are not great lovers of the Murdano. Some wish to leave Nedarra and live in Dreyland."

"Traitors?"

"You may call them that," Elexor said. "Though they would not use the term."

"We're supposed to believe you're helping refugees from Nedarra?" Khara asked.

"Yes," Elexor said, his palms upraised.

Khara turned to me. "It is a lie," I whispered, feeling, strangely, like a traitor to my own species.

"Tell us about these Nedarrans you transport," said Khara.

"They are . . ." A furious glance at me. "They are Nedarrans who may have reason to flee the Murdano."

Renzo spoke for the first time in a while. "And why should you help them?"

"I work for the Kazar Sg'drit," Elexor said, torn between putting on a proud front and some deeper shame. "My task is to question others. To discover whether the tales they bring are truth or lies."

"You were expecting new passengers here," Khara said. "Dreylanders?"

Elexor shifted uncomfortably. "Yes, some go from Dreyland to Nedarra. I also question them. And sometimes those same Dreylanders return, and I question them again."

Renzo laughed aloud. "Traitors one way and spies the other direction!"

"Those are your words," Elexor said. But he offered nothing more.

I sank onto one of the cots and put my head in my hands.

The dairne I had strived desperately to find, endangering not just myself but my friends, was a servant of Sg'drit.

He used his dairne abilities to check the stories of those claiming to defect to the Kazar's cause. And he transported spies into Nedarra, verifying their stories when they returned.

This was the dairne I'd dreamed so long of meeting?

"But how do you cause the island to obey your wishes?" Khara pressed.

"I don't, of course," Elexor said, trying to recover some fragment of his original arrogance. "No one commands the island but the natites."

Renzo narrowed his eyes. "The natites allow . . . support this?"

Elexor didn't answer. He didn't need to.

Khara looked at us. "If the natites are conspiring with Dreyland, and the terramants are controlled by the Kazar as well, there is no hope for Nedarra."

"Does it matter?" Renzo said cynically. "The Murdano or the Kazar, they're both power-hungry madmen anxious to start a war."

"I can never take the side of a valtti like this Sg'drit," Gambler said. "And my own family, my brothers and sisters, live in Nedarra."

"My family as well," Khara said. "Though I would be loath to do anything to aid the Murdano." She turned back to Elexor. "Your passengers heading south, when are you expecting them?"

"The galley should be coming at any time. I was only hoping to rouse my son to clean up. But he is a lazy child and not always obedient."

"Then we must leave if we are to avoid a fight we may well lose," Khara said.

Tobble raised his hand, a habit he had when interrupting.

"He mentioned a galley. In deep water a sailing boat may outrun a galley, but only if the wind is in our favor."

"What is a galley?" I asked.

"A boat that uses thralls to drive the oars. Some galleys have as many as twenty men, ten to a side. A galley cares nothing for wind. They have very shallow drafts, and thus may be hiding in a channel beyond our sight."

"What is this?"

It was a new voice, and we all spun to discover its origin.

My heart leapt.

There in the doorway stood another dairne.

27
Attack!

Elexor had said he had a son, a child. For some reason, I'd been expecting a much younger dairne, but this one appeared to be close to my own age.

He was a bit shorter than I, but broader in the shoulders, with glossy wheat-colored fur and large, teardrop-shaped ears.

Elexor, looking aggrieved and worried, said, "This is my son, Maxyn. As you see, he is just a child."

Maxyn rolled his eyes. He looked us over, one by one, settling at last on me. We stared at each other with frank curiosity. He was the first young dairne I had seen in a very long time.

It should have been a momentous occasion. The air should have been filled with songs of joy. But faced at last with two other members of my kind, faced with the undeniable evidence that I was not, in fact, an endling, I saw only Maxyn and his father.

They were not just an abstraction, the proof my species might yet survive. They were specific individuals.

It occurred to me, after what must have been an uncomfortably long pause, that Khara was waiting for me to say something. When I did nothing but gape openmouthed like a fool, she spoke up.

"I am Khara." She pointed to the rest of us. "Gambler, Renzo, Tobble, and, of course, Byx."

"Byx," Maxyn repeated.

I nodded my head too vigorously. Speech was still beyond me.

"But what is going on?" Maxyn asked.

"It seems your father is being used to assess the veracity of spies and traitors for the Kazar Sg'drit," Khara said bluntly.

"I know that. But . . ." Maxyn frowned. He had interesting eyes, darker than mine, storm-colored and hard to read. "But what does that have to do with all of you?"

We were, I admit, a motley crew, and I could well understand Maxyn's puzzlement.

"We have been . . . ," I said at last, my voice strange in my own ears. "We have been seeking dairnes. In Nedarra it is said that we are all gone, wiped out by the Murdano. I thought I was—"

I choked on the words. Embarrassed, I shook my head and looked pleadingly at Khara.

"Byx believed, feared, that she was an endling, the last dairne. We have been searching for more of her kind. We spotted this island in Nedarra and followed you here."

"But we are not the last of the dairnes," Elexor said.

It took a moment for his words to sink in. "We are . . . not?" I managed, and I feared I'd forgotten how to breathe.

"True, there are few of us left," Elexor said. "And what was once a small colony on this island is now reduced to just us two. But I am surprised you know nothing of the Pellago River colony. I've never been, but—"

"The Pellago River?" Khara interrupted. "But that's in northwest Nedarra, beyond my family's lands. That area is populated by fell beasts and monsters. No one goes there. Or if they do, they do not return."

"Perhaps," said Elexor. "But if that's what you seek, be on your way before the Kazar's men come. Time is short—"

Gambler's ears flicked, and the fur on his back stood up. "Too late," he said, unsheathing his claws. "They are here!"

Gambler was the first through the door, with Khara right behind, sword drawn.

Entering the clearing were a finely dressed man and woman, four men-at-arms, and what looked like a ruffian, carrying a wood staff with a heavy, knobbed end.

They spotted us at the same time we spotted them, but Khara was the more decisive commander. "Attack!" she cried.

Four men-at-arms, three others. Between them, they had five swords and one cudgel, plus anything that the woman might be hiding.

On our side, we had a young girl with a fabled sword, a thief with a shield and a knife, a wobbyk with nothing but his own unpredictable capacity for anger, and me, with a knife I liked to think of as a sword.

And Dog, of course.

But we had one other thing: a felivet.

I will never understand how Gambler can move like lightning and still seem graceful and almost relaxed. He ran, leapt, let loose a terrifying roar, and hit the nearest man-at-arms while snagging a second with one extended paw.

Khara swung her sword at a third soldier. He parried well, but his weapon was no match for the Light of Nedarra. Khara's sword broke his in half, and with a backhand swipe, she sent him running.

The woman screamed, clutching at her male companion as he struggled to draw his bejeweled sword.

Renzo smashed the edge of his shield down on the man, who crumpled to the ground. Just like that, the odds were better. We now faced one soldier and two civilians.

The big one with the staff was brave, an experienced fighter, and he caught Renzo in the back with a wide swing of his staff. Renzo cried out in pain and fell hard.

I had my knife out, but I'd learned only one move. I shouted in a mix of terror and determination and ran straight at the big man as he aimed his staff toward me. But I can be quick when I need to be. I threw myself at the ground between his legs and slashed at a knee. I felt the blade encounter resistance.

Hitting the dirt knocked all the wind from my lungs. I lay helpless, struggling for air. Out of the corner of my eye, I noticed the remaining soldier turn tail and run, yelling, "Help! Help!"

With effort, I crawled a few feet and rolled over. To my relief, the big man with the staff was teetering. Blood soaked his pant leg. He looked at me in surprise, blinked, as if unable to believe what he was seeing, and fell to his knees.

Gambler had an expression on his face that I was glad had never been used against me. Khara's blade was stained red. Renzo was getting awkwardly to his feet, clutching his back and wincing in pain.

I heard something fly past, just as Renzo threw himself into Khara. An arrow, right where Khara had been a split second before. Someone cried out in surprise, and I saw the arrow's feathered shaft protruding from Elexor's chest.

"Father!" Maxyn screamed. As Elexor fell, Maxyn caught him. A second arrow flew and grazed Gambler.

The fleeing soldier had come back with an archer.

It might take an experienced archer three seconds to fit a new shaft, draw, and aim. But it took a fraction of that time for Gambler to leap and sink his teeth into the man.

The remaining soldier dropped to his knees and held his hands high in the air. "I yield, I yield!"

Khara had her blade at his throat in an instant. "Are there any more soldiers coming?"

"N-n-no! No!"

"How did you come here?"

"The galley," the soldier yelped.

"Tobble, tie him up," Khara ordered. "Gambler, with me!" The two of them raced off toward the water.

I knelt next to Elexor, across from Maxyn. Elexor still lived, but I doubted he would for long. The arrow was buried deep in his chest and every breath was an effort.

"My son," Elexor gasped.

"Father!"

I said, "We can try to pull the arrow out."

"Sg'drit's men use barbed arrowheads," Maxyn said bitterly.

The two civilians, the expensively dressed man and woman, remained. The man had struggled to his feet after the hit from Renzo, but seeing how things were going, he threw his sword to the ground. "I am not a soldier!" he declared.

"No, just a spy," Renzo snarled, grunting at the pain in his back.

Khara and Gambler came running back, looking relieved. "The galley is moored just a hundred yards over there," Khara said. "There are six rowers, all captured Nedarrans who would be glad to row back to Nedarra."

I tried to focus on their words, but all I could think about was the old dairne lying on the ground nearby, cradled by his son.

"How is he?" I asked gently.

Maxyn looked at me with pure hatred.

"He's dead," he said. "He's dead because of you."

28
The Galley Chase

Tears poured from my eyes. Losing a parent was unbearable. And in such a violent way . . . I knew, all too well, how it felt.

"I'm so sorry, Maxyn," I managed.

"Spare me your pity."

"I know what you are feeling," I said, wiping my cheeks with the back of my hand.

"How could you possibly know?" His voice was harsh, but his hand on his father's arm was tender.

"I know," I said simply. "You can't stay here. I know you want to, but you just can't. You have to come with us for your own safety."

"I take no orders from those who cost my father his life," Maxyn said, fighting back his own tears.

"Stay here only if you wish to die," Renzo advised.

"Do you threaten me?" Maxyn demanded.

"No," Renzo said as he helped Tobble tie up the men and woman. "But when the Kazar's soldiers get here, they may well blame you for what's happened. When people are angry, they tend to focus on the nearest available suspect."

I was about to tell Maxyn that Renzo spoke the truth, but of course he knew.

"Listen, please, Maxyn," I said, taking his arm, only to have him shake me off. "For all we know, you and I may be the only surviving dairnes—"

"Nonsense. My father spoke often of the Pellago River colony."

"And he surely believed that. But are you certain he was right? And without us, how would you ever reach that colony?"

Maxyn didn't answer. His eyes were cold. I expected no more: he had just lost his father. But he knew I spoke the truth.

"We need to get moving," Khara said.

"Maxyn, please," I said.

"Leave me," he whispered, stroking his father's head. "Leave *us*."

Reluctantly, I followed Khara and the others to the galley. I must have turned around a dozen times to check on Maxyn, hoping against hope that he'd realized he should join us.

"Give him a moment," Khara advised. "He may yet come."

The galley was low-slung, long and sleek. Twelve oars stood tall like small masts, resting in their oarlocks. Between the oars were six men, all kept imprisoned by chains around their ankles.

Khara climbed aboard. Without saying a word, she brought the edge of the Light of Nedarra down on the central chain lock.

For a moment the rowers sat in stunned paralysis, followed by loud rattling as they pulled the chain through their shackles. Cautiously, still fearful, they stood.

Khara hopped onto a barrel set amidships and, in a loud, confident voice, said, "You are free men. You may stay or leave, as is your rightful choice. But know that we are taking this galley to Nedarra. If you stay, you will row, and row hard. But you will row as free men going home!"

All six men chose to stay. But one, older and gray-bearded, said, "I am called Norbert. Our gratitude knows no bounds. We are, and will always be, in debt to you. But in Nedarra, many of us have oaths of long standing to fulfill. Do you call on us to forsake our oaths and swear loyalty to you?"

Khara took a moment to consider. We were heading to Nedarra, but we would need to sneak in around the Murdano's patrol boats, and perhaps around the natites.

"Yes," she said. "You have a debt to me and to my companions. To repay that debt I require the following: that you obey my orders—all my orders, without hesitation—until we reach safety in Nedarra. Once we are safely ashore, you will go your own ways, and we will go ours. That will erase your debt, and from then on you must each do as your conscience directs."

Norbert looked around at his companions, who nodded vigorously. "We swear to obey all your orders without hesitation, until we are safely ashore in Nedarra."

"Good," Khara said. "Because we have little time." She pointed her sword toward a second galley in the distance. It was far larger, and pulling quickly toward the island.

"Norbert," Khara instructed, "take three of your men. Gather up any weapons you find, and any food, as well. Renzo, take the remaining men and fill every water bottle or barrel you can find from the stream there. Tobble, familiarize yourself with the workings of this boat. And quickly! Quickly! That galley will be here all too soon."

Khara turned to me. "Byx, you must deal with Maxyn."

I nodded. "I will try," I said.

Maxyn was still by his father's side, where we'd left him. He was crying softly.

He didn't seem surprised that I'd returned. "I beg you to respect my father's . . . my father's body," he said when I knelt next to him. "If you could perhaps build a fire. It doesn't have to be large. We are small creatures, after all." He met my eyes, and it was like seeing a mirror of my own pain. "We dairnes."

Maxyn managed to make the request without breaking down in sobs, but my own eyes spilled tears.

One more dead dairne, and with so few to spare.

Gambler, passing by, overheard Maxyn's request. "It will be done," he said.

I held out my hand. "Please come with us, Maxyn," I said. "There's nothing for you here. Not anymore. And there are so very few of . . . of us."

He took a steadying breath and stood, refusing my hand. As he trudged toward the galley, he glanced back only once, to the spot where Gambler was gently preparing Elexor's body.

When Maxyn and I climbed on board, Khara gave me a small nod.

It wasn't long before Norbert and his crew were back at the galley, carrying heavy loads of weapons and armor. Renzo and the other men returned at the same time, dragging waterskins and canteens.

The oncoming galley had cut its distance from the island by half. Even without Tobble's Far-Near, we could see that it had twenty-four oars and carried at least a dozen soldiers.

How had they come to realize what was going on here? I glanced up and saw that most innocuous of seaside sights: gulls wheeling. Perhaps one of them had carried tales? Or had a treasonous raptidon passed overhead?

"Gambler!" Khara cried. "Tobble! Are we ready to push off?"

"Yes!" Tobble confirmed from his position at the tiller.

One of the freed men came up to Khara and said, "I am called Aloish. I know these waters well."

I nodded, confirming that this was the truth, and Aloish went to confer with Tobble.

I smelled something and turned back to the island. A small tendril of smoke rose from the trees.

"Gambler is coming," I said, glancing at Maxyn.

"Men, to your oars! Shove off!" Khara cried, and just as we cast off, Gambler came bounding toward us. He sailed effortlessly through the air, landing with perfect nonchalance on the deck.

"Gambler," Renzo chided, "now you're just showing off."

"I might deny that, if we had no truth-telling dairnes with us," Gambler said.

Maxyn met Gambler's eyes. "Thank you," he said, staring back at the twirling ribbon of smoke.

Gambler nodded solemnly. "I am sorry for your loss."

"Down oars!" Norbert commanded. He took an oar himself and yelled, "Will someone work the drum and set the pace?"

Near the stern sat a large drum covered in stretched animal skin. As I had no other job to perform, I settled on the tiny round stool next to it, lifted the mallet, and banged the drum once, producing a satisfying sound.

"Like this," Norbert said, clapping. "Beat . . . beat . . . beat!"

I mimicked the rhythm, and the galley surged so suddenly that I nearly fell off my stool. I continued at a steady pace until Norbert called, "Double time!"

Renzo took the place temporarily left vacant by Aloish, the man who'd claimed knowledge of the waters. He was pulling hard, muscles straining, and making rueful remarks about his own relative weakness compared to the rowers near him. They were smiling now, rowing with all their might.

We raced through the water, sending up a fine bow wave. But the other galley veered to intercept us, and they were faster still. The border of Nedarra was many leagues to our south, around the mountains that ran down into the sea. We would not be safe from the Kazar's troops until then, and to my unpracticed eye, it did not look as if we would make it.

Khara and Tobble conferred with Aloish, and after a moment, she came to me as I beat my drum. "Aloish says there's a shoal ahead, a submerged reef. If we can reach it before the Kazar's galley gets to us, we will clear it. The other galley, which sits lower in the water, may be stopped."

"Let us hope," I said, pounding away.

"Let us do more than hope," Khara said. "Norbert? Give us the beat for full speed."

"Beat, beat, beat, beat!" he yelled.

I copied the rhythm, and the galley, which had already seemed to me to be moving with unsafe speed, seemed to fly across the water.

Khara occupied her time carrying water to the rowers. They seemed shocked by the gesture, and I doubted they'd ever been shown such courtesy. I'd seen the whip lying on the deck near my feet.

After a while, Maxyn took over the water duties from Khara. His face betrayed no emotion, but I knew what he was feeling, and I wished there was something I could do or say.

The chase was not a matter of minutes, but of hours, as the two boats, coming from different angles, raced to an intersection that would mean our doom, if it came even a few seconds too soon.

The men were weary, but they kept rowing, sweat pouring as they grimaced at the pace. I was doing a mere fraction of their work, and I was exhausted.

Beat, beat, beat, beat, beat. The distance between us and our pursuers lessened with each stroke. We were two sides of a triangle, converging on an apex. They were near enough that I could differentiate the determined faces of the men, glaring at us from beneath their silver helmets.

I watched as one of those men stepped away from the others. He had something in his hand. Was it—?

"Arrow!" I yelled.

The arrow flew in a low arc and struck the water. But it was only twenty feet short. Soon we would be within range.

Sure enough, the next arrow hit the side of the galley with a thunk.

"Khara!" Tobble cried. "The wind has shifted. We can raise sail!"

Aloish ran to comply, but now there were two archers firing at us, and the arrows flew with terrifying speed and increasing accuracy. One of the rowers was hit in the leg. Grimacing in pain, he kept rowing, despite the shaft sticking out of him.

An arrow hit the mast, just missing Maxyn, who erupted in sudden fury. He jumped to his feet, yanked the arrow out of the mast, and threw it back toward our pursuers.

A brave gesture, but it did not stop the arrow that pierced a rower's arm. Aloish jumped to take his place, so we lost very little speed, but we had no speed to spare.

And then came a beautiful sight. The sail Tobble had called for filled with wind and billowed to life.

Off we flew, an arrow in our own right, straight and true and deadly fast.

29
Dabyrro

The wind was our friend. The next volley of arrows struck only our wake.

"The reef is ahead!" Aloish yelled to Tobble. "Veer two degrees to port!"

We turned sharply, toward a line of troubled water flanked by two black rocks protruding from the sea. Tobble sent us straight into the trough of white foam between the rocks.

I kept up my drumbeat, while the exhausted rowers kept pushing and pulling their oars. When I glanced at the pursuing galley, I saw anxious looks. They knew these waters, too, and knew we were racing toward a submerged reef.

No doubt they were calculating their own odds. Perhaps if they caught a wave just right, they could manage the maneuver. The alternative was to sheer off and lose us.

"Oars up!" Tobble cried.

The oars rose clear of the water, but not before one oar struck a submerged rock and splintered.

My stomach dropped as we flew through the gap like a sled on an icy hill.

"Oars down!" Tobble cried. "Byx! Regular time!"

I began beating again, but more slowly. *Beat. Beat. Beat.*

It was painfully clear that if the other galley cleared the reef, it would catch us. All of us, even the straining rowers, watched with dread as the galley rose on a wave, surging forward.

I heard a sickening crunch, a rending of timbers. The galley had come to a stop. The next wave lifted it off the reef and seemed poised to send it through, but the galley did not move quickly enough. The wave slipped away and the galley's stern landed hard on the rocks.

"Yes!" I shouted, and cheers broke out from all of us— cheers that ceased altogether as we watched the galley come apart like a flimsy toy. Men spilled into the water, screaming with terror.

Maybe a few would find wreckage to keep them afloat. Maybe a few could swim well enough that they had a chance to reach shore. But most, we feared, would drown.

Gambler seemed to read my thoughts. "It is good to survive," he said. "But that does not make it any easier to watch men die."

We sailed on quietly after that. The weary oarsmen, including Renzo, rested and ate, while Khara tended to their wounds and blistered palms. Gambler settled onto a sunny spot near the bow, like a carved figurehead at the prow of a great ship. Tobble leaned against the tiller, enjoying the calm waters, his big ears fluttering in the breeze.

I joined Maxyn in the stern. He was gazing back at Tarok, now just a spot on the horizon, and stroking Dog's head.

I passed him a waterskin. "Thank you," he said, without meeting my eyes.

Many questions filled my head, but I knew to hold my tongue. Instead I simply said, "I'm sorry for all that's happened."

Maxyn took a long swig from the waterskin. "I know it's not your fault," he said flatly. "Not any of yours." He looked so much like my oldest brother, Avar: same skeptical gaze, same dense, golden fur. "It's nobody's fault. This is what happens when there's war."

"There's no war yet," I said.

"There will be." Maxyn turned, leaning against the polished wood rail so that we were face-to-face.

"Only fools know both the beginning and the end of the story," I said.

Maxyn frowned. "What?"

"My father used to say that. He liked sayings and proverbs and such."

"All I know is, I've spent the past year watching spies come and go. Trust me. A war is coming, and soon."

For a few minutes, we didn't speak, but curiosity quickly got the better of me. "Have you always lived on Tarok?" I asked.

Maxyn nodded. "I was born there. My mother died giving birth to me."

"I'm sorry."

"Again: not your fault."

"It must have been strange, floating from place to place for all those years," I mused. "And on a carnivorous island, no less."

Maxyn smiled for the first time since I'd met him. "Carnivorous? Rooklets like Tarok live on seaweed. Every now and then they'll eat baitfish like smelt."

"But we've heard stories—"

"That's all they were. Old tales. Probably started by the natites. They love their legends." He nodded. "Impressive, you and your friends going to an island you thought might eat you."

"My friends are loyal indeed. They knew how important it was to me to find more dairnes."

We shared a smile, and I realized, with a sudden pang,

how long it had been since I'd been able to do that with a fellow dairne.

"Were you and your father the only dairnes on the island?" I asked.

Maxyn shook his head. "Not when I was growing up. There were maybe a dozen of us. Some moved on, some died, and these past couple years, it's just been my father"—he paused, his voice catching—"my father and me."

"We learned a poem about a colony of dairnes that lived on an island." I reached into my pouch and withdrew my smudged map. Shyly, I handed it to Maxyn.

"Dairneholme, yes. At the center of the island. About all that's left of it is that barracks building you saw." He nodded, studying the worn playa leaf. "My father told me stories about it. Many generations ago, there was a thriving colony on Tarok." He gave a little shrug. "Sorry to disappoint you. It's just down to me, it seems."

I tucked the map back into my pouch. "But perhaps there are more dairnes at the Pellago River colony?"

"Perhaps." Maxyn sighed. He looked weary, and I realized what a terrible toll this day must have taken on him.

"You should rest," I said. "I'll get a blanket."

I scrounged through our supplies, tossed into the galley in haste during our frantic escape, until I located a worn blanket. By the time I returned to the stern, Maxyn was curled up in a tight ball on the deck, eyes closed. When I covered him with the blanket, his lids flickered.

"Dabyrro," he murmured.

It took me a moment to realize what I'd heard.

Dabyrro. *Thank you* in Dairnish.

"Rhen eh taber," I whispered back.

Glad to help.

And I was. So very glad.

As we wafted south on a mild breeze, with Aloish trimming the sail, I joined Tobble at the tiller. "Captain Tobble," I said, "you did some fine sailing today."

"Thank you," Tobble said, eyes on the waves. Whitecaps spread before us like an endless blue meadow of snow-frosted hills. "How is Maxyn faring?"

"As well as anyone might," I said.

"I am happy for you, Byx," Tobble said. "Happy and relieved. I was so afraid we might not find another dairne after all we've been through. I know he is but one. Still, it means hope. For you. And for all dairnes."

What had I done to deserve such a fine and loyal companion? I wondered.

"Dabyrro, Tobble," I said softly.

"What's that mean?"

"It means I shall never be able to repay you for your friendship."

"I know how you can repay me."

"How?"

"Take the tiller for a moment. My paws are weary." He stepped aside. "Don't worry. I won't leave your side."

I felt the ancient pull of the sea in my hands as I gripped the tiller hard. My heart felt strangely full, as if my chest might burst, and I realized what the unfamiliar feeling was.

Joy, plain and simple.

I had a gentle wind at my back.

A dear friend at the helm.

A band of loyal companions at the ready.

And one of my own, a kindred soul, a dairne, by my side at last.

30
The Natites

By late afternoon, we'd passed the invisible line between Dreyland and Nedarra, feeling content that our worries were over for the moment.

We knew, of course, that our eventual landing would mean renewed danger.

But that was down the road. For the time being, we had good wind and calm seas.

Unfortunately, Khara's earlier worry about the natites proved true.

The seas belonged to them.

They arrived just as the sun was dropping beneath the horizon like a gold coin tossed into the waters. I caught a flash of movement starboard: a dolphin, I assumed.

But this dolphin shot up out of the water and landed on the deck, dripping wet. Another came, and then another, and in seconds the galley was hosting half a dozen natites, all armed with deadly javelins.

Khara drew her sword, but the first natite aboard held up a hand, palm out, and said, "Before you threaten me, kindly look around you."

Khara did—we all did—and what we saw were a dozen or more natites in the water, heads and shoulders in the air, javelins at the ready.

"If those are not enough," the natite said confidently, "I can always summon more. You will lower your sail."

"Take the sail in," Khara muttered to Aloish. He did as instructed, and instantly the galley slowed.

"I am called Emecktril in the Common Tongue. I've come to investigate you, as this craft is not known by us to be native to these waters. Who speaks for you?"

Most eyes turned to Khara, some to Norbert. But the man deferred to Khara with a gracious nod.

"I do," Khara said.

Emecktril was the height of a man, somewhat larger and stronger-looking than the first natite I had seen back on the Isle of Ursina. He had the bow-front face and head of his kind, tentacles that rose from his back, and dark green and turquoise scales. I was surprised to see his two wide, webbed feet. I'd thought Natites only used fishlike tails.

"I know that you have paid the blood tax," Emecktril said

to Khara. "But that entitled you to passage only to and from the Isle of Scholars."

"We intended no disrespect or violation," Khara said. "But we had no choice. We were pursued by enemies and—"

Emecktril cut her off with an impatient wave. "Yes, and those who pursued you threaten you no longer."

None of us could hide our surprise. We all knew that natites had some means of communicating over vast distances at impossible speeds. Still, it was disturbing that Emecktril, like the terramants, knew of events that were mere hours old.

"What we do not yet know is your purpose, Kharassande of the Donatis."

I noticed Norbert glancing sharply at Khara, but he said nothing.

Khara took a deep breath. "We have been searching for living dairnes to join with our friend, Byx."

Emecktril looked me over and nodded. "Yes, we know of this one." He turned his semi-opaque gaze on Maxyn. "This one we recognize from Tarok. And these humans would be the galley thralls."

"They are free men now," Khara said firmly.

Emecktril sniffed. "That is a land affair, and none of our concern."

I saw the dangerous light in Khara's eyes and knew she was becoming angry. "Yet you *do* concern yourselves with the affairs of land by allowing the sentient islands to move spies and traitors between Nedarra and Dreyland."

Her words earned a natite smile, which looked almost comically like a gaping fish mouth. "Do you now wish to lecture me on political matters far above your station?" Emecktril asked with a sneer.

"War is coming."

"A land war. Which is of no concern to us."

Khara shot me a look. "Byx?" she asked.

I swallowed hard and said, "The natite lies."

Emecktril didn't seem overly upset. In fact, he laughed, a low, liquid, gargling sound. "I see the dairne talent is more than a myth. I will amend my statement. We do as we choose, when we choose, for reasons that are our own."

"Actions that may result in tens of thousands of deaths," Khara said.

Emecktril considered for a moment, nodded, as if to himself, and said, "This matter requires further thought."

With that, he waved his back tentacles in a pattern that must have had meaning, for there was a sudden flurry of activity from the natites still in the water. Those aboard, all but Emecktril, leapt over the side to join them.

All at once, to my utter shock, the deck fell away below my feet. The galley sank with sudden, plunging speed. But even as we all cried out in panic, it became clear that the entire galley was sinking within a massive bubble of air. The water rose, blue-green and foaming, around us, but it did not even touch us.

As the sea closed over our heads, many of the rowers wailed in terror. I was just as frightened, but I bit off the screams rising within my throat.

The water grew murkier as we dropped, but I could easily make out dozens of natites swooping and diving. They looked as at home in the water as the curious fish cruising past to investigate the odd disruption in their neighborhood.

I made my way to the railing of the galley and looked down. Far below us was what looked like a submerged city, as if an island had been swallowed by the sea. It was not as vast as Saguria, nor even as extensive as the Isle of Ursina, but it was greater than a village. Strange, spiraling buildings made of pink coral and gold stone rose up from the sandy bottom.

Behind the village was a jagged crack in the sea floor, and from this crack rose a furious bubbling. I had the sense, though I couldn't be certain, that a peculiar yellow glow emanated from the bubbles.

Soon we were sinking past the tallest of the coral-and-stone buildings, aiming, it seemed, for an open square facing a grand palatial structure.

The palace, like all the natite buildings, was a lattice of structural beams resolving into floors. There were no walls, meaning that water could flow through unimpeded. I saw no doors, either. The effect was eerie, but strangely lovely.

On some floors, adult natite groups were visible, busy at work I could not begin to comprehend. Other floors housed great nets filled with smooth eggs the size of a dairne's head. In a few areas, I could just make out what looked like dense schools of tadpoles, guarded by sturdy-looking, heavily armed natite warriors.

"That's a nursery," Renzo said. "It may be that this entire, impossible town is a nursery."

We came to rest in an open space, the galley crunching loudly on coral paving stones. I looked at my companions, all of whom shared an expression of utter disbelief.

We were in a bubble on the ocean's floor. If the bubble popped, we would all die.

We were in the land of the natites. And we were completely at their mercy.

31
Grendwallif

"I will take two humans as well as the dairnes," Emecktril announced. He squinted at Gambler. "And the felivet and wobbyk, I suppose."

"What about Dog?" Renzo asked. "He stays with me, no matter what."

"Fine. Bring the canine as well," said Emecktril with a wave of his hand.

"Where are you taking us?" Khara demanded, trying to assert her authority in a place where no one but a natite could have any sway.

"Surely we cannot leave this bubble?" Maxyn asked, sounding as afraid as I felt.

"We have our ways," Emecktril said smugly. "Stand before me."

We all stood nervously. The natite closed his eyes and

began to mutter strange, indecipherable words in a dialect I had never heard.

"Tamak on maaginen colloitsu, joka trojuu vett'ank antar simulle heng itsken," he murmured.

"He's weaving a theurgic spell," Renzo said.

I suppose he meant to reassure us, but his words failed. I felt something spreading across my body, as if someone were covering my fur with jelly. It was at once invisible and disturbingly slimy. When the goo made its way to my face, I felt a moment of panic.

"Now, follow me." Emecktril stepped directly through the side of the huge, transparent sac surrounding our galley. Amazingly, the bubble remained intact.

Emecktril turned and gestured impatiently.

Khara went first. Safely on the other side, she took a wary breath. Her eyes widened, and she motioned us to follow.

It was perhaps the strangest thing I have ever experienced. Slipping through the bubble barrier was painless. There I was, underwater—far underwater—and yet my fur remained dry. When I took a tentative breath, I tasted only cool, clean air.

My feet touched wet sand and I found I could walk, but with the resistance you might expect from water. Each step was slow and laborious. Emecktril floated in his natural element, swimming forward in a leisurely fashion with little kicks from his webbed feet, while steering with his webbed hands.

It was like having a savrielle dream, strange and unreal without being frightening. Shimmering fish fluttered past my face. An octopus scuttled across the sea floor, raising a small cloud of sand. Natites passed us alone or in groups, while others busied themselves in what seemed to be large birthing rooms in separate buildings. Maxyn nudged me, and I followed his gaze to see a collection of eggs, perhaps a hundred, held in place by a loose net. While we watched, the eggs hatched, extruding tendrils of purple liquid. As the tadpoles swam free of their egg casings, three natites used small nets to shoo the newborns to the next level of the nursery.

Emecktril led us into a large building. It was open on all sides but contained a sort of building-within-a-building, a windowless cube with a single entrance. Emecktril opened the door and moved through. So did we, and all at once we were in air again. The absence of watery resistance made me stumble, and Maxyn caught my arm.

The room was absolutely bare, with no sort of furniture or adornment. "What is this place?" Khara asked.

"It is called an interface. A place where natites can allow air breathers to be at ease."

I was definitely not at ease. In fact, I was still verging on panic each time I remembered the hundred feet of water between me and the atmosphere. But I was quickly distracted by an arrival.

The door swung open, and a large natite head poked inside. "Ah! I see you are already here!"

The head, broader, less sleek, with startlingly blue eyes, was followed by a long body, three times the length of Emeck-tril. Once inside, the creature filled a quarter of the space.

"Welcome, welcome," the new arrival said cheerfully. "I am Grendwallif, the Elect of this hatchery."

I had never met, seen, heard of, or imagined such a thing as a cheerful natite. But cheerful she was.

"Emecktril! Have some refreshments brought for our honored guests. And what are those things . . . I forget what they're called. Humans use them. They place their rear fatty sections on them and—"

"Chairs, Elect," Emecktril offered. "They are en route."

Two new natites appeared, hauling what were arguably chairs fashioned out of coral.

"Ah, there! Do please use them," Grendwallif the Elect said.

As soon as Khara had seated herself, Grendwallif cried, "Oh, I want to try one!" She settled into one of the far-too-small chairs uncomfortably for a moment before ceding it to me. "Well," she said ruefully, "to each her own, eh?"

Soon food appeared: raw fish, something green that was

bitter to the taste, and, to our delight, a teapot and cups. The tea was hot and a little sweet—not wonderful, but drinkable and most welcome.

Grendwallif waited impatiently while we ate, moving back and forth, two strides in each direction. Every so often she muttered, "I must practice my dry-walking skills."

Finally Khara said, "Grendwallif the Elect, may I know the reason for this meeting?"

"Oh, of course!" Grendwallif exclaimed. "Mind you, I am no diplomat, nor am I a warrior, nor yet a leader, except of this small hatchery. Still, I have been tasked with discovering your purpose." She clapped her webbed hands together. "And so let us begin, shall we?"

32
A Curse and a Prophecy

"We are on our way to Nedarra," Khara answered cautiously, "having freed some galley thralls who wished to return home."

The Elect's brilliant blue eyes blinked. First a translucent lid closed, then an opaque lid. Then they opened in reverse order. "That does not explain why you are traveling with two dairnes, a wobbyk, and a felivet."

I wondered why, if Grendwallif was a mere hatchery supervisor, she was questioning us, but realized I was probably seeing more evidence of the natite ability to share information over vast distances.

Khara shrugged. "We had a common purpose: to find living dairnes."

"And you found these two?"

"Byx"—Khara indicated me—"has been with us from

the start. The slaughter of her people left her without home or family."

Grendwallif winced. Insofar as I could read natite facial expressions, it seemed to me she was genuinely sympathetic. "What a terrible thing!"

"The Murdano's Seer, Araktik, declared dairnes extinct. We endeavor to see whether this is true."

Grendwallif nodded. "To preserve a species is a noble cause. But is it your only cause?"

For once, Khara was caught off guard. "It is the cause that unites us."

It sounded evasive, and Grendwallif's smile was tolerant. "Ah, this is when I wish I were a diplomat. I would perhaps find a better way to say what I must, which is that your answer is . . . incomplete. Is that not so, my dairne friends?"

Now I was the one caught off guard. As I hesitated, Maxyn spoke. "Her answer is true but incomplete."

"Perhaps you will complete the answer, Maxyn the dairne."

"After they came to my home, my father was killed."

Grendwallif recoiled in horror. "Can this be true?"

"It was not their doing," Maxyn said.

"We never meant any harm to come to Maxyn's father," said Khara. "We were searching for dairnes on the sentient island of Tarok."

"And what do you know of Tarok?" asked the Elect, her tone grave.

Khara said, "We know it is used to transport spies and traitors. We know that Maxyn's father was used by the Kazar Sg'drit to test the veracity of all passengers and report back to the Kazar."

"Ah. And you surmise that we natites allowed this to go on, yes?"

Khara nodded.

"Drench me," Grendwallif said. A hatch opened directly over her head and seawater cascaded down like a tiny waterfall, wetting Grendwallif's drying scales. The water pooled around our feet, then vanished.

Grendwallif heaved a sigh and said, "We do not interfere in the affairs of air breathers. This means allowing the passage of boats or even islands, so long as the blood tax has been collected and tariffs have been paid. Sometimes that tariff is in the form of an object we cannot make ourselves. Other times the tariff is . . . information."

Khara understood before I did. "You were being kept informed of what happened on the sentient island."

Grendwallif nodded and smiled. "Understand that this is not my usual function. I am here to watch over the young ones. To protect them. But here I am, and here you are, so the unpleasant duty of questioning you falls to me. I don't wish or intend to be rude."

Khara nodded. Renzo rolled his eyes. Gambler studied a paw intently.

"Here is the thing," Grendwallif said regretfully. "Your story is still incomplete. Will you, Kharassande of the Donatis, show me your sword?"

Khara had no choice. She drew her sword and handed it hilt-first to Grendwallif. The big natite examined it with care.

"Great and ancient theurgy hangs about this sword," Grendwallif pronounced. "This is no sword for a simple girl leading a small expedition to find dairnes. This is a sword of great significance, is it not?"

"Yes," Khara admitted.

"Will you name your sword for me?"

"It is called the Light of Nedarra."

Grendwallif's face lost its cheerfulness. "It is as we suspected. So. War comes, and soon our waters will be poisoned by the bodies of dead air breathers."

"But I am not the cause of a war," Khara protested.

"No," Grendwallif acknowledged. "But I see you do not know the spells that surround your sword, Kharassande of the Donatis. Air breather theurgy is crude but powerful. Its secrets are not secrets to natite eyes. We see what air breathers merely feel."

Khara exchanged confused looks with us. "What spells are you talking about?"

"A destiny spell woven by a sorcerer of great power and deep understanding. The sword has power of the conventional kind. It is sharp and heavy and made of a metal whose secrets have long been lost. It carries smaller spells as well, the kind that hide its glory and make it appear a simple, rusty object until drawn in anger."

Khara nodded. "I know of those spells."

"A spell of destiny underlies all other magic, a curse and a prophecy. This sword will be drenched in blood in a great war. I feel the awakening of this ancient magic. Its time is coming." Grendwallif used one of her tentacles to hand the sword back to Khara, as if anxious to rid herself of it.

For a while the Elect stood silent and unmoving, her eyes focused on nothing in particular. I guessed that she was conferring with other natites, perhaps many leagues away.

When she spoke again, her tone was stern. "You must tell me what you intend, Kharassande of the Donatis."

"I . . ." Khara shook her head. "I have no plans."

"Perhaps, but you have a dream, do you not?"

Khara seemed to debate with herself, her expression by turns angry, worried, and, finally, accepting.

"Yes, I dream," she said. She did not look at any of us as she spoke. "I dream of returning to my father and raising an army."

I glanced at Renzo and Gambler. Neither looked entirely surprised.

"And for which side would this army of yours fight?"

"For neither side!" Khara said hotly. "I would stop the fighting. I would use whatever power I have, whatever power this sword holds, to stop the war."

"A peacemaking sword?" Grendwallif was skeptical.

"Yes," Khara said. She was flushed, as if embarrassed by this admission, her voice soft but edged with resolve.

Perhaps I should not have been surprised. I had never asked Khara directly whether she had plans, beyond keeping us all alive.

But Grendwallif's face did not convey disbelief or scorn. On the contrary, she seemed saddened. "So much blood will be spilled to make what you air breathers call 'peace.'"

"We had heard . . . we had come to believe . . . that your people were not neutral," Khara ventured.

"No, we are not neutral," Grendwallif said. "We oppose any who would poison the seas or the rivers that feed it. We know that the Murdano fights for human dominance, even if it means destroying all other species. And we know that if the Kazar prevails, he will do no better. Fools, both! Do they not understand that every creature is connected to all others? Do they imagine that annihilating some species and enslaving others will not spread sickness and despair through all living things?"

"But—" I blurted, before shutting my mouth.

"Speak, Byx," Grendwallif said.

"But don't you natites have the power to stop the war by yourselves?"

"We could try. But by interfering in the affairs of air breathers, would we not then become their enemies? The oceans are vast, but not endless, while the greed and ambition of humans"—she glanced at Gambler—"and, it seems, felivets, is without end."

Renzo cleared his throat. "What, then, will you do with us, Elect?"

Once again Grendwallif fell silent, listening to soundless voices. At last she looked at Khara—only at Khara—and said, "We will not interfere in this, your destiny. But hear this, Kharassande of the Donatis: if you come to power, remember this day. Remember your vulnerability. Remember that you owe your life to the natites."

I expected Khara to deny such a possibility, to dismiss the idea as an absurd fantasy. But I was wrong.

"Grendwallif the Elect, so long as I live, I will remember not just your kindness, but your words of wisdom as well. For I, too, believe that all living things are connected, each dependent on the others. And I will be a friend to your people."

33
Khara's Dream

The natites returned us to the surface, our bodies and our boat intact. The relief of being back above water, breathing actual air, left us all grinning. Quickly we skimmed away on a strong breeze.

Norbert approached me and said, "Friend dairne, I would speak with Khara, and I desire your presence to say whether I speak truth."

I agreed, mystified.

Sitting before Khara, Norbert looked extremely uncomfortable, but also extremely determined. "I have something to say."

"Of course," she said.

"I did not know that you were of the Donatis. I must tell you that I am sworn to the Corpli family."

The Corplis. Luca's clan.

Khara nodded cautiously. "I see."

"The Donatis are sworn enemies of my liege lord."

"Yes, sadly. We would not have it be so."

"Your father and some of his people still raid on Corpli land," Norbert said.

Khara's jaw clenched dangerously, but she took a steadying breath. "There have been many transgressions on both sides. But in a time when terrible war threatens, I would . . ." She stopped herself and frowned. "My father would that we were allies."

Norbert shook his head. "That is not a decision for me to make, Kharassande of the Donatis. I can only obey my liege lord."

"I understand."

"But I have also sworn to obey your orders until we reach safety. I will honor that oath. Still, I must tell you that I am bound to report to my lord all that I know."

"Then I would have you tell him something, if you will bear the burden," Khara said. "His son, Luca, is dead. It was not by my hand, nor by my will."

Norbert looked grave and seemed to age ten years before our eyes. "I will carry this terrible news to my lord."

"Tell him this, as well. That we Donatis . . ." She stopped and frowned again, as if frustrated by her own words. "Tell him that I, Kharassande Donati, would offer him my hand in friendship, and bring an end to this feud between our families."

Norbert nodded. "I shall."

I was relieved to find Khara alone in the bow a few minutes later. I had many questions to ask, and few answers. "You have changed, Khara," I began.

She did not disagree.

"You hesitate to speak for your father. Now you speak more boldly for yourself. When we first met . . . when you captured me"—I smiled to show it was said in jest—"you appeared to be a poacher and a guide. Slowly it became clear that you were more, that you were the scion of the Donatis. That you carried the Light of Nedarra."

Khara pursed her lips. "Do you have a question for me, Byx?"

"More like a request. Tell me your dream."

"My dreams?" She looked puzzled.

"No, Khara, not your dreams. Not the fancies of your sleeping mind. I mean your *dream*. You come from a once-great family. You carry a sword wreathed in magic and myth. I believe that when we started this journey, you wished only—or at least mostly—to help me find others of my own kind. But I no longer believe that is your only goal."

Khara was silent for a long time. "I have no siblings," she began. "As you can imagine, that was a great disappointment to my father."

I frowned.

"Oh, I forgot that dairnes do not assume that only males can lead." Khara gave a small laugh. "We humans are not all so enlightened. There has never been a female head of the Donatis. There has never been a female warrior in our clan, aside from figures of myth and legend."

"But you are a warrior," I objected. "And you have led us over hundreds of perilous leagues. These rowers have accepted your leadership. For that matter, even Renzo acknowledges that you lead us."

Khara looked pained. "Ah, but the rowers accept me because I freed them. Gambler seems to follow me, but in truth, Gambler follows no one." She smiled wistfully. "As for Renzo . . ." She shrugged. "Well, he is a puzzle."

I kept my face carefully neutral. Poor Khara actually did not know why Renzo followed her. His feelings seemed plain enough to me, and to Gambler and Tobble as well, I suspected—and we weren't even human.

Still, it was not my place to explain such things to Khara. She would have to figure that on her own.

"You still have not told me your dream," I pressed.

"My dream? It's a fantasy, an absurd fantasy. I sometimes imagine returning home and uniting the dispossessed families against the Murdano." She winced, as if expecting me to laugh, and seemed surprised when I only nodded. "But for now, it's not about uniting to overthrow the Murdano. Now my fantasy—my dream, as you call it—is of stopping this war." She threw up her hands. "Beyond that, Byx, I do not know. There is a great deal I do not know."

"Then I will tell you what I know," I said. "I trust you. I believe in you. And I will follow you. So will Tobble and Gambler and Renzo." I glanced back at Maxyn. He was sleeping, propped against the mast. "I don't know about Maxyn."

"He has no reason to follow me," Khara said. "If he follows anyone, it will be you, Byx."

I laughed out loud at the thought of me leading anyone. I'd had my brief taste of that. And I had not enjoyed it.

Khara leaned close and said, "Remember, Byx: you are all Maxyn has in the world. He puts on a brave face, but you know all too well what he's been through."

"Too much death," I whispered, not even intending for Khara to hear it.

"Far too much," Khara agreed grimly. "And there will be more. Much more."

34
Return to Nedarra

It was the dead of night when we ghosted along the Nedarran coast and passed Landfail, the peninsula where I'd first
glimpsed Tarok and felt a thrill of hope that I might not be the
endling of my species. Once past Landfail, a great bay called
Rebit's Sound opened on our right, and Tobble ordered the
sail to be taken in.

"Norbert," Tobble called, "wake your men. We've lost the
breeze."

We glided into the sound to the soft shushing of oars in
water. The darkness was so complete that as we crunched
ashore, I could barely see my hand before my face. Norbert
and some of his men leapt out and ran a rope to a stunted
tree. The rest of us followed, feeling the strange reassurance of solid land after so much time on a moving, tilting
deck.

Khara spoke to the rowers. "Men, you have all fulfilled your oaths to me. Go with our gratitude."

"We owe our freedom to you, Khara," Norbert said, clearing his throat, "to you and to your companions. We serve various masters, and each of us will now make his way home to rediscover wives and children. But we shall not forget."

"Go in peace," Khara said. One by one, the rowers went to Khara, bending their knees and lowering their heads, before disappearing into the night.

Khara turned to Maxyn. "Maxyn, you have been dragged unwillingly into our party. Your father was killed—not by us, no, but in part because of us. You have no reason to follow me as the others have chosen to do. You are free to go, or to stay with us."

Maxyn started to look at me, but caught himself. "Do you still intend to reach this supposed dairne colony on the Pellago?"

"I do," Khara said. "But . . ." She paused and looked at me with a question in her eyes. "I had a talk with Byx."

I was surprised to hear my name and wondered where Khara's words were heading.

"She forced me to admit my"—Khara managed a self-conscious smile—"my 'dream,' I guess you'd call it."

"Dream?" Renzo repeated, one brow raised, leaning closer.

"My dream to stop this looming war," Khara said, and Renzo looked a bit disappointed.

She shrugged. "I know. It's insane to think that I could change the future of Nedarra. But I must try. And before I can decide what my next steps should be, I should first see my father. His will may be different from mine." She sent me a pained gaze. "There is an urgency to this I cannot ignore, Byx. I'd like to see him as soon as possible. But if my plans change after speaking to my father, I might not be able to—"

"If necessary," Gambler interrupted, "I will undertake to guide Byx to the dairne colony."

"And I will be right by their side," Tobble added. I gave them both a grateful smile.

"I understand, Khara," I said, although secretly I felt crushed that we might have to delay our plans to find the colony—or even go on without Khara. "You have to follow your heart in this matter."

Renzo didn't speak and looked as if he hoped no one would ask his plans. But I had no doubt that his first loyalty was to Khara.

Maxyn seemed to be considering his options. "I have no great love for Dreyland, nor do I care what happens to Nedarra. I want no part of anyone's war. I saw what taking sides did to my father."

"Sometimes taking sides is necessary," Gambler said, his pale blue eyes sizing up Maxyn carefully.

"Perhaps," said Maxyn. "But sometimes taking sides gets you killed. For now, I will stay with Byx and help her search for more dairnes. That seems to me to be the best choice in a world of bad choices."

"All right, then," said Khara. "We shall connect with my father and his followers. And from there, we'll decide where our futures lie."

The uncertainty and danger hiding in Khara's words worried me deeply. But what choice did I have? She was our leader.

It will all be fine, I told myself. We would find her father. We would decide our next steps. And eventually we would find more dairnes.

We had to.

We spent the rest of the night near the beach in a small grove of dendro trees. I went in search of wood for a fire, as the serrated yellow dendro fronds create too much smoke when they burn. The snow was gone, now that we were south of the mountains. But it was still chilly and damp.

It was not easy to find anything, let alone fallen branches, in the dark. I heard someone moving near me and called out, "Who is it?"

"Me," Maxyn said.

"Oh. Good."

"It would be easy to get lost out here."

"Yes, it would," I agreed.

After that, our conversation was limited to things like "Can you give me a hand with this branch? I need to break it," and other exchanges on the topic of firewood. Still, it was sweet to have a fellow dairne by my side.

Together, Maxyn and I were finally able to cajole the fire into burning. But by then it was so late, and we were all so weary, that it was a race between fire making and rest. The fire was small and sputtering, and I fell asleep as soon as it was going.

The next day we set out at dawn and walked along the beach, hoping to find a fishing outpost. When that proved futile, we headed inland. We soon spied a prosperous-looking village, where we exchanged another jewel from the crown for supplies.

Two days later, the weather had warmed, and we found ourselves walking through a league-long path lined by vivid purple nossit trees, their boughs twining overhead to create a breathtaking, sweet-scented tunnel. We were well away from any true roads and hadn't seen a soul in days, so we soon were singing—the echo created by the tunnel proving irresistible.

We taught Maxyn Tobble's worm song and shared our harrowing tale of the Crimson Forest. Gambler sang a lovely felivet ballad about lost love—surprising, given the solitary nature of his species. His gorgeous baritone vibrated the very boughs above us.

Khara and Renzo attempted a human song, harmonizing nicely at the outset. It seemed to be about a man who exploded after eating too many strawberry pies, but I couldn't be sure. Despite several attempts, they kept dissolving into laughter before they could reach the end of the chorus.

When they'd given up, breathless and flushed, Maxyn began singing an old dairne song about an obstinate pup. I remembered my parents singing it to my siblings and me—over and over and over again, as we begged for one more chorus. Together, Maxyn and I translated the lyrics from Dairnish so that our companions could join in:

Tiny pups, please sleep, we pray.
Tomorrow there'll be time for play.
Slumber in your leafy nest,
and let your parents get some rest!

Maxyn, I learned, often built and slept in tree nests on Tarok, the way dairnes had done in the time of our ancestors. My parents had taught me and my siblings how to construct a nest, as they felt it was important for us to be familiar with our heritage. But in the past few years, with dairnes constantly hunted, tree nests had been abandoned in favor of hidden places on the ground. The nests left us far too vulnerable and easy to spot.

We continued to stay off main roads, hewing instead to cattle paths, and guided only by the sun. Day followed day, and though we had to hide more than once to avoid soldiers marching north, it was a blessedly uneventful hike across gently rolling hills.

Again and again we were saddened to see forests that had been cut down, reduced to fields of oozing stumps. The wood, Khara suspected, was being sent southeast to Saguria to build the Murdano's invasion navy. What would happen, I wondered, to the birds, animals, insects, and reptiles who'd called those woods home? Where would they go? Were they wandering the world like I was, in search of someplace to begin again?

One evening, we stopped near a small creek bordered by gnarled gray trees with thick trunks and cascades of thread-like dark blue leaves on pliable branches. "I'll bet we could rig up a nest with those branches," Maxyn said. "Willows are best, but we could make do."

I looked at Khara. "Would it be safe?"

"Those are botwort elms," Khara said. "Sturdy as they come. The branches could hold you, no doubt. But a tree nest could be seen from a long distance. It would be a dangerous signal that we have dairnes in our presence."

"Perhaps we could just make one on the ground, then," I suggested. "And we could take it apart before we decamp tomorrow morning."

For the next hour, we gathered orb webs, moss, thistledown, and long branches. Once our collection was complete, we set to work.

My job was to strip the branches bare, while Max wove them into a circle that kept growing in size. Together, we pressed the softer items, like moss, into the crevices between the branches.

I noticed Tobble watching from a distance and motioned for him to join us.

"Come help, Tobble!" I called.

He held up his round paws. They looked like the tiny mittens I'd seen human children wear on cold days. "You forget that I lack opposable thumbs. You dairnes are lucky."

"Yes, but your paws are small and nimble," I said.

Tobble stepped closer, watching us work. "Remember when we first met, Byx?" he said. "We joked about your having thumbs."

I grimaced as I tried to bend a too-thick branch to my will, then gave up and tossed it aside. "And then you showed me your wobbyk ear trick."

Maxyn looked intrigued. "May I see it?"

Tobble set his giant ears spinning like tornadoes, then untwisted them just as quickly.

Maxyn laughed. "All things considered, I think I'll stick with thumbs," he said.

The night fire was dying by the time we finished our

nest. It was a work of art, I thought, strong and spacious. I stood back to admire our handiwork, and a memory of the nests I'd practiced building with my siblings tightened my heart. One glance at Maxyn told me he was feeling just as melancholy.

"Khara," Renzo said, "I'll bet they could fit their nest in the crook of that largest tree. See where the bottom branches split? I doubt it would be visible, except perhaps to a resident squirrel or cotchet."

"*Now* who's going soft?" Khara teased. But she nodded to Maxyn and me, and with Gambler's aid, we managed to wedge the big nest in the arms of the tree, just the way dairnes would have done in the old days.

We clambered up easily—dairnes have large, sharp claws—and found ourselves surrounded by a whispering curtain of leaves. It was almost impossible to see past the interlaced branches, which meant, of course, that it would be equally difficult for anyone to sight us, especially at night.

"Tobble," I called down, "come up and see! It's wonderful up here!"

"I believe you," he said. "But a wobbyk is more tunneler than tree dweller."

"It's incredibly soft," I said. "Are you sure you don't want to join us?"

"I'm quite sure."

"Khara," Maxyn yelled down, "do you suppose Byx and I could stay in the nest all night?"

Khara looked at Renzo, who gave her a sheepish grin. "I suppose," she said, "but you need to take it down well before daylight."

"We promise," Maxyn said.

"Tobble"—I tried again—"are you sure you won't come up?" It felt wrong not to have him there with us, like a song out of tune. And I wanted to be certain that he felt included.

"I'm sure. Sleep well, Byx," he called.

Eventually, we would reach the Cruacan Pass, the gap between the two converging mountain chains. The pass, Khara warned, would be guarded, and we would not be able to rely on bluffing our way past.

But that was still days in our future. For now, for tonight, I was going to sleep in a tree nest with another dairne, the way my ancestors had done for endless generations. I would feel the soft warmth of our fur, listen to a lullaby of creaking branches, and feel, for once, what it must have been like to be a dairne, free and hopeful, before the world forever turned against us.

35
The Pass

"Getting through the Cruacan Pass," said Khara a few days later, "will not be easy. It's the old dividing line between the more densely populated east and the wilder west of Northern Nedarra. In the old days it was guarded lightly, and only brigands were stopped. Lately, though, the Cruacan has been more heavily fortified. When last I passed through, the Murdano's men were building a fort on a cliff ledge that looks down over the pass."

Tobble groaned. "Then how do we get through?"

"Yes, that is the question," Khara said. "There are four approaches. You can be an innocent farmer or miner, transporting goods under an imperial license."

"Not us," Renzo said.

"Then there is armed attack."

"Also not us," I said.

"There is stealth," Khara offered.

Renzo nodded slowly, allowing that this was a possibility. "And then there is bribery."

"Ah," Renzo said. "Pry more stones from the crown?"

Khara shook her head. "These are not villagers. These are hard men and eagle-eyed officials. The sudden appearance of a ruby or emerald will only convince them to search us closely and take all we have."

"So it's stealth, is it?" I asked.

"Or a different type of bribery," Khara said. "Just this side of the Cruacan is the land of the Belthassans. They're a rich, greedy family, dishonest and unscrupulous. And firm allies of the Murdano."

"Indeed?" Renzo said. "And what business are these Belthassans engaged in?"

"They are ranchers, mostly. Struzzi."

"What are struzzi?" Maxyn asked.

"A type of large bird that walks on three legs and provides delicious meat," Renzo said. "They're very valuable. A single struzzi can fetch as much as three horses."

"True," Khara said. "Even a small handful of the creatures would constitute a fine bribe. But one not likely to stir up too much attention."

Renzo rubbed his hands together. "I sense my skills may soon be called upon. I suppose I could grab a few struzzi and bribe the guards at the pass."

"Are we common thieves now?" Maxyn said in my ear.

"When we have no choice," I said, but the truth was, it did bother me.

"Perhaps we only need to *borrow* some struzzi," said Renzo, tapping his chin. "Temporarily."

"What do you mean?" I asked.

"I'm merely considering my options," he replied. "Bribery is so"—he feigned a yawn—"boring."

"Just don't get too creative," Khara warned.

We had begun to veer southward, closer to the Perricci mountain range. When the sun was high, I could now see the distant Cruacan Pass, two enormous, sheer mountains separated by a valley no more than a quarter league across. The trees were dense enough to shield us from prying eyes and provide some shade, the breeze cool but not cold.

We also began to see fences of stone or wood enclosing large fields. Some contained cattle or horses. Others held the strange, gawky struzzi, craning their long orange necks while they gaped at us with foolish, wide-eyed expressions.

"Gambler," Khara said, "we are in Belthassan land. Any humans we see must be considered dangerous."

She did not give Gambler orders, but he took her unspoken suggestion. "I will scout ahead."

He doubled his pace and soon drew away from us.

Darkness was falling when Gambler returned to report. "There is a camp of humans, ranchers with horses, a league to the east. If we hug the foothills, we will pass by unseen."

We spent the night in a grove of trees watered by a swift, icy-cold stream. It fed a small pool, half-covered by silver lily pads, and there I braved the water to take the first bath I'd been able to manage in some time. Maxyn jumped in, too, somersaulting and diving happily.

I noticed Tobble standing by the edge of the stream, watching us. "Tobble!" I called. "Come join us! It's freezing, but you get used to it."

Maxyn splashed me and I yelped. "Well, maybe you *don't* get used to it," I conceded. "But it still feels good to get clean."

Tobble shook his head. "Tomorrow, perhaps," he said. "I'm off to sleep."

"You're missing out," I said, but he had already headed back to join the others. Watching him trudge off, I felt a stab of sadness and even guilt. Was he feeling jealous of my new-found friendship with Maxyn?

I resolved to do better. Tobble was my dearest friend.

I owed him everything.

But it was hard to know how to have two friends at the same time. When I'd been a pup, my siblings and I were always together. They were my only friends, and they were all the friends I needed.

This was different.

Khara woke us all once the moon had set. As we neared the Cruacan Pass, she noticed two new fortresses had been constructed. One, round and squat, was on the northern face of the pass. The other, a smaller, more slender watchtower, was perched improbably atop a rock outcropping.

In the round fortress, Khara suspected, were engines of war. Trebuchets capable of flinging stones weighing hundreds of pounds. Cross spears, with pleated garivan tendons used as bowstrings. Fire-spitters, which Renzo suspected used theurgic ingredients to launch sprays of liquid fire. And buckets, trebuchets that launched not stones but great quantities of burning oil.

"I wish we still had Tobble's Far-Near," Khara said. "But from the little bit I can see, the siege weapons are aimed toward the east, as though they expect an attack from that direction."

"But can they still throw rocks at us?" Tobble asked.

"Yes, they can."

"How do we get through?" Maxyn asked.

"Excellent question," Khara allowed. "There is surprisingly little traffic on the Cruacan Road. That bodes ill. It means the Murdano is not buying goods—lumber or foodstuffs or leather—from the families in the Nedarran plains."

"Perhaps the Murdano has all he needs," I suggested.

"Could be," said Khara. "Or it could mean that things are more hostile between the exiled families and the Murdano."

A mere trickle of people and horses moved through the pass itself. Any notion that we could sneak past in a rush of caravans evaporated.

"Remind me, thief," Khara said, with a sideways glance at Renzo. "Just how good is your theurgy?"

Renzo shrugged. "I can cast spells that confuse the eye, but not invisibility spells. I've used them to take food—and sometimes more than food—but they only mislead, so that a shopkeeper will look past Dog and me. Still, with an effort of will, they can see me."

"I can pass unseen," Gambler said, drawing every eye to him. "Felivets are nearly invisible when we wish to be, simply because we are felivets. However, I also have some theurgic powers."

"Really, Gambler?" I asked, surprised. "You've never shown us any."

Gambler gave his version of a confident smile, a sort of combination smirk and whisker-twitch. "I'm a felivet. We rarely need to resort to theurgy."

Khara considered this carefully. She looked at the pass, at Gambler, at Renzo, at me, then back at the pass. She repeated the sequence before saying, "We need a distraction. A big one. If we had a distraction, we could race to the northern fortress. See how the land blocks it? You can't see the round fortress from the watchtower, I'd wager. And men in the fortress would be unlikely to catch sight of us. We'd be directly below them."

"A big distraction, eh?" Renzo said, looking speculatively at Gambler. "I'll chance it if you will, friend felivet."

"Be careful, you two," Khara warned as they headed off.

"Careful? That'll make for a change of pace," Renzo called over his shoulder with a laugh.

We sheltered from view in some tumbled boulders, afraid to build a fire, dining on cold food and muttering in soft voices. After eating, we dragged ourselves behind boulders and into gullies, getting as close as we could to the north fortress. It seemed to be directly above us, though it was in reality a hundred yards or more away.

We waited in a state of agitated readiness, ready to move instantly. Khara scanned the area before us intently, chewing on her thumbnail.

"Khara?" I whispered. "Don't worry. They'll be fine."

"I'm not concerned about Gambler," she whispered back. "He can take care of himself." She rubbed her eyes. "It's Renzo I'm worried about. He takes risks."

"So do you," I pointed out.

"Yes, but my risks are smart ones," she replied with a half smile.

The hours wore on. All we could do was wait, and hope the diversion would be a good one.

We were not, as it turned out, disappointed.

36
A Diversion

First came the deafening cry of the struzzi, a screech that ventures from high to low and back again, seemingly without end.

There is a reason why no one wants to be a struzzi shepherd. Struzzi wallow in their own filth, steal other birds' nests, and often eat their own young. Any time they are startled, they emit a hideous, earsplitting warble.

But that's not all they emit. Frightened struzzi release a bitter, noxious odor that makes a skunk's scent seem like a delicate rose perfume.

Next we noticed the orange glow.

"This is it!" Khara hissed, and we were all instantly ready to run. "Hold . . . hold . . ."

A herd of three dozen struzzi came racing through the pass, pursued by a moving wall of flame.

"Now!" Khara yelled, and we were off, running, stumbling over stones, fighting to keep steady on the steep slope.

Torches flared on the battlements of the round fortress, followed by shouts of alarm.

We were making plenty of noise ourselves, as our clumsiness sent cascades of loose shale rattling down. Still, we knew nothing would be heard over the noise of the crazed struzzi pursued by . . . well, barrels.

Barrels. Burning barrels, rolling down the gentle slope of the pass road behind the struzzi.

This was the moment the Murdano's men would realize they were witnessing a diversion. But we were already passing the round fortress, running as fast as we could, given the terrain. Our only advantage was that the guards would assume the danger was coming from the same direction as the struzzi.

We rounded an especially difficult slope and I fell, cutting both my knees. As Maxyn helped me to my feet, we saw two men in the shadows. I could just make out the silhouettes of helmets and spear tips.

Khara held up a hand, stopping us. Then she walked forward alone, saying, "Is this an attack?"

"We don't know yet," a male voice replied. Then, in a tone of dawning suspicion, he asked, "Who are you?"

By then, Khara had drawn her sword. She struck hard

and fast, and the man who had questioned her spoke no more. The second man panicked and ran, as Khara yelled, "Now, now, now!"

We tore after Khara as she pursued the fleeing man. They disappeared from view for a moment, and when we reached them, Khara was panting and I saw a smear of blood on her face.

Wordlessly, we hugged the wall of the pass, edging along the cliff base, terrified of being spotted. We bumped into a small trading caravan coming the other way, passed through them, and came to a checkpoint set up to guard the other side of the pass.

"If we get past that checkpoint, we may just survive," Khara whispered.

The checkpoint was a stone barracks that held perhaps ten soldiers, and it sat beside the narrowest part of the pass, a spot where the gap between walls was a mere fifty feet. Ten soldiers, we all knew, were far too many for Khara to take on single-handedly, and Maxyn, Tobble, and I would not be of much help.

"Is that a stable I smell?" Tobble asked.

I rose cautiously to see better and yes, there in a hollow, just this side of the barracks, was a stable. I'd smelled it, too, but hadn't realized its importance.

I saw a flash of Khara's teeth in the dark. "Follow me."

We ran, hunched over, our steps louder now as the struzzi shrieks diminished behind us. But there could be no turning back. We were exposed to anyone in the watchtower who cared to look down.

A single guard was on duty outside the stable, but he was staring at the still-burning, if no longer rolling, barrels. Khara came up behind him and smashed the hilt of her sword against the base of his skull. He would have a terrible headache when he woke up, but at least he would wake up.

Inside we found six horses, unsaddled, in stalls.

"Get harnesses on them—no time for saddles," Khara said. Tobble, Maxyn, and I untangled a mass of leather straps, managing, after some confusion, to get harnesses over the heads of all six horses.

"Tobble, with me," Khara said as she swung herself up and onto a bay mare's back. "Byx and Maxyn, up on that spotted gelding. Each one of you grab the reins of two spare horses."

"Why are we taking the spare horses?" Maxyn wondered aloud, as he and I climbed up a stall door to reach the gelding's broad back.

"You want soldiers chasing you on horse or on foot?" Khara said. "Byx, grab the mane. Maxyn, grab Byx. I'll open the gate. Ready?"

If I were indulging in dairne honesty, I'd have answered,

"Absolutely not. Not even close to ready." But what I said was, "Yep."

Khara leaned down from her horse, pushed the door open, and said, "Ride, and don't stop for anything!"

She kicked her horse and I followed suit, though I doubt my horse even noticed. Fortunately, he was willing to follow Khara's steed, and we blew out of the stable at an accelerating trot.

A soldier ran from the barracks, spear held at the ready, trying to cut us off as he yelled for help.

Khara swung the Light of Nedarra and sliced the thrusting spear in half as she shot past.

It was giddy madness, six horses all at a full gallop, unable to see where their hooves were landing. Ours stumbled once and I nearly slipped off, taking Maxyn with me. Behind us came the furious shouts of the soldiers, running on foot with no chance of overtaking us. It was dreamlike: the speed, the flashes of cliff face, the loom of boulders, the sudden snag of unseen brambles.

After a few more minutes, I felt openness and scented the clean smell of a breeze coming from the north. We were out of the pass, racing downhill over pastureland. Ahead I saw two riders, armor glinting in the light of the rising moon, racing from the north to cut us off.

Not just soldiers: knights.

Professional killers, with every kind of weapon imaginable.

Suddenly one of the knights flew sideways off his horse, shouting in surprise and alarm. His horse reared and shied away, panicked. The second knight's horse slowed, and his rider, too, fell in a heap.

Both horses, having had more than enough, went whinnying off into the night.

We galloped on, although my horse was clearly feeling reluctant, and I had to urge him on. "Don't worry, good horse, it's a friend," I said.

We had gained a new traveling companion. He ran along at a distance until we were certain that our soothing had calmed the horses enough to overcome their initial terror.

"Well done, Gambler," Khara said.

"Horses," Gambler said with a sneer. "They have no stomach for facing felivets, especially at night."

Behind us, the fallen knights bellowed threats, but unhorsed, they were no concern of ours. And just ahead of us, on a small rise, sat Renzo on a stolen horse.

"Like our diversion?" Renzo asked as we reined in.

"It worked," Khara allowed.

"And I know you must be very relieved that I survived unscathed," Renzo said, flashing a grin.

Khara said, "Enh," but you could see her obvious admiration.

"I . . . I did not like it," Tobble said from his perch behind Khara.

"You're unhappy I survived?" Renzo teased.

Tobble looked chagrined. "I mean to say," he said in a small voice, "that it was incredibly brave, what you did, and it saved our lives, so naturally, I shall be eternally grateful to you, Gambler and Renzo. But—"

"There's always a 'but'!" Renzo moaned, but he was smiling, still giddy from his success.

"But," Tobble said, "those struzzi must have been terrified. I know they are unlikable birds, what with their squawking and their, um, odor, but still . . ."

"You forgot their habit of eating their young," Renzo said.

"Still—"

"And the fact that they steal nests," Maxyn added.

"*Still*—" Tobble said.

"And the way—" I began, but Gambler cut me short.

"Silence!" he snapped. "Let the wobbyk speak. We may all have something to learn."

Tobble cleared his throat. His big eyes glimmered in the pale starlight. "I just feel that even though struzzi are not the most charming of species—and, oh my, yes, they do smell atrocious—they should be treated with, well, kindness. Those big barrels on fire—what if one had hit a struzzi?"

"I was very careful to time the moment I let the barrels roll," Renzo said.

"But if one of the birds had tripped," Tobble said. "Or if a baby had been too slow—"

"There were no babies. And struzzi can fly brief distances if they need to," Renzo said, but he was starting to sound a little deflated.

"Is my life more important than that of a struzzi?" Tobble asked. "Just because I am cute and cuddly?"

We all fell silent, as the horses trotted along.

"I suppose, Tobble, I could argue that we are in a kind of undeclared war," Renzo finally offered, his tone much subdued. "And that in a war, necessary sacrifices have to be made."

"But who decides that?" I asked aloud. The randomness of it all suddenly struck me—not to mention the unfairness. So few in the world had power. So many had none.

"Was my father a necessary sacrifice?" Maxyn said.

"And my pack?" I added, a catch in my throat.

We looked to Khara, as if she would solve the problem for us. But she was gazing straight ahead, as if she weren't even listening.

Gambler, loping beside us, said, "Tobble, you are a wise young wobbyk. In any war, it is good to have someone ask the hard questions, the ones that defy easy answers."

"It's just so complicated," Tobble said. "Nothing is black and white. It's all shades of gray."

Khara spoke for the first time. "You are right. But don't let the complications stop you from taking a stand, Tobble. When you know in your soul that something is evil, you must fight it. But you fight with honor. With mercy. With fairness."

"Tell that to the soldiers who've felt the point of your sword," Renzo said.

Khara flashed a glance at him. "Do you doubt my leadership?"

"Never," Renzo said sincerely. "I just doubt that war can ever be waged with honor, mercy, and fairness."

"Given the path ahead of us," Khara said, "let us hope you are wrong, my friend."

37
The Baron

After coming down from the Cruacan Pass, we had to cross the Telarno River. All the bridges were sure to be guarded, and we knew we had already stretched our luck to the breaking point.

Khara decided we should travel north for a day into an area where the mountains loomed to our right like a great wall. Luckily, she knew of a ford, and we crossed the river at a place so shallow that the water barely rose above our horses' knees.

We plunged into dense woods after that, and I asked why this forest was untouched, unlike the many we'd seen razed.

"Many of these are witch oaks," Khara explained. "The wood is as hard as iron, very hard to cut, and the trees don't grow straight enough for masts or planks. Then, too, these woods are not uninhabited, and some of the locals might object to tree cutters."

"Are there fell creatures in this forest?" Tobble wondered.

"Oh, some of the fellest," Khara said, but her tone was light. Indeed, she seemed unusually relaxed.

It was slow going, riding through the trees. The witch oaks spread horizontally, their thick branches often right at face level. We had to constantly duck and detour. But all the while, Khara seemed to have a clear idea where she was going.

Then a *flit!* sound cut the air and an arrow appeared in a tree, quivering. Gambler growled and Renzo wheeled his horse around, looking for an enemy. But Khara rode casually over to the arrow, which had passed just inches from her head, and pulled it out to examine it.

Speaking in an elevated voice not meant for any of us, she said, "Look at this. Now you have a bent arrowhead. Another minute's patience and you could have fired into that pine just up ahead."

Two men and a woman slipped into view, where seconds before I'd have sworn there were only trees and bushes. The three wore jerkins and leggings cunningly dyed in green and brown, so that the clothing blended in perfectly with the forest. All three carried bows with arrows nocked, but not drawn.

"You have your next breath to explain why you have entered this land." This was from one of the men, a blond-bearded, middle-aged man with deep-set eyes.

"Well, Archer Maccan, if you can't recognize me, I have to assume your eyesight is far too weak for you to be running around the forest with a bow."

The archer gaped and slowly lowered his bow. "Lady Kharassande?"

Khara slid lightly from her horse, took two quick steps, and leapt at Maccan, who caught her and twirled her around, both of them laughing.

"Oh, you're much heavier than when I last saw you," Maccan chided. "I can barely spin you around without breaking my back!"

"And you're even more bald than the last time I saw you, old man. With a bit of beeswax I could shine your head to make a mirror."

"Oh, you spoiled little—"

Khara shoved him hard. "Where's the respect I'm owed?"

"I apologize," Maccan said, displaying a sweeping bow. "I'd taken you for a poacher or perhaps a tramp." Then his wide grin faded. "I am glad word reached you. The baron has little time left, I fear."

Khara grabbed his arm. "What are you saying?"

"You don't know?" His eyes widened. "Ah, you *don't* know. Your father, my lord Baron Donati, has taken ill, and"—he looked away—"and I am sorry to say ... the physicians do not expect him to live."

Khara blinked. "His heart?"

Maccan nodded sadly. "In the last month he has had two heart seizures and is much weakened."

"My mother can tell me the rest," Khara said with urgency. "Where is the camp?"

"Your mother?" Maccan repeated.

"Yes. Isn't she tending to him?"

"We haven't seen the baroness in many months."

Khara's fists were tight balls. "I don't understand. Where is my mother?"

"We do not know. The baron will not say."

"Enough of this. Point me to the camp," Khara said.

"You know old Humber's meadow? Follow the stream north from there. I would guide you, but . . ." Maccan waved his hand toward the forest behind him.

"Your duty is here," Khara said, patting his shoulder. "Mine is with my father."

Without a further word to us, she dug her heels into her horse's flanks, and we hurried to catch up. She did not gallop—that would have endangered the horse in these woods full of exposed roots and shrew holes—but she moved quickly, urging her horse on. We came to a meadow of tall golden grass, rippling in the wind like a gentle sunrise sea. From there, we followed a small stream.

Khara had talked from time to time about her family, the

Donatis. I knew they had once been a great and powerful family with extensive lands and a fine castle called Watersmeet. I knew that they had resisted the rise of the first Murdano and had been dispossessed.

Given all that, I don't quite know what I expected, but I certainly did not expect what I soon saw.

We rode beneath gnarled, thick witch oaks, and it was a while before I looked up and realized, to my amazement, that the trees bore platforms and rope walkways. Hammocks hung from branches, and rope lines carried fluttering laundry, all in the eye-fooling green-and-brown livery we'd seen on Maccan and his people. The forest pushed right up against a large rock outcropping so tall that it poked out of the forest canopy.

We stopped beneath a witch oak so thick that ten men holding hands could not have formed a ring around it. A young man sank from the branches above, silent as a spider dropping on a line of silk.

He bowed to Khara and said, "I will see to your horses, lady."

"My father—?"

"He is abed. Will you ascend?"

Khara nodded. Instantly a rope with a loop on one end was lowered from the tree above. "Come with me, Byx," she said. "Please, everyone else, food and drink will be brought to you."

Khara set her foot in the loop and gripped the rope. I did the same, and we rose through dense foliage. We passed a platform surrounding the great tree, patrolled by bowmen, continued aloft through a hole framed by timber, and stepped onto a rectangular platform.

The platform was wide and long enough to accommodate a sizable house. But instead of a fixed building, I saw three tents, one twice the size of the other two. All were tall enough for a human to stand erect inside, but with mere inches to spare.

"We build nothing permanent," Khara said, by way of explanation. She hesitated at the opening to the central tent. "At any time, we can break everything down and move within an hour."

"I understand," I said. "It was a little like that for my pack."

Khara's expression was opaque, her voice flat, but I knew her too well to be fooled. I saw the flexing of her jaw muscles, heard the shortness of breath and the uncertain beat of her heart.

"My father . . . ," she began. "My father . . ."

"You don't have to explain anything."

Khara nodded. "Just know that he was once the strongest, wisest, and kindest of men. He may appear—well, you heard that he is ill."

I understood. Khara did not want me to be disappointed

by what I saw. I put a comforting hand on her shoulder and gave a small nod.

We pushed aside the canvas flaps and stepped inside. It was quite warm, with a fire burning in the center of the tent under a chimney hole cut in the top. A bed, fashioned out of rough-hewn branches lashed together with vines, sat near the small blaze. Beneath a pile of furry animal skins I saw a head with thin, straggling gray hair.

Two older women acting as nurses bowed to Khara and stepped back. I stood with them, hidden in the shadows, feeling like an intruder on an intensely private moment.

"Father. It's me, Khara. I am here with a friend, Byx."

The old head rose from pillows and I was shocked, not by how ill and decrepit he looked, but by the sense of what he must once have been.

Khara's father was much reduced, his cheeks hollow and colorless, but I almost laughed on seeing his eyes. They were sharp, intelligent, and unwilling to suffer fools. In short: Khara's eyes. And he had a jaw that spoke of iron determination. The similarity between the sick old man and the healthy young girl was undeniable.

"Kharassande," Baron Donati said, trying for a robust tone that was subverted by a wheezing cough.

Khara bent over and hugged him, her head on his chest. Her father wrapped thin arms around her.

"I feared you were dead," he whispered. "The last of the Donatis."

"No, Father, I live."

He wiped away tears with the back of his hand. "It is good to see you, my child. You have been much missed. I only wish your mother could be here to share my joy."

"Father," Khara said, "where is she?"

The baron glanced my way, clearly worried about speaking openly in my presence. He squinted, and I sensed that his eyesight, too, was failing.

"I would trust Byx with my life, Father."

He nodded. "Your mother is in a safe place."

"A safe place? What does that mean?" Khara stood, hands on her hips. "I know my mother. Sabrinei Donati would never willingly leave your side."

Her father managed a small smile. "No one said she was willing."

"Meaning?" Khara tilted her head, waiting.

"Sabrinei is in the Western Uplands with a handful of servants and guards." He sighed. "She is slower than she used to be, unable to travel without assistance. But her powers of theurgy have grown stronger. And her tongue is every bit as sharp. I convinced her—with great effort—that she was slowing us down." The baron gave a rueful laugh. "And look at me now."

"At least she is safe," Khara said. "That's a comfort." She wiped quickly at a tear and squared her shoulders. "Well, then. I have much to tell you, Father. Much indeed. Let me begin by introducing my traveling companion and friend, Byx." She paused. "Byx the dairne."

38
Another Kind of Endling

The baron managed a wan smile. "For a moment, I thought you said 'dairne'! I haven't seen one of those creatures in many a year."

"You heard me correctly, Father." Khara crooked a finger in my direction.

As I approached his bedside, the baron gasped. He clutched my forearm with his hand, and I could feel his fingers trembling. "I'd thought dairnes were nothing but a memory, thanks to the Murdano's father. Are there many more of you, Byx?"

I shook my head. "We know of only one other living so far. But there are rumors of a colony near the Pellago River."

"A dangerous location, it would seem." The baron squeezed my hand. "But let us hope the rumor is well-founded."

Khara's father was a weak and dying man, but his curiosity was still strong, and once he had heard his daughter's lengthy story, he asked sensible, perceptive questions.

"Ferrucci betrayed you?" he asked. "That saddens me. We trusted him as a scholar and a confidant."

Khara had gone to Ferrucci in the hope of finding an ally who could help protect me—the presumed endling dairne—but he had been far too afraid of the Murdano and his Seer.

"That the Murdano's father," the baron continued, "was behind the attempt to annihilate the dairne species—well, that I have long suspected. The felivets"—he paused as a cough racked his thin frame—"will be next. Nor does it surprise me to learn that the young Murdano would belatedly discover the advantage in having a dairne or two of his own—so long as no one else has one." He shook his head. "As for this tunnel with the terramants . . ." He grimaced, trailing off.

"Yes. It's very bad," Khara said. "I don't believe anyone in Nedarra is aware of it. It seems preposterous, and yet we saw a portion of the tunnel. If—when—they finish it, they can attack with complete surprise. And send thousands of terramants ahead as a vanguard to terrorize any defenders."

"A Dreyland victory is not an outcome to be desired," the baron said dryly. "Unfortunately, a victory by the Murdano would be as bad for us." He tilted his head and looked shrewdly at his daughter. "You are always welcome, dear Khara, but you have not come here simply to keep me informed. Open your heart to me. What is it you wish?"

Khara started slowly pacing, arms crossed over her chest. "I don't know, Father. I know only what I would do if I were older. And a man."

The baron coughed for a while before sputtering, "When have I ever taught you to limit yourself to womanly things, Khara? You are *the* Donati."

"No!" Khara said too loudly. Then, in a calmer voice: "No, Father, *you* are the Donati."

"I will not last a season," the baron said. "And I will never again lead good men and women into battle. The world will not wait for me to die and for you to adjust to your new role. War is coming, a war that will kill not thousands, but tens of thousands. The world has no use for a sick old man, nor any patience with those who can still act to stop this madness."

"But Father, I have with me a thief, a felivet, a wobbyk, and two dairnes. Am I to face and defeat both the Murdano and the Kazar with an army of six?"

"You know what you must do, Lady Kharassande Donati."

Father and daughter looked at each other, both so full of suppressed emotion, both so aware of unspoken words and unacknowledged fears.

"Will I be challenged?"

"Yes."

"By whom?" Khara asked, voice like lead.

"Your cousin Albrit. He is captain of the guard. He's a fine warrior, but he lacks the temperament for a leader. He's proud, though. And he will challenge you."

In an aside for my benefit, Khara said, "Albrit is practically twice my size. And a brilliant warrior, an expert with sword and bow."

The baron nodded. "Yes, Albrit is mighty."

"I would not wish him dead," Khara said.

"You will not convince him, and thus will have to accept his challenge. And Khara"—the baron's voice quavered—"you may be killed, and Albrit Di Tarzo will rule what remains of the Donatis. He will form a new dynasty on our bones."

Khara was silent and so was her father. I waited, feeling small and irrelevant, a minor character witnessing what could well be a momentous decision, a decision on which the fates of two nations might turn.

But even as I tried to absorb their words, all I could think of was how I simply could not bear to see Khara die.

"Father, you're wise in battle, as in all things." Khara tilted her chin and drew in a breath. "Do you believe there is any chance that I can defeat Albrit?"

Her father stretched out a bony hand and touched hers.

"With the Light of Nedarra? Yes, of course I believe you have a chance." He smiled through tears.

With that, the baron's lids dropped, and he fell asleep without another word.

As we walked away, I asked Khara, "Do you want to know whether he was telling the truth?"

"About my chances against Albrit?" Khara barked a short, bitter laugh. "No, Byx. I already know."

"And yet you're thinking of accepting this fight?" I asked, trying to rein in my panic.

"What choice do I have? I'm the last Donati. I owe it to my family. But far more important than that is the fact that my father doesn't think Albrit is ready for the fight we face."

"But . . ." I had nothing more useful to say.

Khara shouted down for our friends to join us. "It seems, Byx," she said, "that I am a sort of endling myself. The last of my family, if not my species." Instantly, she winced at her own words. "Forgive me, friend. Your pain is infinitely greater, I know."

"Don't apologize, Khara," I said firmly. "There are many kinds of pain."

Even as I spoke the words, I shook my head in disbelief. Little Byx, the runt of the litter! A few months ago, would I ever have dreamed I would know so much about the world?

We slept that night in one of the smaller tents that shared

the baron's platform. There were comfortable cots for each of us, appropriately sized for human, dairne, and wobbyk. Gambler rested on a bed of soft branches and silken leaves.

In the morning, as we drank tea and ate a cold but filling breakfast, we heard the sound of heavy footsteps. A moment later, the tent flap opened on a rather imposing fellow. He was tall and broad-shouldered, his dark hair threaded with gold. I immediately guessed his identity.

"Albrit," Khara said, embracing him. They smiled at each other—not enemies, at least not yet.

"You've grown taller and stronger since last we met," Albrit said.

It was true enough, but Khara was still a head shorter than he, and barely more than half his width. I could not bring myself to think about the two of them in battle.

"I've been on a long journey," Khara said. "How are your wife and your sons?"

"Fiona is as beautiful as ever," Albrit said, "and my sons are nearly grown now."

We listened as they chatted about shared experiences and common acquaintances, but it was obvious that they were only going through the polite motions. Finally, it was Khara who broached the topic on both their minds.

"My father is dying, Albrit," she said, in a strong, clear voice. "I mean to claim the leadership of the Donatis."

Albrit nodded. He seemed to be suppressing a smile. "You are brave and clever. But you are only a woman, Khara. The Donatis have never been led by a woman, and these are perilous times."

"Yes, they are perilous times indeed. I will open my heart to you in this, Albrit. I do not wish to fight you. I would far rather have you as my strong right arm. But I intend to rally the Donatis, make peace with the other exiled families, and move to stop this war with all the power I can assemble."

"You would go to war to stop a war?" Albrit smiled skeptically. "Why should we not welcome this war? Let the Murdano fight this rogue Dreyish felivet! Let them destroy each other." He spoke with passion, and as yet I'd detected no falseness in him.

"I know what you do not, Albrit. I've been to Dreyland. I've seen preparations for war that will bring untold slaughter and misery to Nedarra."

"Not here," Albrit said flatly. "War between the Murdano and the Kazar will unite the exiled families. Together we can hold the Cruacan Pass and make a new kingdom here in the west. A more just kingdom."

"With you as king?" Khara asked.

"Perhaps."

"I would not see tens of thousands torn apart by rampaging terramants."

"Terramants?" Albrit frowned.

"There's much you do not know," Khara said.

Albrit shook his head sadly. "Your plan is foolish, and your readiness to face me in battle is insanity. You cannot defeat me, Khara." He nodded down at the sword hilt protruding from Khara's scabbard. "At least let me loan you a decent weapon. I'd hate to prevail simply because your shabby sword snapped in half."

"You're generous, Albrit. But I'm accustomed to this sword, and with it, I'll face you at the traditional time. You and one of your followers against me and one of mine."

"The setting of the moon, then," Albrit said. "On this very evening." He stuck out his hand. "I will shake your hand one last time as a friend."

"I hope our friendship will be renewed," Khara said, taking his hand.

As he left, the others stirred. Renzo spoke quickly, with an urgency I'd never heard before. "I can sneak into his tent and use a file to weaken his sword so—"

Khara put a hand on his arm, silencing him. "No, my friend. I will not cheat my way to the leadership of the Donatis."

"Doesn't Albrit know you carry the Light of Nedarra?" I asked in a whisper.

"Of the Donati clan, only my father and mother know," Khara said.

Renzo gripped Khara by the shoulders. "Khara." For once, there was no humor in his tone. "He will kill you. And with you will die all our hopes."

"I do not need a reminder of how serious this is," Khara said. She looked him in the eyes and smiled. "But don't despair. I have a plan."

39
Khara's Surprise

The battle, we learned, was to take place in the trees on two separate platforms, one nearly as long and wide as the baron's, the other much smaller, no larger than the bed of a wagon. Both platforms were built high above the ground so that a fall would bring almost certain death. The smaller platform was separated from the larger one by a space a strong warrior could leap across.

Spectators—far more than I'd imagined the Donati clan could muster—filled the trees on all sides. Branches sagged and even large trunks swayed with the weight of expectant bodies.

A rope walkway led from the baron's area to the larger of the two fighting platforms. My friends and I, sick with dread (with the possible exception of Khara herself), stood in a helpless, frustrated gaggle on the baron's platform.

Renzo had spent the evening begging—and probably stealing—weapons, on the assumption that he would be Khara's second.

For my part, I assumed Khara would name Gambler. There were few human warriors who could stand against a felivet. Many a swordsman believed himself to be quick, but no human has the speed to match a felivet.

Khara ignored us. She sat at a small makeshift table, bent over scraps of paper on which she was penning notes. I imagined these to be her last will and testament, or perhaps farewells to her family and to us, her companions. But I was quickly proved wrong when she summoned messengers, lean men and women, skilled at evasion, with the fastest of horses. Khara sent them off with whispered commands.

Only then did she rise, stretch, force a shaky smile, and say, "Well, I suppose it's about time."

Khara borrowed the shield from Renzo, the one from the Subdur natites' realm. "I will now name my second," she said, "who will fight beside me."

Both Renzo and Gambler stepped forward.

"If I name you, Gambler, any victory will be yours and not mine, and the Donatis will deem it a cheat."

"Maybe," Gambler growled, "but you would perhaps survive."

"And good thief Renzo, you are brave and resourceful.

You fight well . . . but you fight well for a thief. You aren't yet a warrior."

"But what are you thinking of?" Renzo cried.

"I am thinking," Khara said with a smile, "of asking my fine friend Tobble to fight beside me."

A yelp, not unlike the noise you might make if someone stepped on your toes, came from Tobble. It was followed by a squeaky "Me?"

"Yes. You. Will you join me and share my fate?"

I expected Tobble to state the obvious: that he was the smallest of us, the weakest, the least like a warrior. But when he spoke, it was not to offer excuses. Once again, I realized I should never underestimate my dear wobbyk friend.

"I w-w-will j-join you," Tobble said. "It would be a g-great honor."

From our place on the baron's platform, we had a clear view of the larger fighting space, and a somewhat more obscured view of the smaller platform.

As Khara and Tobble crossed the rope walkway, I felt Maxyn's hand reach for mine. I squeezed back. My whole body was trembling. How, I wondered, must Khara be feeling?

Above the fighting platforms hung thick ropes that could be used to swing into or away from an opponent. Torches in the trees and around the edges of the platform cast a shadowy, flickering light. There were no railings.

Albrit appeared, walking confidently across the rope bridge to the larger platform. He was stripped to the waist, revealing thick muscles and blade-scarred skin. He wore leather trousers and high boots.

"I'm nervous for your friend Khara," Maxyn said. "I'm no judge of humans, but this one looks very strong."

I couldn't speak. My throat was tight as a fist.

Behind Albrit came his second, an even larger man. He stood a whole head taller than Albrit, who in turn stood a head taller than Khara.

A jester, a scrawny fellow in colorful rags, slid down one of the ropes and landed in the middle of the platform, performing a comic somersault as his feet touched the planks. This drew appreciative laughter.

In a loud, whining voice he said, "We come to witness a challenge! Kharassande of the Donatis, daughter and sole heir, asserts her right to rule in her father's stead."

The onlookers in the trees murmured and muttered. I was heartened to hear a few shouts of support for Khara.

"Challenging her is Albrit of the clan Donati, but of the family Di Tarzo. His second is his cousin. You know him, you love him: Mountain Morgoono!"

Mountain Morgoono, which I assumed was some sort of nickname, was obviously a crowd favorite. I noticed that the cheers for Albrit had ranged from enthusiastic to perfunctory. But Mountain was liked by all.

"And now, please welcome Kharassande Donati and her second, Tobble the wobbyk!"

Khara stepped nervously across the rope bridge. I'd never before seen her so affected by fear. It was as if her feet were refusing to move. Behind her came Tobble, nimble enough, but with his tail braid sticking straight back, clearly trembling.

Khara earned cheers, but cautious ones. Tobble, on the other hand, set off gales of laughter and some shouted insults.

"Khara brought her pet cat!"

"Be careful, little one, that Mountain Morgoono doesn't eat you!"

They reached the platform and stood in one corner, opposite Albrit and Mountain. Khara and Tobble together were not half the weight of Mountain alone. To make matters even more dire, both Albrit and Mountain carried heavy swords and had knives in their boots. Mountain also had a knobby mace hanging from his belt.

Tobble had a small knife Khara had given him. For her part, Khara had only her shabby-looking sword in its sheath. She was dressed more lightly than I'd ever seen, in a simple cotton shift over leggings. Her feet were bare.

"Call this off, Kharassande," Albrit shouted. "I have no desire to kill you. Withdraw your claim and serve me!"

"I fear death," Khara said, and she definitely sounded like she meant it. "I fear death, but I will not submit."

Her eyes were wide, her shoulders hunched, her hands visibly trembling. It was painful to see, and hard to believe that this was the fearless fighter I'd seen in battle so many times.

Hard to believe, I realized with a gasp, because it wasn't true.

Khara was acting.

The seeming clumsiness, the way her choice of outfit accentuated her small size, the tremble in her voice: it was all planned.

"I could deal with them both!" Gambler raged by my side. "Why did she not make me her second?"

"Because then the victory would not be hers, but yours, Gambler," Renzo reminded him.

"Victory?" Gambler gave his hoarse, coughing version of a laugh. "I hope only that she—and Tobble, of course—will survive. There is no possibility of victory."

Renzo shrugged. "You're almost certainly right," he said. "But only *almost*."

At that moment Mountain started in, hounding Tobble. "Am I to fight an overgrown rat? You're scrawnier than the plucked chicken I ate for dinner!"

This ritual abuse was expected, I realized, but Tobble did not find it amusing. I could see the anger building in him, and a tiny tendril of hope began to grow within me.

No creature is sillier, weaker, less threatening than a wobbyk. Unless.

Unless the wobbyk in question is enraged.

"Come, rat thing, you can nest in my pocket and I'll keep you as a pet and feed you treats!" Mountain guffawed, and the whole audience, above, around, and below us, laughed heartily.

"That was a mistake," I said.

Without a word of warning, Mountain charged right at Tobble, his teeth bared, his hair flowing, one massive hand reaching, the other wielding a dagger.

And that was an even bigger mistake.

40
Treetop Battle

Mountain Morgoono shook the platform with each massive footfall. There were already sounds of pity coming from some of the audience, and one voice cried out, "Don't hurt the little fellow!"

"I'll make it quick. You'll barely have time to know you're dying," Mountain said, laughing heartily as Tobble backed across the platform. He teetered on the edge, and I thought he might leap off in sheer terror.

I was already calculating a glide path for rescue when my thoughts were interrupted by a high-pitched scream.

With a babble of enraged and incomprehensible speech, Tobble ran straight at Mountain, leapt, and grabbed onto his belt. He scampered up the great man's body as if he were a real mountain and Tobble was in a great hurry to reach the summit.

Mountain cursed and swatted, slapping himself in an

effort to grab the swift wobbyk. But Tobble was already atop Mountain's head, legs wrapped around his neck, riding him like a child on his father's back.

And then Tobble went berserk.

Even Albrit froze, watching the insanity as Mountain staggered and roared. Tobble yanked out Mountain's hair in tufts, tore one of his nostrils, and bit a sizable chunk out of his right ear.

After that, Tobble went after Mountain's eyes, poking and prodding enough to leave his adversary squinting and dripping tears. Mountain, temporarily blinded, was like a great bear, plowing this way and that. He veered wildly, heading for the edge of the platform. Tobble gripped the sides of Mountain's mouth with his paws, as if he were reining in a horse, in an effort to stop him from falling to his probable death.

Mountain stumbled backward just inches from the edge. Tobble scrabbled down, grabbed Mountain's ankles, and held on tightly.

Like a toppled tree, Mountain dropped. The impact on the platform nearly knocked Khara off her feet.

Tobble drew his knife and held it near the man's throat. His voice reedy and shrill with excitement, he yelled, "Yield! Yield or die!"

Not twenty seconds had passed from the moment when Mountain Morgoono had charged against Tobble to the moment when the flustered, humiliated man cried, "I yield!"

A shocked and sobered Albrit faced Khara.

Under the rules, Tobble was free to help Khara, and it was clear to me that Albrit feared the outcome. But Khara held up one hand and said, "I will fight alone."

I suspect that statement, spoken with calm and confidence, may have worried Albrit even more than the prospect of having Tobble chewing off his ears.

"Come then," Albrit said. "I fear you not! You are but a small girl!"

He was reassuring himself. He was also lying about not fearing Khara. He hadn't lied before. Now he wasn't so sure.

And his apprehension was about to get much worse.

Khara strode toward him, her bare feet showing none of the awkwardness she'd feigned. She stopped near the center of the platform, widened her stance, straightened her pose, and drew her sword.

"Come, Albrit, and face me. Face me . . . and the Light of Nedarra!"

The shabby sword had vanished, and in its place was a razor-sharp blade. Its jeweled hilt glowed with an unnatural light.

The audience cried out in shock, amazement, and a sort of bloodthirsty anticipation. What had seemed likely to be a one-sided slaughter now looked like a real contest.

A murmur began and was repeated, growing louder with each repetition.

"The Light of Nedarra!"

"The sword!"

"I thought it lost!"

"The Light of Nedarra has returned!"

Albrit shook his head, as if to throw off his own doubts, but he had little time to think, for now it was Khara who attacked. Silent on bare feet, with the swiftness and agility of youth, she snatched one of the hanging ropes and swung toward Albrit.

Albrit dodged right, but as Khara passed, she managed to slice a red line in Albrit's shoulder.

She dropped from the rope at the end of its arc, spun, and faced Albrit, who charged, his own sword swinging horizontally with such force that it could have cut Khara in two.

Khara ducked under the swing and came up too near Albrit for him to make another attempt. Instead of thrusting her sword into Albrit's heart, she reached, took hold of his dagger, drew it from its scabbard, and flung it away, over the side of the platform.

"No!" Renzo cried. "She's not fighting to kill!"

"Foolish girl!" Gambler murmured.

Albrit backed away fast, and Khara, overbalanced, tumbled toward him. He brought his sword around with startling speed, but Khara flung herself forward through his legs. She rolled, stood, and ran to the edge, grabbing a rope and swinging to the smaller platform.

Albrit had a choice. He could either come after her, to his disadvantage, or refuse to attack and look like a coward. With such a choice, a brave warrior had but one option. When Khara let her rope swing back, Albrit took hold of it with one hand. He backed up to get room, ran, and swung, with a terrible war cry, toward Khara, sword extended to pierce her.

Too slow. Too ponderous.

Khara sidestepped easily and swung her sword high. It sliced through the rope and Albrit fell. His chest slammed the lip of the platform, legs dangling over the edge. He had to let loose his sword in order to claw at the wood as he tried to regain his footing.

Khara stood over him, looking down. With the side of her foot, she pushed against his right hand as he clawed, and all at once Albrit was hanging above the forest floor by one hand.

"Go on, kill me!" Albrit said in a ragged voice.

Khara had the warrior completely at her mercy. I held my breath, simultaneously longing for and fearing the sudden downthrust of her sword that would drive through his neck and into his heart.

"No, I will not kill you," Khara said. "Not unless you leave me no choice."

"Kill me and be done with it," he snarled. "Isn't my humiliation already complete? Will you make a mockery of me?"

"No," Khara said. "I would never mock so courageous and able a warrior. I have other uses for you, Albrit."

"Uses?" He was a strong man, but his fingers were white with strain, and the muscles of his arms and shoulders trembled.

"Yes," Khara said. "I have need of great warriors. I have need of a general."

41
A Three-Part Plan

Dairnes have few heroes of the sort humans seem to revere: strong, willful, sometimes even violent people. But we do have one, the Great Gerel. The Great Gerel was reputed to be twice the size of any other dairne and ten times as strong, able to wrestle even a giant swamp bear to defeat. When dairnes did something especially brave, they'd be complimented as "another Gerel."

Khara and Tobble's conquest of Albrit and Mountain Morgoono was, in the eyes of the Donatis, impossible. It was as if I had beaten the Great Gerel.

And yet it had happened.

There was simply no conceivable way that a girl and a wobbyk could defeat two big, powerful, experienced warriors.

And yet.

As I strolled along the leaf-strewn floor of the forest with Khara, I was very aware of Donatis whispering, pointing, and staring at Khara as if she were herself a creature from myth.

"You are quite the hero," I said.

"Yes." Only Khara could acknowledge her rise to hero status while sounding neither impressed nor pleased.

"What do we do now?" I asked.

Khara walked silently for a while, head down. Then she sighed, glanced around to make sure no one was within hearing, and said, "My plan has three parts. Part one: Albrit has sworn allegiance to me, and he will keep his word. He will send out riders—and head out himself—to rally our people from all over Donati lands."

"You're sure he won't betray you?"

"If I'd had any doubts about his honor, I'd have let him fall."

She delivered this bit of ruthlessness without apparent qualms, and once again I was reminded that there were hidden depths to the girl I'd once considered my captor.

"Part two?" I prompted.

"Part two is that I go to the Corplis and propose peace between our two peoples. And a union against our common foes."

"Will they join you?"

Khara shrugged. "Perhaps. Perhaps not. Luca's father is an honorable man. If I go to him under a flag of truce, he will hear me out. I can ask for no more."

"Do the Corplis have enough warriors to make a difference?"

"Yes. We Donatis will rally four, maybe five thousand soldiers, though I use the term 'soldier' very loosely. Most are farmers or herders or tradesmen. The Corplis can match that number."

"Ten thousand sounds like a great many," I said. "But we've heard that the Murdano's army is five times that and growing."

"Other families of the west will join us if the Corplis do. We may hope to assemble fifteen thousand armed men."

"But still—"

Khara held up her palm. "No, you're right. It's not enough to face the Murdano, let alone the Kazar. And certainly not both. But if I can get through to the Corplis, I'll speak with other . . . groups."

It wasn't a lie, but Khara wasn't being entirely open, either. I suspected that she didn't mean other humans, but rather, other species.

"You said you had a three-part plan. What is part three?"

Khara turned to face me. "Part three is about the future, Byx. The future of all Nedarra, and Dreyland as well.

Stopping the war won't be enough. We must change the way we are governed."

"Will you be Queen, then?" I asked, thinking I was teasing. But her expression remained solemn.

"A mere title alone won't matter. For too long, our leaders have ruled with lies and deceptions. The people—the common folk who farm and fish and make things with their hands—are never consulted, merely controlled. I would change that, Byx. But nothing is possible without truth. Truth is everything."

I felt a cold chill wrap around my heart. I knew before she said them what her next words would be, and the knowledge filled me with dread and sadness.

"This world needs dairnes," Khara said. "But I can't look for the Pellago River colony, not now, Byx. If this dairne colony exists, then they have survived against very long odds. They will be wary and afraid, and they would never trust a human interloper, with good reason." She put her hand on my shoulder. "But they would trust a fellow dairne."

I swallowed past a lump in my throat. "But what are you asking, Khara?"

"I am asking, Byx, whether you will journey to find these lost ones. And, if possible, bring them to understand their importance in the world."

"I—it's a very long way, and I don't know . . ." I petered out, hearing the cowardice in my voice.

But in truth, fear was only part of what I was feeling. The rest was loss.

I did not know how to be, how to live, without the support of this strange new family of mine: Tobble, Gambler, Renzo, and especially Khara herself. They—and Maxyn, though I still did not know him well—were all the pack I had now.

I wanted to beg Khara to change her mind.

I wanted to remind her that I was merely Byx, the smallest and least important of my pack.

I wanted to tell her I was not a leader and never could be.

I tried out the words in my frantic mind. *I can't, Khara. I won't.*

Khara was waiting, gazing at me with her dark, wise, penetrating eyes.

I couldn't say those words to her.

Never.

"I will do my best," I said miserably.

"Of course you will," Khara said. "And Byx, dear friend, you will not be alone."

42
Sabito Seventalon

Khara's words sent a wave of relief through me. I wouldn't be alone on my journey! I would at least have a chance of success, with Gambler and Renzo and—

"I plan to send Tobble and Maxyn with you," Khara said, interrupting my plans. "I wish I could add Gambler and Renzo as well, but I may yet need their help. I could send a handful of Donati warriors with you as well—"

"Yes," I said urgently, "*please* do."

"—but whatever number I send, it will not be enough in the event of a battle," Khara finished. "I think you would fare better as three—forgive me—small, unthreatening creatures."

I considered for a moment. Yes, she was no doubt right.

With effort, I managed a smile. "True. The three of us will have less reluctance to run away from danger."

Khara smiled back, but her gaze was serious. "You'll be given fast horses, food, weapons, and one other companion."

I frowned. "Another companion?"

"Do you remember Rorid Headcrusher?"

"How could I possibly forget him?"

We had encountered Rorid, a wise and enormous raptidon with a thirty-foot wingspan, as we were fleeing the Knight of the Fire. Rorid had provided us with much-needed information and had allowed us to pass through his lands. Later, at a dangerous moment when all seemed lost, a flock of crows had appeared and saved us. We'd never been certain that Rorid had sent the birds to help us, but we all believed it to be true.

"Well, after our encounter, old Rorid sent a representative to see what was happening with my family."

"Clever old bird. He sensed that you were important."

"Perhaps. What *is* important is that a young hawk has been in the area for some weeks. He has orders to observe and, if called upon, to aid me in any way that seems useful."

"So this bird," I said, "is to accompany us?"

"If you allow it."

The odd phrase echoed in my head. If *I* allow it? Me? The youngest in my family, the one called "runt" and "whelp" by her siblings?

Not until that moment did it truly dawn on me that I was

to be the leader of this expedition. It would be my task to make split-second decisions the way Khara did, weighing life and death in the process.

"Of course," I said. My voice sounded small and silly to my ears. "I'm told hawks have excellent sight. Flying high, one could—"

I heard a faint whoosh of air as a feathered blur shot past my face. A riverhawk flared his wings, pivoted like an acrobat, and landed on Khara's outstretched arm. He had a white underbelly, blue and brown feathers trimmed in black, and an indigo tail.

"Our hearing is rather good as well," said the hawk.

"Byx," Khara said, "meet Sabito Seventalon."

I did what I'm sure everyone who'd ever heard the nickname "Seventalon" had done: I peered at the hawk's talons. Normally, all types of raptidons have four talons on each foot—three in front and one behind—all strong enough to crush the head of a small mammal in an instant. Sure enough, he was missing one talon on his right side.

Sabito held up his right leg to show me. His stare was intimidating, a black dot within a brown iris on either side of a yellow, hooked beak.

"I am pleased to meet you, Byx of the dairnes," Sabito said with a more mellifluous voice than is common in raptidons.

"I as well," I answered.

I was surprised at how easy it was to understand Sabito. Raptidons have their own language and dialects, but when speaking the Common Tongue, they tend to struggle with the sounds of *w*, *b*, *d*, *f*, and *m*. I'd had to work to understand Rorid Headcrusher, but Sabito's accent was excellent.

We sized each other up—he with those intense, unforgiving eyes, and I with . . . well, I don't really know how I look to other people. Although I suppose my eyes look rather like those of any dog. (Only smarter, of course.)

"You will have concerns," Sabito said easily. "You have suffered betrayal and will be suspicious, with good cause. You will wonder if I have a secret agenda. And you will wonder whether I, a raptidon, a species renowned for its arrogance, will submit to being led by a dairne."

I couldn't help but smile at the self-aware remark about his own kind. "Well then," I asked, "what are your answers to those questions?"

"One: my agenda is no secret. I serve Rorid Headcrusher, but my wise chief has instructed me to obey Kharassande. You may trust me to obey Rorid, and thus Kharassande, and thus you. However—"

"Yes?"

"However, if I think you're making a foolish decision, I will challenge you relentlessly, until you tell me to shut up and do what I am told."

"And then?"

"And then I will shut up and do what I am told." Sabito swiveled his head back and forth in what seemed to be an avian shrug. "However—"

I smiled. "However?"

"However, if your decision turns out to be wrong, I will tell you so, and do it in an arrogant and even obnoxious way. However—"

"However?" I asked again.

"However, if your decision is the correct one, I will praise you."

"And admit that you were wrong?"

"Wrong? We raptidons are never wrong."

"Of course not." Despite my desire to remain suspicious and vigilant, I found I liked the self-mocking hawk. "Well then, Sabito, I welcome you to our"—I glanced at Khara, remembering our earlier words—"doomed and pointless enterprise."

"Doomed and pointless?" Sabito repeated. "If it's not doomed and pointless, what fun would it be?"

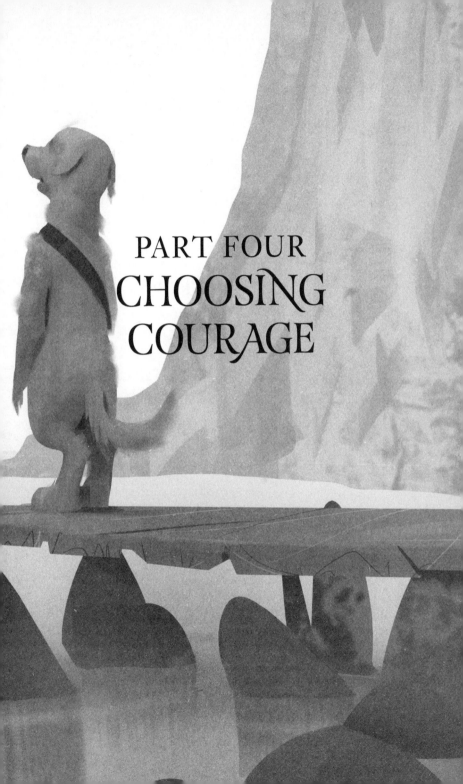

PART FOUR
CHOOSING
COURAGE

43

In Truth Lies Strength

We planned to set out early the next morning. It was chilly, and the forest was smothered in a thick shroud of fog that muted the whole world, muffling bird chirps, dulling footfalls, and gentling words to whispers. I hoped, somehow, that the mist would also mask my fear and sorrow.

I didn't want my companions to see how unready I felt.

How unready I *was*.

While I double-checked my pack, Gambler approached me. His forehead was furrowed, his eyes downcast. It was a look of concern I'd never before seen on the felivet's face. Most of the time his expression was unreadable, although every now and then he looked vaguely bemused, especially when it involved Renzo's antics.

"It was my intention to accompany you on your search for the colony," Gambler said. "I regret deeply that I may have given you false hope."

"Khara needs you, Gambler," I said. "She wouldn't ask you to stay unless it was absolutely necessary."

It was the right thing to say. And the true thing. But I desperately wished Gambler could come with me. Not just for his incredible speed and strength, but also for his cunning, his calm, and his wisdom. He knew the world in a way I simply did not.

Gambler leaned back on his haunches and raised his right paw, placing it gently on my shoulder. His claws, even sheathed, were terrifying to behold, the paw itself huge and heavy.

"Trust your instincts, friend dairne. You are wiser than you know."

I tried to speak, but found tears instead of words.

The Donatis gave us four small horses. They were an improvement over our previous steeds—still large for dairnes, but manageable. Maxyn rode a sturdy lilac roan, while mine was dappled silver with a flowing white mane and long, feathered hair on his fetlocks. Tobble sat behind me, as no horse is docile enough to be handled by a wobbyk, at least not well. The other two horses carried food and weapons, along with gifts from Khara to present to any dairnes we might find.

As we prepared to leave, Renzo ambled over to Tobble and me, already astride our horse.

"So. What's your horse's name?" Renzo asked with a forced grin.

"He's called Havoc," I said.

"I like him already." Renzo gave a laugh, then went silent. "You're going to be fine, you know," he said at last. "The way Tobble took down Mountain Morgoono . . . well, trust me: you have nothing to worry about."

I glanced over my shoulder to see Tobble's ears fluttering at Renzo's compliment.

"Just don't annoy that little wobbyk, Byx," Renzo added, "if you know what's good for you."

"There's a reason his family called him Tobble the Terrible," I replied.

Again Renzo fell uncharacteristically quiet.

"We will miss you, Renzo," I said to fill the emptiness. "Who will steal for us when the need arises?"

I expected a joke in response, but Renzo looked at me with complete seriousness. He glanced furtively to his right, where Khara was adjusting Maxyn's stirrups, then returned his gaze to me.

"You know I would go," he said under his breath, "if I could. But she"—another quick look at Khara—"she needs me."

I nodded. "It's true."

"We'll be fine," Tobble said. "You take care of Khara, Renzo."

"With my life," he whispered.

Were his eyes damp with tears? Renzo, of all people? He stepped away before I could be sure, and Khara took his place.

She looked from me to Tobble and back again, then gave a terse nod, as if assuring herself she'd made the right decision.

"The journey you undertake could change the future of Nedarra," Khara said.

"Khara, I . . ." I trailed off. I was a leader now. Wasn't it my job to say something profound? "I don't exactly know what to say."

"I do," Tobble said, with all the certainty I lacked. "When wobbyks head off to sea on a long voyage, we always say, 'I wish you fair winds and following seas.' It means 'Have a safe journey.'"

"I wish you the same," said Khara, a catch in her voice.

It was time to go, but I couldn't seem to bring myself to urge Havoc into a walk. Instead I reached into my belly pouch, where I kept my small array of treasures.

Most of them were things Tobble had rescued from the spot where my pack had been destroyed. Shards of a world I'd lost forever.

A bit of seashell, pink as summer sunrise.

A frayed playa leaf, the map I'd drawn as a student that had led us to Tarok.

A well-loved toy, a replica of a dairne pup made of tightly woven zania reeds.

A small leather-bound notebook, the one Luca had given me, and a feather, shed by a blue grouse, that I used as a pen. (I made my own ink from berries and leaves when time allowed.)

A small, flat rock with words carved into it.

I passed Khara the black stone. "I want you to have this."

She examined the tiny letters, then looked up at me, frowning.

"It says 'Xial renarriss,'" I explained. "Our pack motto in Old Dairnish: *In truth lies strength*. I think it belonged to our pathfinder, Myxo."

Khara rubbed her eyes. "I can't take this, Byx. You're the one who's pathfinding now."

She held out the rock cradled in her palm, and I realized that her hand was trembling.

It should have terrified me, seeing the obvious evidence of her fear. But somehow it gave me the surge of confidence I required at that moment. Perhaps Khara needed me as much as I needed her. I owed it to her to be strong.

Or at least to pretend to be strong.

"It appears we're both pathfinders now. Keep the stone until we meet again," I said. "Think of the stories we'll have to share with each other!"

Khara tightened her fist around the stone and nodded tersely. Before I could say anything more, she gave Havoc a nudge, and off he took. I allowed myself only one backward glance, as Khara, Renzo, Gambler, and Dog faded into the fog like a waking dream.

We hadn't gone far before the heavy mist quickly demonstrated Sabito's value. Again and again, he flew well above the fog, then dropped down through it, zooming close to yell directions and warnings.

"Veer north to get around a bramble patch!" he'd cry. Or: "There's a stream just two hundred yards away where you can water the horses."

By late morning, the fog had burned off and we began to emerge from the forest onto the great plain of Nedarra, thousands of square leagues of cultivated land. From this wide expanse came most of Nedarra's food crops: wheat, maize, sagrash, oats, and irridin.

This, Khara had explained to me, was part of the ongoing struggle between the exiled families and the Murdano in the east. Armies need food, and the Murdano (and his father before him) had always insisted on keeping the exiled families in line in order to ensure that his soldiers were well-fed.

But all this food traveled to the east by way of the Cruacan Pass, and we had noticed surprisingly little traffic there.

Either the Nedarran plain had already been stripped of crops, or families were keeping food from reaching the pass to begin with.

If the latter was the case, then the exiled families were already acting against the Murdano. If the Murdano wanted Nedarra's bounty, he would have to send troops to enforce his will—something that greatly concerned Khara, but not me, not right now. I had other worries, starting with the crushing realization that I was solely in charge.

Me. Responsible for a dairne, a wobbyk, a raptidon, and four horses. It wasn't an impressive army, perhaps, but it was more authority than I had ever carried, and it was intimidating, to say the least.

At first I found myself getting short-tempered with my companions, who seemed far too sanguine about the task that lay before us. I felt paranoid and anxious, constantly scanning the horizon for signs of trouble. My sleep was fretful, filled with terrifying dreams I could not control, despite my best attempts to savrielle.

But as the days wore on and we rode through endless tilled fields awaiting their next planting, I began to relax. We saw no signs of pursuit, and Sabito was always a thousand yards up in the sky, floating nonchalantly on updrafts of warm air. It seemed unlikely that we would be attacked by surprise.

Still, I had my responsibilities.

"Tobble," I chided, as we settled for the night in a deep gully cut by a swift stream, "remember, just one ration! We have to make this food last."

"Plenty of water, though," Tobble said cheerfully.

"For now," I grumbled. "We should all keep our waterskins topped up, in case we have to move quickly. And Maxyn, make sure to give your horse a thorough brushing and check his shoes."

I said a lot of that sort of thing.

Tobble was remarkably tolerant. Maxyn less so.

"Listen, Queen Byx," he said at one point, "I follow you. I obey you. But I have to tell you that you are growing a bit annoying."

"This isn't easy, you know!" I shot back. "It's my first time as a leader. And I'm responsible for all of us."

Tobble and Maxyn responded with weary sighs and a bit of eye rolling.

I resolved not to be a bully, and to try to project Khara's calm assurance. But I wasn't the scion of a great family. I didn't wield a fabled sword. Authority didn't come easily to me. My entire puphood had been nothing but me doing what others told me to do.

Most of the time, anyway.

With each passing day, I admired Khara more. She had

far greater responsibilities. How had she maintained discipline?

I only had three "followers." I knew Tobble loved me, Maxyn grudgingly liked me, and Sabito at least pretended to care what I said. How had Khara dealt with the formidable Gambler and the permanently independent Renzo?

Better than I was doing. That was the embarrassing answer.

44
My First Test as a Leader

Our fourth day began as the others had, with Tobble and me on the lead horse. Maxyn rode behind us with the two pack-horses tied to his saddle. The vast plain spread before us like a rippling golden lake.

Havoc, despite his name, proved to be a calm steed—perhaps even too calm. He had no trouble ignoring my commands if he felt like nibbling on a tuft of rengrass, or gazing at a herd of gamboling clouds. Sometimes, when I requested a gallop, all I got was an aimless stroll. I feared what might happen in the heat of a battle, when I needed him to heed my every command.

We hadn't gone far that morning when Sabito came swooping down out of low-hanging gray clouds.

"A hunting party of men is approaching from the south," he announced. "Five men on horses, armed with bows."

Everyone turned to me. *Tell us what to do,* their eyes demanded.

How many times had I looked at Khara with that same question, certain she'd have the right answer?

"Is there a place we could hide?" I asked Sabito. To our north were bare, rolling hills, but they were several leagues away.

Sabito landed on one of the packhorses. "There's no hiding place that I have seen. Do you have a theurgic concealment spell, by chance?"

I shook my head.

"Then we must either try to outrun them or face them," Sabito said. "They'll spot you within minutes, if they haven't already."

He didn't seem overly concerned. But then, Sabito had less reason to be afraid: the sky is a big place.

"Are they simple, honest hunters, or bandits? That's the question," I said. "Maxyn?"

"Yes?"

"Untie the packhorses."

"*Untie* them?"

"Odds are they'll follow us," I said, not at all sure I was right. "Tobble, hang on tightly."

"Will do!"

"Maxyn, spur your horse, and let's see if we can outrun

these men," I said with brittle confidence.

I nudged Havoc in the ribs. Maxyn did the same to his horse, and with our shouts of encouragement, both broke into a gallop. The packhorses kept pace with us, to my great relief. And Havoc surprised me with a newfound sense of urgency.

Perhaps he smelled my fear.

The hunters were coming from the south, and we could either flee in a straight line north or keep to our westward course. "Keep west!" I cried over the thunder of hooves, as if I were sure of my choice.

I sat low, hunched forward, one hand on the reins, the other on Havoc's mane, and we flew over the ground.

It was a wild, exhilarating run. Weeds whipped our flanks, and the air grew colder as a storm closed in. We galloped until our horses' mouths foamed and their backs were sheened with sweat.

At last I raised my hand, signaling Maxyn to slow, and Sabito went aloft to spy out the situation. He returned with the welcome news that the hunting party had headed north, even after crossing our highly visible tracks.

They were not after us. I had made my first important decision as leader, and amazingly, it seemed to be the right one.

I felt pleased, even a little proud.

But far more important, I felt relieved.

By early afternoon, we had come within distant view

of Mirror Lake to our southwest. We traveled across more wind-teased fields before I held up my hand to signal a pause. In all the excitement of our frantic ride, I'd forgotten to stop for a meal.

We dismounted near a hedge of dense, prickly bushes bordered by a tiny stream. Tobble set out a simple meal while Maxyn and I watered the horses.

When we were done eating, I reached into my patchel and retrieved the notebook Luca had given me. It had been ages since I'd written in it, but I still had a small vial of ink, along with my quill pen.

Maxyn leaned back against a rock, hands laced behind his head. "What are you going to write about?"

"I thought I'd keep track of our journey," I said. "So I can tell Khara and the others about it someday."

I winced as soon as the words were out of my mouth. It seemed wrong, just assuming that we would all meet again. I felt as if I were tempting fate. What were the odds, really, that we would ever see our dear friends again, given all we faced?

"Luca told me that I should write down everything I know about dairnes," I said, pushing past my dark thoughts. "Our myths and music and history. For scholars and such, in case we really are the last of our kind."

"I suppose it's as good a way as any to make the time pass," Maxyn said.

"I'll probably start with our family stories," I said, twirling the feather in my fingers as I considered. "Then move on to what we remember from our history lessons."

Maxyn laughed. "Well, that'll take about two lines! When my father tried to teach me history, it was the surest possible way to put me to sleep."

"I liked history. But now I really wish I'd listened even better." I flashed on a memory of white-muzzled Dalyntor discussing dairne lore while I daydreamed about adventures.

Well, I'd gotten my share of those, hadn't I? As my father liked to say: "Dream greatly and you may be challenged greatly."

For the next hour, Maxyn and I reminisced about our old lives. We talked of family lore, of folktales and songs, of favorite holidays and comforting foods. (We both adored roasted blue honeycorn and fish-eye pie.)

We shed a few tears, but we also laughed: wonderful, straight-from-the-belly laughs that left us breathless. I was relieved to be able to venture back to my old life with someone who understood the dairne world. For a long time, I hadn't let myself dwell on all that I'd lost.

I filled six pages of Luca's notebook with my hasty scribblings. Tobble, who, with Sabito, had been listening attentively, said, "You'll be out of ink soon, Byx. I'll go see if I can find any berries or herbs to mix up a new batch."

"Thank you, Tobble," I said. "That's very kind. I have the

feeling we are going to need a *lot* of ink."

Maxyn laughed, a husky, full-throated sound that reminded me of my brothers. "More ink? We're going to need more notebooks!"

"No doubt," Tobble said softly as he retrieved a small pouch from his saddlebag. "No doubt at all." He gave a little wave. "I'll be back in a few minutes."

"Don't dawdle," I said, falling back into my role as occasional leader and frequent nag, but Tobble had already turned his back on us and was heading downstream.

"Is everything all right with Tobble?" Maxyn whispered. "Of course, I don't know him as well as you, Byx, but he seems . . . distracted."

I tapped a finger on my chin. "I'm not sure. But you're right."

"Perhaps he's afraid of what lies ahead," Sabito offered. He cocked his head, one brown eye, shiny as a chestnut, trained on me.

"Tobble is braver than the three of us put together," I said. "No, it's something else. I wonder if he's pining for home."

"At least," Maxyn said with a shrug, "he has a home to pine for."

I nodded. I knew what Maxyn meant, although I also knew it wasn't fair to resent others just because they had families, and we did not.

He smiled at me, a lopsided grin that warmed my weary

heart. I am looking at another dairne, I told myself for what had to be the hundredth time. At one of my own. Someone who understood my life, and my pain, in a way no one else could.

Not Khara, not Gambler, not Sabito. Not even dear Tobble, busy gathering berries, just so that I could hold on to my precious memories a little longer.

45
Mud and Misery

The storm that had threatened since daybreak finally struck late that afternoon while we were still riding.

Sabito came streaking down out of the sky. "Hail!" he screeched, landing on one of the packhorses and covering his head with a wing.

The hail came, hard pellets as big as my fists. They flattened the field we were passing through, bounced merrily on open ground, and even drew blood when a huge ice chunk grazed Maxyn's ear.

The hail lasted several minutes, then stopped, but we had no rest from punishment. Rain gushed down in torrents, instantly drenching us. The ground turned to thick sludge, sucking at our horses' hooves and slowing progress to a crawl.

Before long, all four horses were clearly exhausted. We

dismounted and walked beside them, our feet booted in icy mud.

And then things got worse. The temperature dropped dramatically and the wind picked up, hurling flecks of ice and fat raindrops into our faces. With stiff, numb fingers I extracted three blankets from a saddlebag and passed one each to Tobble and Maxyn. When I wrapped mine around my shoulders, I realized it was no help at all. Instantly it was soaked, and weighed as much as I did.

"We have to stop!" Maxyn shouted.

"But where?" I called back.

Our visibility was down to a few yards. I saw no trees to shelter beneath, no convenient gullies or rock outcroppings to hide us from the wind. We were in a plowed, fallow field, with muck that rose to the horses' fetlocks.

Maxyn reined to a halt. "I have an idea!" He explained it in gasps and shouts, and while it sounded unlikely, it was better than nothing.

While Sabito watched, Maxyn, Tobble, and I tied the lead rope of each horse to the tail of the horse before him. Carefully, we shepherded all four into a circle and tied the rope to the last tail, forming a tight ring of snorting, unhappy horses.

Finally, we stretched our canvas ground cover over the horses. They were a bit protected and so were we, although it made for a windy, muddy, freezing shelter.

We four—even Sabito joined us—crawled under the legs of our horses to enter. The rain pooled onto our makeshift tent, so periodically Maxyn or I would stand on tiptoes, stretching our hands up into the canvas to make a sort of tent pole, in an attempt to shed accumulating water.

The horses did what horses do, and in copious amounts, so that in addition to our other discomforts, we also had to smell horse urine and . . . other things. Still, I reminded myself, the horses were doing us a favor, and they were certainly no happier about the circumstances than we were. It was an endless, exceedingly miserable night.

Morning was little better. We were greeted with wan sunlight and snow falling thick and fast. It was certainly prettier than rain, and less immediately terrifying than hail, but the mud that surrounded us like a vast brown pudding hadn't yet frozen. We slogged on in silence, encased in slush and muck. Visibility was terrible, and Sabito wisely chose to ride on the back of Maxyn's horse, Zara, rather than attempt to fly.

After just a few hours, we stumbled upon a small, burned-out building made of boulders and wood. Two walls were steady, a third wall was mostly gone, and the fourth wall was nowhere to be seen. Part of the roof remained, covering one corner, and we huddled there together, with the horses once again drawn close.

We spent two days in that charcoal wreckage, feeding

the horses with oats from our saddlebags, and ourselves with cheese and soggy bread. We had nothing to burn—the remaining timbers of the shack were soaked—so a fire wasn't a possibility.

We passed much of the time lost in our own thoughts. Every so often one of us would ask a variation on two questions: "How are Khara and Renzo and Gambler doing?" or "Do you think we'll really find more dairnes?"

While Maxyn and I kept up a constant stream of complaints about the mud and slush, Tobble was subdued. "I'm starting to wonder if you actually like this miserable weather," Maxyn said to him, as darkness wrapped around us like a sodden black cloak.

Tobble gave a smile. "I'm from Bossyp. It's a journey of many days from here, but the weather is quite similar."

"I've flown over Bossyp," said Sabito. "Veered off course during a storm. Beautiful place."

"It is," Tobble agreed. "This time of the year we do something called 'warren watch.' When you live in dens underground, weather this wet can be dangerous indeed. During warren watch, we took turns doing night patrols, looking for water leaks or signs of collapse. Of course, with one hundred and twenty-seven siblings, we had plenty of help."

"One hundred and twenty-seven?" Maxyn exclaimed.

"Wobbyks have several litters a year."

Maxyn shook his head. "I wouldn't know what to do with that many siblings."

"True, my parents sometimes forgot our names." Tobble smoothed his braided tails. "Well, *often* they did. But having so many warm bodies in our tunnels made things nice and toasty."

He sounded wistful, so I said, "Perhaps when we're done with our search, we could visit Bossyp, Tobble."

Tobble's long whiskers quivered, and his big, round eyes glistened. "I would like that, Byx. Very much indeed."

It was a relief to see Tobble's smile return, though it didn't last. He fell quiet while Maxyn and I played a silly pup game called Jip-Jop-Nop. It involved making three different shapes with your fingers and thumbs, but since we barely recalled the rules, we made up our own.

I offered to teach Sabito and Tobble, but Sabito said it was beneath his dignity to play pup games. Tobble simply held up his paws and shook his head. "I seem to be a bit short on fingers," he said.

I felt badly I hadn't considered that before asking. It was thoughtless of me, and I promised myself I'd be more careful in the future.

The next morning dawned cold and gray, but free from hail, rain, or snow. I could barely move after sitting cramped for so long, and the others seemed equally miserable.

Through chattering teeth, I ordered everyone to pack up. We led our horses from the wrecked home and discovered that the ground had begun to freeze and was firmer underfoot.

"Have patience," I told my friends. "When the horses warm up, we should be able to mount again and make better progress."

What I should have done before departing was ask Sabito to take to the air and scout our surroundings.

What I should have done was assess all possible threats, then plan accordingly.

What I should have done was be the leader I was supposed to be.

But I didn't do those things.

And I would forever regret it.

46
The Chase

As we slogged along, Sabito surveyed our path from the air. Moments later, he veered back, screeching a warning—one that came too late, for even I could see that not a quarter league away was an encampment of six large tents, with a dozen horses tethered beneath a long canvas lean-to.

It was not a hunters' camp. Nor was it a camp set up by a traveling caravan. No, it was the one thing that, above all else, I didn't want to see.

It was, unmistakably, an army camp. Already two riders in the Murdano's livery were galloping toward us to see whether we were friend or foe.

I couldn't drop to all fours, stay mute, and pass myself off as a dog. That works if no one looks closely. But dogs do not ride horses or lead expeditions.

"Everyone stay calm," I whispered, despite the fact that

"calm" was the last thing I was feeling. "Remember: we are adventurers seeking a fabled lost diamond mine."

That lie had seemed plausible enough when Renzo had cooked it up. But now the idea that anyone would accept it seemed ludicrous.

We stood still and waited. That's what the innocent do. Only the guilty flee.

The soldiers clattered up, their huge warhorses towering over our steeds. Both riders stayed in their saddles, unconcerned that their animals were kicking up mud and snow and frightening our horses. Not to mention us.

"State your names and business," the smaller of the two men snapped.

"Yes, of course," I said, trying to locate a steady voice. "I am Byx, this is Maxyn, and this is Tobble."

"And what are you?"

"Me? I am from the far, far south."

"I didn't ask where you came from. I asked what you are."

"Ah, I see. Yes, I must look strange to your eyes, but I am a . . . a . . . southern felivet."

"A what?"

"We are an offshoot of felivets." I clenched my hands into fists to hide their trembling. "A subspecies of small, harmless catlike animals."

The large man scowled. "You look more dog than cat."

"Yes, well, as I said, we come from a distant land. A strange land with strange creatures. Creatures like us."

I was babbling, and my fear was getting the better of me. I could only hope he assumed my teeth were chattering because of cold rather than guilt.

The two men consulted for a moment. Then the larger one spoke in a commanding voice. "You will come to our camp. The captain can question you."

I knew we couldn't refuse. Two armed men, soldiers, would cut us down in less time than it took to draw a breath, let alone draw a weapon.

"Of course," I said, defeated.

We set off, following the soldiers.

"Byx," Maxyn said in a whisper, "if they sense anything wrong, they will torture us for information."

I gritted my teeth. Surely not? We were harmless enough.

Except.

Except that we carried too many weapons to be mere adventurers. Except that someone in the human camp might know just enough to recognize us as dairnes.

"Warhorses are big but slow," Maxyn said. "We can outrun them."

Could we? But where would we run? And would the soldiers pursue us, or would they pass us off as irrelevant? They might assume we were mere poachers—lawbreakers, but not the sort of lawbreakers that a common soldier would care much about.

However, if they learned we were dairnes . . .

I glanced to the west. Just a few leagues ahead was a forest, but what forest? We'd wandered so long in such poor visibility that I had no clear idea where we were. Was that the Mirror Lake forest? Was that a hazy hint of water I saw off on the horizon?

If we ran for it and reached the woods, would the soldiers follow us?

I looked at Maxyn, met his eye, and with my heart in my throat, nodded. "In three seconds," I whispered.

"One."

The smaller soldier twisted in his saddle and said, "Shut your traps back there."

I mouthed the word "two" and added, "Hold on tight, Tobble."

With a slashing motion of my hand, I kicked Havoc's ribs, cried, "Run, boy, run!" and yanked his reins to the left.

We were off at a quick pace, but that wouldn't be enough. I needed Havoc to live up to his name. "Now, now, now!" I screamed, and he stretched out into a full-on gallop.

Almost instantly, both soldiers turned in shock. One of them shouted a curse, and they wheeled to come after us.

Maxyn had been right: our horses were faster. They'd

been well-fed and watered recently and welcomed the chance to stretch their powerful muscles.

It would have been thrilling, if I hadn't been so terrified.

Sabito swooped close and kept pace beside me. "You're making progress, but they have bows!"

Bows? I hadn't seen any bows.

I searched my panic-scrambled memory and recalled seeing a long leather pouch strapped across the haunches of one of the warhorses.

I risked a backward glance. Maxyn, hot on my heels. The packhorses off to the side, but keeping pace. The two soldiers falling slowly back.

Fifty feet became a hundred. A hundred became two hundred.

And then the first arrow flew by my head, so close I felt its feathers brush my cheek.

"Faster!" I cried.

A second arrow stuck hard in the back of my saddle with a sickening thud. Moments later, I heard a horse's scream. I jerked my head back just in time to see Maxyn's horse stumble, catch herself, then trip into a somersault that sent her rider flying.

The soldiers were on Maxyn before Zara could even try to stand. An arrow was embedded in her right flank.

"Maxyn!" I yelled.

I tried to rein in Havoc, but he ignored me, frenzied with terror, while Tobble was in my ear shouting, "You can't help him, Byx! You can't help him!"

Both soldiers gave up the chase. They rode in circles around the fallen horse. I watched for as long as I could without losing my seat, but I did not see Maxyn rise.

Tears froze on my cheeks. I could think of only two possibilities: Maxyn had been crushed by his horse. Or he was a prisoner of the Murdano's men.

Either way, I knew with a sinking heart, I might have prevented it.

And either way, there was nothing I could do now to save him.

47
Retreat

I rode on in a fog as dense as the one that had enveloped us the morning we'd left our friends behind. But this one was entirely of my own making, an impenetrable cloud of questions without answers.

Was it possible Maxyn was still alive? If so, was he in pain? Was he terrified? Did he fear we would abandon him forever? How could I have let him down—my responsibility, my friend, my fellow dairne—so utterly? Why had Khara trusted me to lead?

Why had I trusted myself?

I had failed, catastrophically, in my first duty as a leader: to keep my charges alive. Or at least free.

If Maxyn was really dead, my heart would be broken, but the Pellago River colony—if it even existed—was safe for now. If Maxyn was alive and being tortured for information, the Murdano's soldiers might soon be pursuing us. Should I attempt a rescue, despite the likelihood—no, the certainty—that we'd all be put in prison for the rest of our lives, or killed?

We galloped on, simply because I didn't know what else to do. Tobble and Sabito kept silent, no doubt waiting for me to come to a decision. The two packhorses followed behind us.

Soon we were heading into lands that were unmistakably wild, as we skirted Mirror Lake, a deep and gloomy body of water. Finally I called a halt. The horses were exhausted and so were we. Tobble and Sabito ate a small meal, but I had no appetite for food. No appetite for conversation, either, but Tobble was insistent.

"Byx," he said, as always reading my mind, "what happened to Maxyn is not your fault."

"Of course it is." I rubbed my eyes. "I'm in charge. What happens to you and Sabito and . . . and Maxyn . . . is my responsibility. Maybe if I hadn't decided to attempt an escape, Maxyn would be alive right now."

"We don't know if he is dead," Sabito said.

"If he's alive, I have to try to save him," I said, even though I had no idea how. "Not just for Maxyn. For the colony, too. The Murdano's soldiers will show no mercy, and if Maxyn reveals our true goal, the last remaining dairnes will be in danger."

"There were six tents at the soldiers' encampment," Sabito reminded me. "And twelve horses. You're talking about pitting a dozen of the Murdano's heavily armed men against a dairne, a wobbyk, and a riverhawk?" He repositioned a wing feather with his beak before continuing. "That's a fool's errand, plain and simple."

I paced back and forth, my hands behind my back, something I'd seen Khara do in moments of crisis. "There must be something I can do. *Something*."

"When I joined this expedition at Khara's request," said Sabito, "I warned you I would speak the unalloyed truth, as is my way. And the truth, Byx, is that Maxyn is quite likely already dead. The further truth is that if you attempt to rescue him—assuming, by some miracle, that he is still alive—you will be killed, tortured, or imprisoned. It's that simple. There are no other options."

I looked at Tobble. I don't know what I wanted from him. A brilliant plan? A tendril of hope? Some kind of absolution?

"Sabito is right, Byx," Tobble said in a whisper. "I'm so sorry."

I stopped in my tracks. "I can't risk your lives. I've already done enough damage. But I can go back alone." My pulse raced, along with my plans. "I'll sneak into the encampment, see if Maxyn is alive, and if he is—"

"This isn't just about Maxyn. Your duty is to Khara," Tobble interrupted. "She needs you to find more dairnes. For the inevitable war."

"And for the possible peace," Sabito added.

"Just a day or two," I said, almost pleading. "I owe it to Maxyn."

"You will never return," Sabito said flatly. "And our mission will end."

I shifted from one foot to the other, my hands clenched. "But you could go on alone, you and Tobble."

"We need a dairne to approach the colony," Tobble reminded me. "It's the only way they'll listen."

Tobble and Sabito were right, and for a moment, I hated them both for it. I slumped against a tree trunk, my shoulders sagging. There had to be something I could do before simply giving up and moving on.

A tiny seed of hope planted itself in my mind. "Sabito," I said. "Fly back to the camp. Search for any sign of Maxyn and report back here."

"And *then* what?" Sabito asked, with precisely the arrogant tone he'd warned me I'd be hearing.

I straightened up, met his gaze, and forced an edge to my voice. "And then," I said, "I will decide what happens next."

He gave a little flick of his wing tips, which I took to

signal his reluctant agreement, and flew off without another word.

For the next hour, Tobble and I set up camp and cared for the horses. I could feel his huge eyes boring into me, and I found it annoying. I was supposed to be the leader. The strong one. The wise one. I didn't need a little wobbyk overseeing me like a fretful nanny.

"I'm fine, Tobble," I snapped when I caught him glancing at me yet again. "You don't have to coddle me."

Tobble's ears drooped, and I instantly regretted my words. "I'm sorry," I said. "I'm just so . . . tired."

I busied myself with the task of pulling a burr from Havoc's tail so that Tobble wouldn't see the tears pooling in my eyes.

Maybe I wasn't so fine, after all.

"I know how much Maxyn meant—means—to you, Byx," Tobble said, joining me at Havoc's side. "With him, you weren't the only dairne anymore. And now, well . . ."

Strangely enough, the possibility hadn't occurred to me until that moment. Was I really an endling once again? If the Pellago River colony proved to be a myth, then the answer was obvious.

I shrugged. "You know what's odd, Tobble? I don't even care about that." I waved a hand. "I mean, of course I don't want to go back to being an endling. But what I can't bear is the idea of being responsible for what's happened to Maxyn."

"You did your best," Tobble insisted. "Isn't that what you would tell Khara?"

"Khara wouldn't have made such an error."

"Would it help," Tobble asked, "if I told you that I trust you completely to lead us?"

I moved to Havoc's mane, searching for more burrs. "You're my friend, Tobble. You have to say that."

"And so was Maxyn," Tobble said. Without warning, to my shock, he began to cry, great, rib-heaving sobs that seemed too huge to be coming from such a small body.

"Tobble!" I exclaimed, giving him a hug. "What's wrong?"

"I feel s-s-so bad," he managed. He pulled a leaf from his pouch and blew his nose. "Poor Maxyn. I . . . I was jealous of him, Byx. I felt like I was losing your friendship, because how could I compete with another dairne when I am just a wobbyk, and sometimes I wished he would just leave and now he's gone and"—he paused for a quaking breath—"and I hate myself for even thinking that and—"

"Tobble," I interrupted, "is that why you've been so quiet lately?"

He found another leaf and blew his nose again. "Yes."

"I thought you were homesick for Bossyp and your family."

"I am. A little. But *you're* my family now, Byx. You and

Khara and Gambler and Renzo. And maybe Sabito. I'm not so sure about him yet."

I took Tobble by the shoulders and looked into his shimmering eyes. "Tobble, no one could *ever* take your place. Ever. Do you understand?"

He sniffled, then nodded.

I started to say more, but just then Sabito dropped from the sky, silent as the moon. He landed on Havoc's saddle, adjusted his feathers, then looked at me. Hawks have rather impassive faces. Nonetheless, I felt certain he had bad news.

"Nothing," he said, before I could ask. "No sign of Maxyn anywhere, though his horse survived. They're preparing to move camp."

I let the words lie there. "I have failed him, and failed you all," I finally said.

Sabito hopped closer. He held out his right leg, with its missing talon. "You know how I lost that talon, Byx?"

I gave a shrug. I didn't know and I didn't care.

"It was ripped off during a battle last year between Rorid Headcrusher's forces and a competing clan of raptidons. A territorial dispute, nothing more. Rorid miscalculated their strength and we lost many valiant fighters."

"I'm sorry."

"And so was Rorid. But he continues to lead us with wisdom and honor. I would follow no one else into battle." Sabito paused. "With two possible exceptions."

I looked at him, waiting. "And they are?"

"Kharassande Donati," Sabito answered. He cocked his head, taking me in, sizing me up. "And you, Byx. You."

48
Nearing Our Goal at Last

I was relieved that I couldn't sleep that night. I didn't want to face the nightmares I knew would haunt me.

In the morning, Tobble and Sabito looked at me expectantly. "Well, what are you waiting for?" I said. "Tend to the horses and let's be on our way."

The command surprised me. I hadn't been sure what I was going to do until I'd said the words aloud. But I knew in my exhausted heart that Sabito and Tobble were right. My duty was to our mission.

We traveled for two whole days on the narrow verge between dense forest and the foreboding Mirror Lake, its surface smooth as polished armor. On the third day, Tobble and I, with Sabito hovering overhead, made a perilous crossing of the Pellago River.

We cut down a dead tree and used it to float across, both

of us feeling jealous of Sabito's winged talents. (Glissaires are no match for feathers.) Unfortunately, the river took its time delivering us to the far shore, and we lost a league of progress. The horses, of course, handled the current much more easily than we did, but it took almost a day to round them up.

At last we were close to what we hoped was our final goal. But "close" is a relative term. Merely saying "the Pellago River area" did not narrow things down by much. After conferring with Sabito, I realized we had only two paths forward. We could walk up into the valley that was the source of the Pellago River. Or we could head on to the seacoast. Both would take us near the border of Marsony, a little-known land believed to be populated by fearsome beasts and wild men.

"Which would be more likely?" Sabito asked from his perch on a packhorse. "A dairne colony hidden in a valley, or a dairne colony by the sea?"

I considered for a moment. "It's been a long time since any group of dairnes felt safe enough to pursue the old ways. We've become fugitives, hiding during the day and sneaking around in the night. I'm not really sure how dairnes live when they're not under attack."

"These dairnes are still afraid," Tobble pointed out. "Otherwise, why would their existence be only a rumor?"

I nodded. "I suppose if I were their leader, I'd get as far

from the Murdano as possible. As far from any human."

Once again, I was faced with a decision about which direction to take. "I remember Dalyntor telling us that in long-ago times dairnes fashioned boats," I said at last. "It's not much to go on. But let's take the seafront path. I've had enough of gloomy forests."

Our path took us along impressively high cliffs for two days. At times, the passage was so narrow that a misplaced hoof would have sent us falling to our deaths. Still, there was something soothing about the *shush-shush* of the waves crashing below us. The breeze was crowded with vivid scents: shellfish and sea salt, fir and sandbeech, cotchet and squirrel.

Calm weather held until we turned due north, when snow came fluttering in from the sea, frosting the landscape. As we plodded along, we noticed that a channel had formed between the mainland and a pair of narrow barrier islands. Here we encountered more wildlife than I'd ever seen before. Shy coastal deer poked their antlers out from behind trees, while snow-dusted hedgehogs and chillugs waddled fearlessly across our paths.

And there were birds. Thousands of them.

"Razorgulls!" Tobble cried, pointing with a trembling finger at a thick cloud wheeling and diving above a cove.

"Ah, good," Sabito said.

"Good?" Tobble echoed. "They tried to kill us!"

"And nearly succeeded," I added.

"Razorgulls? Pah!" Sabito's voice was disdainful. "Do you really think those scavengers would dare look for trouble with the likes of me?"

With a nonchalant flap of his wings, he caught the ocean breeze and soared off to meet them. Twenty minutes later he was back.

"Interesting," Sabito said. "They have never heard the word 'dairne.' These are rustic birds, you understand. Simple creatures. They serve no one. Yet when I asked them to look at you, they said they might have seen similar animals."

"Encouraging!" said Tobble.

But I stifled any enthusiasm. I was still the leader of this tiny expedition, and I was determined not to let emotion cloud my thinking.

We pressed on, the churning sea and the steep drop on our left, a pleasant grove of hardwood trees on our right. As we turned a sharp corner past a stand of yellow birch, we gasped at a massive obstacle before us: a rock as tall as a small mountain, with unscalable granite on all sides.

Our path along the sea was blocked. With a sigh, I pointed to the woods and we entered, our horses' hooves crunching on dead leaves crusted with ice.

"We must be nearing the border of Marsony," I remarked.

"How can you tell?" Tobble asked.

"I remember from my geography lessons that—"

A blur of movement caught my eye. A bent sapling, one that had been suddenly released, slapped me hard in the side, and I fell off Havoc with a thud. Startled, he galloped away with poor Tobble clutching the saddle for dear life.

As I rose from the ground, brushing snow from my fur, I took in my surroundings. Sabito did the same, with his infinitely superior eyes. Neither of us saw anyone who might have triggered the simple trap.

"See if you can locate Tobble and Havoc," I said. "I'll catch up."

Sabito soon found Tobble trembling atop Havoc, who had stopped to nibble a tuft of grass poking through the snow. I gathered up the two packhorses and joined my friends minutes later.

"Must we turn back?" Tobble sounded more than a little hopeful.

"No," I said, grinning. "Don't you see? A trap means someone is trying to discourage the curious."

"Did you smell dairne?" Tobble asked.

"No," I admitted. "But that may have been set long ago, and triggered by a thread I couldn't see."

I rode on, faster than before, while keeping an eye out for traps. I felt encouraged—even eager. But another day passed without further clues.

Then, just as night was falling and I was looking for a place to camp, Sabito came tearing down through the trees.

"You've almost missed it!" he cried.

"Missed what?"

"Turn your horses back toward the water and you shall see."

We did as instructed, riding carefully through the dark hush of the trees. I let Havoc pick his hoof falls carefully, lest he step in a hole or trip on a root.

We arrived north of the great rock that had impeded our progress, and once again I heard the rhythmic tumult of waves far below us. Had Havoc been a foolish beast, we might well have met with disaster, for with full dark and only a faint, cloud-shrouded moon, we came to a sudden ravine.

"Yes," Sabito said, swooping past.

Mystified, I dismounted and walked to the lip of the chasm. It was a sheer drop-off, less a valley than a tear in the land, no more than two hundred yards at its widest.

I sucked in a breath. Far below, where the ravine met the sea, I saw something miraculous.

Light.

More than one light. Many, in fact.

Enough to brighten a small village.

49
A Treacherous Descent

"How do we get down there?" Tobble asked, peering over the side. "And what about the horses?"

"There must be a path," I said. But the odds of us finding a trail down that sheer drop in the dark were just about nonexistent.

"I could carry Tobble," Sabito offered, "as long as we're descending. Otherwise, I'd need a good, stiff breeze. The wind right now is blowing from offshore, which won't help us."

"I might be able to make it on my glissaires," I said, but I had my doubts. A dairne's glissaires aren't meant for perilous, thousand-foot drops into a narrow ravine. I'd already endured enough airborne acrobatics to last a lifetime.

In the end, I decided we should wait until morning, though my yearning to move forward was nearly desperate. I stared at the lights until my eyes blurred, trying to imagine what lay below.

Was it really the dairne colony? And if so, what could that mean?

For Khara, and for the war, it could mean a huge advantage. Truth tellers might prove invaluable when dealing with the enemy. For my species, it could mean there still was hope that we could survive.

And for me? A colony of dairnes could mean a new beginning. A life with others of my own kind. The thing that I'd wanted most of all.

With a pang, I thought of Maxyn. If only he were here to share this moment!

Tobble approached me with some steaming dorya leaf tea he'd managed to make. I warmed my hands around the wooden cup we shared. "Thank you, Tobble," I said, grateful for his company as much as for the tea.

"Are you excited?" he asked, gazing at the lights twinkling like sunken stars.

"I am," I admitted. "Though I don't want to get my hopes up."

"I am, too," Tobble said. "As relieved as we were to find Maxyn and his father, this"—he gestured with a paw—"would be even more important, if it really is a whole village of dairnes."

I passed the mug back to Tobble, who slurped—Tobble was a big slurper—contentedly.

"If there are more dairnes here," I said, remembering what he'd confessed about Maxyn, "I'll be . . . preoccupied for a while, Tobble. Speaking Dairnish, sharing stories. But don't ever doubt that you are my dearest friend."

"I will never doubt again," Tobble promised. He leaned his head on my arm. "I wish Maxyn could have been here for this. I really do."

I lay awake much of that night. I must have finally fallen asleep, for I was awakened by Sabito, flaring his wings as he landed on a dead branch a few feet away.

"Found it!" he said. "Oh, they were clever, very clever, your dairnes. No one on foot could ever have discovered it."

Tobble was already busy frying the last of a slab of bacon. I wolfed down my food, scalded my tongue with hot tea, and said, "All right, then, let's get moving. Sabito? Lead on, my hawk friend, lead on."

We followed him to the east for a while. When I looked back, I could see that the great mass of rock we'd been forced to circumvent actually formed the southern edge of the ravine. Soon we turned, following the northern edge, but still I saw no path leading downward. Each time I peered over the cliff, I recoiled at the terrifying drop.

Sabito landed, as had become his habit, on a packhorse.

"There! Do you see?"

I saw nothing but a jumble of boulders filling a collapsed bit of cliff. "We can't possibly take horses over those rocks."

"Ah, but we don't need to," Sabito said smugly. "Just beyond those rocks there's a narrow, but usable, trail down the cliff. You would never notice it from ground level."

"Fine," I said. "But I still see a massive pile of rocks, and it looks unsteady. I don't fancy tumbling a thousand feet down in a rockslide."

"You see that first boulder, the big one with the little tree growing on top?"

I nodded.

"I suggest that you and Tobble give it a push."

"Give it a push?" I laughed. "It's bigger than a house!"

Sabito cocked his head. "Indulge me."

Tobble and I reluctantly dismounted. Feeling like complete fools, we placed our hands against the towering rock, a rock that must have weighed more than a dozen horses. We leaned into it, pushing with all our meager strength, and promptly fell on our faces.

The giant boulder swung aside as easily as a door.

In fact, it *was* a door.

"I saw the marks made by the swiveling action," Sabito said. "Quite obvious from the air."

The path through the boulder jumble was narrow. Briefly

I considered abandoning the horses and heading forward on foot. But we needed them. Not just for the supplies they carried, but also for a quick escape.

Nothing I'd endured so far had prepared me for the descent that followed. The trail down was as wide as Havoc's stance, with perhaps six inches to spare. One wrong step, and we were facing a long and deadly fall. I gripped the reins until my hands ached, afraid to move a muscle. Havoc's flanks scraped the rocks on either side, and Tobble and I had to draw up our saddlebags and raise our feet to squeeze through.

A third of the way down, we came to a washout, a place where rain had eroded the pathway, creating a three-foot gap.

Sabito could carry Tobble that short distance, and I could glide. But the horses were another matter entirely.

They would have to jump.

I'd never before tried to get a horse to jump. It wasn't easy. Havoc, sensible beast that he was, had no interest in leaping from one narrow pathway, across a long and deadly drop, in order to land on another narrow pathway. I couldn't blame him.

But I'd already decided that we needed the horses, and in any case, the trail was too tight for us to turn around. With much coaxing and urging, along with Sabito's gentle but strategic pecking, we convinced Havoc and the packhorses to back up fifty yards or so.

"If he misses, spread your glissaires and try to push away from the cliff," Sabito advised.

"As it happens, I'd thought of that," I replied. It sounded more sarcastic than I'd intended, but then, when you're terrified, politeness can be in short supply.

I twisted in my saddle. "Hang on, Tobble," I advised.

"Yes," he said with a smile, "as it happens, I'd thought of that."

I leaned forward and whispered to Havoc, "You must trust me. We'll make it."

With my heart thudding and my stomach churning, I dug my heels in hard and yelled, "Go, boy! Go!"

To my amazement, and his, Havoc broke into a panicked run, hooves pounding. I barely stayed in the saddle.

Even more remarkably, the two packhorses, perhaps assuming Havoc was their leader, followed after him.

The leap—the part where we were actually soaring through the air—seemed to take hours. Breath held, fur flying, I gritted my teeth as Havoc made a hard, but clean, landing on the other side.

The first packhorse had a tougher time, barely scrabbling to safety. Then, to my horror, I watched the second horse miss his footing. He fell, silent, as I cried out. The only comfort was that his death was instantaneous.

Another loss that could be blamed only on me, I thought, my heart breaking for the poor animal.

Deeply shaken, I led on, ever downward. The angles were sharp, and I caught only fleeting glimpses of our objective before we finally reached level ground.

A palisade of stripped, sharpened tree trunks awaited us. The logs were old, graying with age, the bark rotting from ants and termites, although a gate in the center of the palisade appeared newer. I saw no observers anywhere, and no watchtowers. In fact, the whole thing seemed quite abandoned.

"Hello!" I yelled. Nothing. "Hello!" I cried at the top of my lungs, this time in Dairnish.

"Shall I just take a quick peek?" Sabito suggested.

I nodded. He flew off, and a minute later I heard a shout, a yelp, and an angry question.

Sabito reappeared. "The gate will be opened shortly. It seems the guard was having his lunch indoors and did not expect to be disturbed."

I had only one question, of course. Was the guard a dairne? But before I could ask, a small spyhole opened in the center of the gate.

An eye stared, blinked, stared some more. The spyhole closed. After some rustling of chains, the gate squeaked slowly open.

The guard was old, shaggy, and gray-muzzled. "By all the fish in the sea!" he exclaimed. "You're one of us!"

50
One of Us

Us. One of *us.*

I grinned hugely. I nodded frantically.

I must have looked like a lunatic.

"I'm a dairne!" I cried. "And so are you!"

"Well, of course *I* am," the old dairne grumbled, eyes narrowed. He was using the Common Tongue, presumably because of his role as gatekeeper.

"I'm sorry. It's just that I wasn't sure you . . . existed," I explained, laughing as I wiped away tears with the back of my hand.

"Seems I do. Well then, you'd best come on in, and I'll take you to the elders."

Tobble patted me on the shoulder. "Can you believe it?" he whispered, sounding as thrilled as I felt.

"No," I admitted. "I keep waiting to wake up."

We rode behind the slowly shuffling dairne, passing habitations. They ranged from modest, windowless log houses with low doors to two-story buildings leaning out precariously over a narrow paved lane. There were few side streets, and the ones that existed traveled only for a few yards. I was quite aware of our position at the bottom of a steep ravine. Sunlight, it seemed, would rarely reach the cobbles of the street. This was clearly a fishing village, and not a wealthy one. I saw no gold- or silversmiths. And even the finer houses looked worn and somehow fragile.

But everywhere, *everywhere*, there were dairnes!

Dairne couples, leaning out of windows to watch us suspiciously. Dairne children, following behind us in a chaotic procession. Dairne merchants, selling fish, dried seaweed, herbs, and pottery from small stalls.

The old dairne led us the length of the main street. When the cobblestones ran out, we came to a cheerless, gray shale beach. It featured a pier made of boulders, topped by a wooden walkway that was in better repair than the rest of the village. Two small fishing boats rocked in the water, while five more boats lay at angles on the beach, abandoned by the receding tide. All were painted in cheerful, if fading, colors.

"They shouldn't be in the harbor," Tobble said to me.

"What?"

"The boats. I come from a fishing village myself, and on a day without storms, the boats should all be at sea."

"Perhaps it's because of them," said Sabito, who was flying beside us.

I followed the direction of his intense hawk stare and saw two boats. One was a galley of no more than eight oars. The other was a sailboat, much larger, with two masts amidships.

"Whose ships are those?" I called to the old dairne.

"Who do you think?" he snapped.

"Are they the Murdano's?"

The dairne spat. "You must be a stranger to these parts. We've seen nothing of the Murdano's men for many a year. No, those are Marsonians. Marsonian raiders blocking our boats from leaving, and hoping to seize our boats. They arrived a week ago."

At the southern end of the beach was the largest structure I had yet seen. It was an odd building, constructed out of limestone blocks and wood. Clearly some ancient building had been abandoned here by long-ago inhabitants and left to collapse with age. The dairnes had used the crumbling stones as a foundation for a two-story building, topped by a shaky tower that rose another fifty feet. Gazing up, I saw a dairne watching the ships from Marsony.

"Did you notice the fish in the market stalls?" Tobble asked.

"No. What do you mean?"

"It was old fish. Eyes clouded, scales slimy, a rising smell. I think the village is being starved out."

It was a disturbing thought, but the more I considered my surroundings, the more it seemed a real possibility.

We stopped at the stone-and-wood building and the old dairne announced, "This is the hall of the elders. Go say hello to them. I have my duties to attend to."

He left us standing at the bottom of a set of steps that led to an impressive door bound with rusting iron straps.

Sabito landed on a bit of broken stone railing and said, "So. Here we are."

He seemed rather satisfied with himself, but I was too giddy to care. "Thanks to you," I said, "in large part."

"Yes," Sabito agreed. "Thanks entirely to me."

I think he was joking. But you can't always tell with raptidons.

We tied up the horses, and I mounted the steps on trembling legs, followed by Tobble. I touched the door as if it were a holy object.

The hall of elders. *Dairne* elders!

We stepped inside. Sabito chose to wait where he was most comfortable—a few hundred feet up in the air.

The interior, cool and dark, smelled of mildew and time. I sensed that it was a large space, but with just two stingy candles burning, one at either end of the rectangular room, it was impossible to perceive any details.

A dairne female, quite old and leaning on a wooden cane, came out of a side door. She caught sight of us, gaped in disapproval, and said in Dairnish, "Well, what are you waiting for? The elders are over there." She waved a gnarled hand.

I looked at Tobble, his eyes glittering in the candlelight, and nodded.

As we advanced, I heard the soft murmur of voices. At the end of the room we found a shallow, circular pit with benches placed all around the sides.

Four dairnes—two males, two females—sat in dim light. One was knitting. One was reading a scroll. One was throwing dice against a wall. And one was snoring heartily.

They could have been the elders of my own pack, sitting in companionable silence on a peaceful afternoon.

For a moment, I just breathed it all in. The scent of a roomful of dairnes! The sweet, warm comfort of it. The heart-filling familiarity.

The acceptance. The belonging.

"Eh? What's this?" asked the reader, speaking Dairnish, but with an accent I didn't recognize. She was old but not ancient, a grandmother but not a great-grandmother, I thought. Her muzzle and the tips of her ears were silver, but other than that, she was glossy black, a rare, and thus treasured, fur color among dairnes.

I took a deep breath. "I'm sorry to disturb you," I said,

struggling to find the words in my native tongue, "but I am Byx, and we—oh, this is my dear friend, Tobble—" I began to cry, but they were gentle, grateful tears. "We have traveled many leagues to find you."

51
A Roomful of Dairnes

The older female dairne peered closely at me. An aging male, the one who'd been knitting, set aside his needles and joined her.

"That's a wobbyk, as I live and breathe," he said. "Hah! I haven't seen a wobbyk in ages."

"Do you speak the Common Tongue?" I asked, still sniffling.

The male shrugged. "Of course. Not much use for it here, though. Why d'ya ask?"

"So that my friend, Tobble, can join in our conversation," I said. Tobble's ears perked up at the second mention of his name.

"Hard to believe a wobbyk could contribute much," the female said, adding with a gruff laugh, "though goodness knows he'd make a fine meal!"

I decided not to translate her comment for Tobble.

Instead, I changed to the Common Tongue and asked, "How many dairnes live in this village?"

"Not as many as there used to be," the male replied, switching as well.

"All right, then. Let's get down to basics," said the female, in heavily accented Common Tongue. "I'm Larbrik. And that there"—she jerked her chin at the knitter—"is my husband, Figton. Now, who are you? Where are you from? Why have you come here?"

Once again, emotion overwhelmed me and I started to weep. Tears flowing, I rushed over and hugged her as if she were my own mother. She patted my head and said, "There there, now," but with an edge of lingering suspicion.

"Orban!" she called. "Fetch tea! You, wobbyk, does your kind take tea?"

"We do, and most gratefully," Tobble said politely.

The tea came promptly, delivered by a young male dairne about my age. He winked at me as he set down the tea and withdrew.

It was an odd-tasting tea, something made, I suspected, of algae or seaweed, more salty than sweet. Still, it was warm and soothing, and I calmed down enough to share my lengthy story while the others gathered around.

I'd become so accustomed to speaking to different species that I'd almost forgotten what it was like to speak to my own kind. With humans especially, I always had to be aware of their suspicions. Because they couldn't always distinguish truth from lies, they were often wary of an unusual story.

But because dairnes can instantly discern lies, as strange as my tale was, they believed me wholeheartedly. By the time I'd finished, other dairnes had crept in around us, hanging on my every word.

The more questions they asked, the more I realized just how isolated from the world these villagers were. Who was Araktik? Had the old Murdano truly been replaced? What was all this about exiled families?

Some questions were heartbreaking. What news of the dairnes in Urmanland? Had I encountered any dairne of the wandering Blue Sky colony? Did I know anything of the dairnes near the upper Tellarno?

"Don't you see?" I said, my voice breaking. "They are all gone. All dead. My own pack, my family . . ."

For a moment I couldn't speak. It had been a while since I'd cried over my family. I preferred to push those thoughts away, because with the sadness inevitably came rage, and I couldn't spend my life in a state of constant anger.

I gazed from face to face—so many dairnes, so hungry for news—and tried again. "You must understand that until we found Maxyn and his father, I thought I was the last. The endling of our species."

"You've been all alone?" a sympathetic voice asked.

"Yes," I replied. But instantly that answer sounded false to my own ears, as it did, I could tell, to my fellow dairnes. "No, not alone. Not alone at all," I said, and I pointed to Tobble. "I've believed myself to be the last of our kind. But I've made dear friends on my journey here."

"Here to do what?" Larbrik asked bluntly. "To starve with us? Or, when we are weakened enough, to join us as thralls to the Marsonians? We have but a few days of food left. Soon after that, we'll begin to see the first signs of starvation."

"You're certain the boats belong to Marsony, and not the Murdano?" I asked.

"The Murdano has no boats this far north," Figton said. He had long gray hairs protruding from his ears and was missing a few teeth. "Marsonian raiders have come before, but this is their most determined effort. In the past, they stole food and whatever valuables they could find. This time, we feel certain they mean to finish us off."

"We shall soon have no worries about Marsonians," I said, surprised at my sudden confidence. "I have come to lead you out of here. The dairnes must join with Kharassande Donati to stop this war, to prevent the slaughter of entire species, and to bring justice to Nedarra!"

It was an inspiring speech, and some of the younger dairnes in the circle around us applauded. Most, however, young or old, frowned and looked distinctly unhappy.

"Byx," said Larbrik, "this is our home. For ninety-two years we've survived here, and now you tell us that our survival was a miracle, and that we are the last of our kind. Why would we march off to join some distant war? To serve some ambitious new human ruler?"

Several dairnes murmured agreement.

"And how would you have us leave?" a young male dairne demanded. "By the crumbling path? Our old and infirm, not to mention our youngest pups, couldn't hope to make that climb. Would you have us leave them here to the mercies of the Marsonians? Abandon our village? Our boats? Our way of life?"

"But," I argued, "you say the Marsonians have you at the edge of starvation. You can't just sit here and slowly die."

"Better to be a thrall of the Marsonians than to fall from the crumbling path or be eaten by wild felivets!" someone shouted.

"There are no wild felivets waiting to—" I glanced at Tobble helplessly. "I mean, yes, there are some felivets, but they don't eat dairnes. Not anymore. And anyway—"

"This outsider will lead us to our deaths!" a shrill voice yelled.

"Go back to where you came from!"

"We don't need your wild ideas!"

The noise level rose and the shouting verged on hysteria. "Byx," Tobble whispered in my ear, "perhaps we should give them some time to think things over."

"Enough!" A voice cut through it all—a clear, intelligent female voice. She was only a few years older than I, lovely, and quite tall for a female dairne.

The room quieted to a dull hum. "If there exists a way to scare away the Marsonians, we could sail south, find a landing place, and join with Byx's human leader," the young dairne said. She sent me a sympathetic smile. "It's better than dying of boredom in this deadly dull place."

"Oh, is that so, Glynlee?" asked Figton. "Fine, then. Go chase away the Marsonians!"

His retort brought a gale of derisive laughter, and Glynlee hung her head. Still, she muttered, "It's the only way."

The words came out of my mouth before I could think them through. "I can deal with the Marsonians," I said, as certainly as I might have declared, "I can count to ten."

The crowd fell silent. The only sounds were the click of knitting needles and the steady snore of the elderly dairne I'd encountered on arriving.

No one called me a liar, which could only mean that I was not lying. And *that* could only mean that somewhere deep down I believed—actually believed—I thought it was possible.

"How exactly would you accomplish this, Byx?" Glynlee

asked in an encouraging voice.

My stomach whined, and I realized I needed food and, far more important, time to strategize.

"Good question, Glynlee," I said, ignoring Tobble's worried gaze. "I will reveal my plan later this evening. After dinner."

52
Audacious and Quite Possibly Preposterous

"So," Tobble asked when we were in a private place, a hut we'd been given for the night. "What exactly is this plan of yours for dealing with the Marsonians?"

"You know I don't have one."

"But a whole roomful of dairnes believed you."

"That's because in that moment I believed myself."

I sighed. We were sitting on a dirt floor around a meager fire. Half its smoke meandered up through a chimney hole, while the other half lingered in the air. The village elders had offered to feed us, but knowing how dire things were, we'd chosen to eat from our own dwindling supplies.

Tobble rubbed his eyes, which were watering in the murky air. "Then what do we do?"

"I don't know, Tobble," I admitted. "I really don't."

On what should have been a day of joy and triumph for

me, I was as worried as I'd ever been. Two ships bottled up the colony. And only the hardiest of dairnes could escape up the dangerously steep trail. There was no way out.

These dairnes were in a trap. I'd promised to deliver them from it. And I had nothing at all to offer.

Even if I were somehow able to rescue them, what then? I had no way of knowing how Khara was faring. Had Albrit remained loyal? Had Khara been able to make peace with Luca's clan? Had she been able to raise a force capable of stopping the coming war?

I shook my head, trying to clear away the biggest question of all, but it held fast as a poacher's arrow: What if Khara was no longer even alive?

I poked at the fire with a stick. "Do you think Khara is"—I struggled for words—"all right?"

"Yes," Tobble said firmly. "I do."

"How can you be so sure?"

Tobble pulled on a whisker. "Because she's Khara."

I wanted to believe Tobble, but some part of me wondered if this journey had all been a waste of time—and a waste of life. What about Maxyn, and the poor packhorse who had fallen to his death? Had this been worth their pain?

Again I punched at the fire, harder this time. The wood popped, sending a hot ember flying onto Tobble's pack. He batted it out with his tail braid.

It was a commonplace thing, that ember. Fires always spat and crackled. But perhaps because my thoughts were spiraling in pointless circles, I found myself mesmerized. There was something there. Something important . . .

"Byx?" Tobble prompted. "What's wrong?"

I jumped to my feet. "The fire!" I exclaimed.

"I know it's awfully smoky," Tobble apologized. "The wood they gave us was quite damp, and I didn't want to make a fuss—"

"Sabito!" I shouted, flinging open the door while Tobble watched, mouth agape.

Sabito swooped in a few seconds later. He settled on the floor, looking annoyed. (Hawks always look annoyed, but I knew Sabito hated landing in a spot where his talons couldn't manage a firm grip.)

"You shouted?" he grumbled.

"Tell me, Sabito. How far could you carry Tobble?"

"What?" both Tobble and Sabito demanded in unison.

"Tobble," I repeated. "Without his pack."

The riverhawk tilted his head and considered. "Hmm. I could get him airborne, but only for a few feet."

"I've watched you, Sabito," I said. "You seek out rising heat. I've seen you use the warmth of fires, the warmth coming from chimneys, the warmth of the sun on rocks—"

"Yes, yes," Sabito interrupted. "We call them updrafts.

Warm air rises in a column. Raptidons spread their wings and—" He stopped, eyeing me carefully.

"And if you had a column of warm air?" I asked.

"Oh, then I could almost certainly lift Tobble."

"If you rode high enough on a column of air," I continued, waving my hand toward the ceiling, "you could glide then, still holding him?"

Sabito stretched out his wings and gave a perturbed flutter. "I think it's time you told me just what you have in mind."

Tobble nodded. "As the item being lifted, I agree."

And so I told them.

They listened carefully, if skeptically (Sabito in particular had his doubts). There were many questions, and a few groans (mostly from Tobble). Still and all, they grudgingly agreed that my idea just might work.

"It's audacious," said Sabito. "Possibly even preposterous." He gave a little avian nod. "I like it."

The three of us returned to the hall of elders, where many of the same dairnes we'd met earlier were still gathered. I found Glynlee and asked her to assemble the rest of the villagers. Before long, the entire hall was filled to the brim with dairnes, young and old, waiting to hear what I had to say.

I stood on a small wooden pallet, cleared my throat, and began.

"Fellow dairnes," I said, "we have a plan. I'm told it is audacious." I smiled at Tobble and Sabito. "Perhaps even preposterous."

I paused, looking at the expectant, worried, doubtful faces gathered before me. "But," I said, "if there is one thing I have learned from my friends, it's that even the most audacious plan can sometimes work. Will you at least hear me out?"

There were murmurs, a few groans, a bit of laughter.

I spoke.

They listened.

They argued.

I argued back.

At one point, Tobble left the gathering. He returned moments later with one of the saddlebags and passed it to me.

Khara's gifts for the dairnes. I'd forgotten all about them.

"Friends," I said, "I know that you continue to have doubts about my plan, about the brewing war, and about Kharassande Donati. In my haste to talk to you, I neglected to share these small tokens sent by Kharassande to signal her commitment to you, and to our species."

I passed the bag to Larbrik, who examined the contents and handed each item to Figton. A small silver chalice, one I recalled seeing in the baron's treetop hideaway. Two sharp knives with elaborately engraved handles. And most important: a glittering green gem from the natite crown.

Larbrik shook her head in disbelief. "This could feed our village for a year."

"And yet those offerings are useless to you unless you can reach the outside world," I pointed out.

We continued our back-and-forth until my voice grew hoarse. Gradually, I began to sense a shift in the mood. But it wasn't my speech, or Khara's gifts, that made the difference.

In the end, it was Sabito and Tobble who convinced the dairnes to give my plan a try, with two simple sentences.

"I would trust Byx with my life," said Sabito.

"I *have* trusted my Byx with my life," said Tobble.

Whatever their doubts, our audience of dairnes knew one thing with complete certainty: Tobble and Sabito were speaking the truth.

And I knew we were about to embark on my audacious, quite possibly preposterous, plan.

53
Figton's Folly

The next day, the elders dispatched a team of workers to place a temporary bridge over the washed-out section of the trail, the terrifying spot where we'd lost our pack-horse. They also gave us the boat I'd requested. It was small, old, and creaky, and it stank of fish. Its wooden hull had seen better days. But it had a mast and a sail, and for my purposes, rotting wood was perfect.

Tobble took note of the boat's name, painted on the side in chipped paint: *Figton's Folly.* I was grateful indeed that Figton had been willing to sacrifice his boat. But the word "folly" didn't seem like a particularly good omen.

As the day wore on, villagers brought bundles of straw down to the water's edge. "Pile it all belowdecks," I instructed. "But loosely, please."

After a light evening meal, Tobble, Sabito, and I checked

our tired-looking craft one more time. I fretfully rearranged the dry straw in the hull, while Sabito circled the harbor, searching for potential obstacles. The breeze was reassuringly steady, and Tobble held up a moistened paw to gauge its direction.

An old dairne fisherman named Ornyxus joined Tobble and advised, "The wind tends to shift after midnight. Should be comin' from the south, southeast. The tide will be goin' out about the same time."

"Will she lie close to the wind?" Tobble asked, a question that meant nothing to me.

Ornyxus nodded. "Aye, she'll lie close enough. If you know how to handle her, she'll do. You'll be able to tack almost due west."

"Then ride the breeze straight on in," Tobble said, nodding.

"If fortune smiles," the old sailor said.

"What about natites?" I asked.

"Oh, bless me, they're scarce in these waters, and this boat is licensed. The natites don't fool with fishing craft, so long as you pay the fee."

"Is that why they allow the Marsonians free rein? Do the raiders pay a fee?"

Ornyxus shrugged. "The natites rule the seas. They do as they please."

It was well past midnight when, just as Ornyxus had predicted, the wind shifted. Most of the villagers had come out, despite the late chill and a light dusting of falling snow. They lined the pier and much of the beach—all curious, most afraid.

Tobble raised his paw and, with a losing attempt to sound bluff and hearty, called, "Let's go! Time and tide wait for no one."

He and I climbed aboard the boat, which was now stuffed with straw. I'd piled more straw in loose bales on the deck.

"You know you don't have to do this, Tobble." I reached into my patchel and retrieved the all-important tinderbox. "You have nothing left to prove to me or to anyone."

Tobble scratched an ear, feigning calm. "I think it sounds like fun."

I didn't need my dairne ability to know that wasn't true.

"Are you *sure?*" I pressed, hit by the crushing weight of worry and guilt. If things went badly, I would be responsible for my best friend's death.

Tobble put his paw on my arm. "Byx," he said, "I want to do this. It's my choice."

Once again, I wished for my companions and their strengths—Khara's resolve, Gambler's wisdom, Renzo's confidence—at this moment when so much was at stake.

"All right, then." I hugged Tobble close, handed him the

tinderbox, and turned away quickly so he couldn't see my anguish.

"Cast off fore and aft," Tobble yelled, once I was back on the pier. Dairne onlookers rushed to loosen ropes. With a long pole, Ornyxus pushed the boat away, while Tobble raised the sail and ran back to grab the tiller.

The breeze filled the sail, Tobble leaned into the helm, and the boat began to make its way roughly west.

I looked back to see if Sabito was perched atop the elders' tower. He must have known I was nervous, so he flared his wings, the better for me to see him. The height of the tower would, I hoped, provide the riverhawk with early and much-needed speed.

Tobble gathered momentum, aided by the breeze and the receding tide. Soon he was a quarter of a league out, and nearly invisible.

I was powerless to do anything but watch and wait. It was agony. Pacing back and forth, I stared at the black waves, muttering under my breath while the shy moon cowered behind clouds.

Time passed. The crowd grew restless. I began to worry that Tobble had lost his nerve or, worse yet, fallen overboard. But then, far out at sea, I noticed a flicker of light.

The moon chose that moment to reappear. I saw a silver, triangular glow—Tobble's sail—within a few hundred yards of the larger of the ships from Marsony.

The Marsonians had spotted Tobble, too. Faint cries of excitement in an alien tongue floated across the water. I pictured their sailors rushing to small boats, no doubt assuming that Tobble was a helpless dairne in a tiny vessel, making a break for the open sea.

But Tobble wasn't aiming for escape.

He was preparing for attack.

"You can do this, Tobble," I whispered, and seemingly out of nowhere, a tongue of yellow flame appeared, as if the water itself had caught fire.

"Sabito!" I shouted.

"I see," he cried. He spread his wings and swooped from the tower, turned his downward momentum into forward speed, then flapped to gain altitude, heading straight out to sea.

The flames on Tobble's boat were growing rapidly, beautiful and deadly, even as he advanced on the nearest Marsonian boat.

Panicked yells, louder now, carried on the air. The Marsonians would be trying desperately to pull up anchor and flee. Would they have time?

Would Tobble?

Clearly, the Marsonian crew members were quick and well-trained. They had their anchor off the sea floor and were raising their own sails when Tobble's blazing torch of a boat crashed into the side of their own.

I dashed back and forth, hoping to catch a glimpse of Tobble.

Nothing. Nor could I see Sabito.

But I could see one thing: the flames from Tobble's boat as they licked the side of the Marsonian vessel, caught the rigging, and, in a spectacular rush of flame, ate through the sail as if it were parchment.

Cheers from the dairnes filled the air.

Now it was up to the wind.

As I'd hoped, the Marsonian ship, unmoored and aflame, began to drift into the second, smaller Marsonian boat.

Cheers redoubled. There were even shouts of "Byx! Byx!"

But I couldn't seem to breathe. My eyes ached from staring at the sea. My fevered heart rattled in my chest.

Nothing would matter, not this victory, not any victory, without Tobble by my side.

Something plummeted down out of the sky and splashed at the edge of the surf. Dairnes rushed forward, shouting and chanting, and moments later, there he was: Tobble, borne high on the shoulders of grateful villagers.

"Tobble!" I cried. "Tobble!"

He had singe marks on his fur. His face was smeared with soot. But he was grinning.

"Hanadru was kind," he said.

"And you were brave," I replied.

Sabito joined us, perching on a post. He was not one for being touched, let alone carried aloft by a giddy mob.

"It was close," he said. "Very close! The fire was hotter than I expected. When I grabbed Tobble, his tails were smoldering. The updraft was excellent, but the flames shot so high I could scarcely stay in the column of air."

"But you did it," I said, shaking my head in disbelief.

"Yes. I did, didn't I? Well then, I must be very pleased with myself."

We were all very pleased with ourselves—for a few moments, at least. I hugged Tobble and Tobble hugged me and half the village hugged us both, it seemed. Glynlee patted me on the back and said, "You did it, Byx."

"Tobble and Sabito did all the work," I said.

"But you made it happen. And this village will be the better for it."

We were stopped cold by the sucking sound of rushing water, followed by the terrified yells of desperate men. The Marsonian ships were going down, and with them, perhaps, many souls.

We fell silent, chastened and grave. The snow quickened, turning the harbor into a scene of sparkling loveliness and obscuring the horror beyond.

54
Dreams and Departure

My sleep was disrupted by chilling nightmares, though Tobble seemed to doze undisturbed. I awoke repeatedly, each time reminding myself to savrielle and take control of the stories spun by my sleeping brain. "You are the dream and the dream is you," I whispered. "You are the dream and the dream is you."

But the nightmare kept repeating, taunting me with its vividness. Always, it began with Tobble on a boat engulfed in flames. He was clinging to the mast, crying out my name, begging me to save him. And though I swam with all my might through a choppy black ocean, he remained forever just out of my reach.

Three times—for three horrifying dreams—I watched my best friend drown.

I woke the third time screaming for Tobble, only to find

him shaking my shoulder. "Byx!" he said. "Wake up! You're having a nightmare."

I blinked, my chest heaving, my throat dry as ash. "You're alive."

"Quite." Tobble yawned. "I was having a lovely dream about centipede biscuits."

"I'm sorry I interrupted," I said, rubbing my eyes. "I tried to savrielle, but I just couldn't get control."

Tobble responded with an exuberant snore. I looked over to see him already fast asleep. Carefully, I tucked a blanket under his chin. How I envied his ability to sleep under any circumstances!

Lying back on my straw mat, I resolved to stay awake until dawn. I couldn't witness the death—however unreal—of Tobble again. We were leaving in the morning, and I needed to be fresh. But exhaustion was far preferable to the alternative.

And yet fall asleep I did. Once again, the nightmare returned. Once again, Tobble clung to the mast while flames licked at his rear paws. Once again, I swam to no avail, ever closer, but not close enough.

You are the dream and the dream is you.

Tobble's boat began to sink, his eyes wide with terror, my screams swallowed by the indifferent sea.

You are the dream and the dream is you.

There.

There on the horizon.

It was another boat. A boat coming closer, slapping against the waves, filled with three—no, four—individuals. They were shadowy, unrecognizable.

Tobble screamed again. I paddled furiously.

The boat neared. The four shadows took form, grew more distinct.

Tobble yelled, but this time, the sound he made was different.

I fought the waves harder. So close now, so close. The boat was there, and Tobble was yelling, and the yelling was . . . not fear, not pain.

No. Could it be that I was hearing joy?

I stopped, exhausted. For a moment, I sank, swallowed by the sea, and when at last I made my way back to the sweet, cold air and wiped the water from my eyes, I saw them in their little boat.

Khara. Renzo. Gambler. Sabito.

And Tobble, safe, if singed.

"What took you so long?" I said, and then, at long last, I fell into a dreamless sleep.

Before leaving the next morning, we breakfasted with Lar-brik, Figton, and Glynlee, along with several other grateful villagers. "Not much to offer," Larbrik apologized, "but we'll have fresh catch this evening, that's for certain." Indeed, we'd already seen several fishing boats heading out into the harbor.

"Where are you going now, Byx?" Glynlee asked.

I sipped my tea. "Back to find Kharassande Donati and her people. We'll report to her that we've succeeded in finding your colony. And, I hope"—I glanced around the table—"I'll be able to tell her that she will have your support, should it be needed."

"Aye, that she will," said Figton, and the others nodded in agreement.

I clasped my hands together, leaning forward. "You must know, however, that you are not out of danger. The Marsonians may return, perhaps with reinforcements. And it's possible that the Murdano has learned of your existence, which could put you in even greater peril."

"We'll trade Kharassande's gifts and, with the money, do what we can to fortify the village," Larbrik said. "We'll be fine, for a while yet."

"I wish you could all come with me now," I said. "But I know that's not possible. We'll need help before that can happen."

I stood and embraced each dairne in turn. "I hate to leave," I said, "but for all of us, I must."

Tobble and I climbed on Havoc, having tied the packhorse

to our saddle. (We'd decided to call her "Folly.") With Sabito floating along beside us, we clattered down the long cobblestone road through the town, while villagers cheered and waved.

The trip up the steep path was almost as treacherous as our downward effort, but at least the gap had been repaired, and we had a better sense of the danger. Just before we reached the top, we were relieved to hear from Sabito that there was no sign of the Murdano's men.

"Well," Tobble said as we emerged, "at least we know for sure that you're not an endling."

"Not today," I said darkly. "But those dairnes were few in number, and weak and defenseless. I'm not an endling now. But next year? Next month? Tomorrow?"

We rode on in silence. The air was crisp and tinged with balsam.

Tobble was the first to break the quiet. "You have grown larger, Byx."

I glanced behind me. "If anything, I'm probably skinnier than—"

"No, no, not that kind of large. I mean that when we met, you were just a pup. A clever, kind pup, but not one who dwelled on dark thoughts about the future. Let alone someone who could order . . ." Tobble coughed to cover his awkward pause.

I finished for him. "Someone who could order up a fire boat, send his closest companion into great danger, and cause the terrible deaths of dozens of Marsonians?"

Tobble nodded, a movement I felt rather than saw.

"Well, I'm not the only one, Tobble. You've done things no one, including you, could have imagined. I don't know if wobbyks have heroes, but if they do, you're one of them."

Over the next couple of days of travel, it snowed occasionally, but with only a few inches of accumulation. We located plenty of fresh, unfrozen streams for water, but our food was running low. After successfully fording the Pellago River, we found ourselves once again on the Nedarran plain.

Day after day we trudged along, living on meals of dried game and hard crackers. Always alert, on guard for any sign of the Murdano's men, it was hard to relax. Our progress was slowed when we ran out of oats. The horses had to graze, and that was especially difficult when snow covered the ground. One afternoon, I sent Sabito in search of a convenient village where we might purchase some food.

Only minutes later we heard a scream from the sky, the syllable stretched by the speed of Sabito's dive. "Ru-u-u-n!"

I looked up and saw him dropping like a bolt of lightning. He flared, slowed, and yelled, "Men in the Murdano's livery. Seven of them. And they're chasing us!"

Without waiting for further explanation, I released Folly, then nudged Havoc and yelled, "Hold on!" to Tobble.

Sabito, agile as always, managed to flap along beside us, still talking. "I think it may be the same squad of soldiers that captured Maxyn."

I jerked my head in his direction. "Is Maxyn with them?"

"I saw something draped over a saddle and tied down, but I didn't look closely enough to—"

"Then *do*!" I snapped, and Sabito soared away.

He returned as the horses were showing signs of exhaustion. I slowed Havoc reluctantly, knowing that if I pushed too hard, he might founder.

"I think it may be Maxyn," Sabito reported, and my heart leapt. "He, or it, whatever it is, is wrapped in a blanket and held with ropes. In any case, it's alive. I saw it move."

"Have they slowed at all?"

"They'll catch up to us in less than half an hour if we keep to a full-on gallop. If we do not, well . . ."

"Sorry, boy," I said to Havoc, urging him on.

I managed a quick glance over my shoulder. I could see them. Their great warhorses weren't as fast as ours, but they were strong and hardy.

Would they wrap us in blankets and throw us on a horse beside Maxyn? Or would they kill us instantly for having evaded them once before?

Havoc stumbled from weariness but caught himself. I held on tight, berating myself for not having a plan.

I was in charge. It was my responsibility to save us.

To the woods, then. It was better than nothing.

I yanked the reins hard and turned sharply toward a thick stand of firs, but Sabito, surveying the scene, delivered bad news. "You can't reach the woods before they cut you off!"

What was my backup plan? Nothing. I had nothing.

We would be captured. Then killed or made into thralls.

At least I would get to be with Maxyn, perhaps, one last time.

I could see the very eastern tip of the woods ahead. But behind us I could also see, quite clearly now, our relentless, apparently tireless, pursuers.

Then, as I watched, a miracle! One of the soldiers' horses tripped, sending his rider sprawling.

We gained precious yards, as the soldiers paused to collect the horse and return their fallen man to his saddle.

Maybe. Maybe we still had a chance.

That was the moment all hope died.

From the end of the woods rode hundreds—no, thousands—of armed men.

55
Into Battle

I don't know what happened to me.

I'd been filled with fear and despair.

Now, as if by some theurgic spell, all my doubt and terror transformed into something else.

Feel fear. Choose courage.

I slowed Havoc.

"What are you doing?" Sabito screeched.

I had no answer. I had no words.

It was Tobble who answered Sabito.

"She's fighting!" he yelled, voice high and shrill. "And so am I!"

I dug in my heels and drew the long knife I used as a sword, ready to make one last, desperate stand.

To my absolute amazement, the Murdano's seven soldiers, the ones who'd been closing in, reined hard, stared in apparent confusion, and turned their horses away, spurring them on.

"Yes!" I roared. "Run, you cowards! Ruuuuun!" I turned Havoc yet again, intending, in my rage-addled mind, to attack the great force of armed men streaming from the woods.

I'd abandoned the idea of surviving. Now I was just determined to take some of them down with me.

It's wonderful how recklessly brave you can be once you give up on life.

I charged the mass of soldiers racing to meet me. Two in front carried fluttering banners with a strange, ornate pattern rendered in several colors. I picked out one fellow, a big man with streaming red hair beneath a gleaming helmet, and decided he was my target.

I would die, yes. But I would die fighting.

"Aaaaarrrrggghhhh!" I shouted, teeth bared as we came together.

I stabbed my knife at him, and he knocked it aside easily with his huge sword. My blade twirled away like a moth pursued by a raptidon.

My opponent's heavy horse blocked mine, and he grabbed for my reins, while Tobble tried to fight him off.

"Kill me, then!" I yelled.

Despite my madness, despite the red veil that seemed to come down over my sight, I noticed that the mass of horsemen were streaming past us, swords drawn, spears aimed, yelling in the crazed fervor of battle.

"Kill you?" the red-haired man cried. "We have come to rescue you. Unless there is some other doglike creature in company with a wobbyk."

I gaped at him. I was panting. The throbbing of my own pulse was deafening.

I managed the one thing I could think of to say, which, as it turned out, was not particularly clever. As last words went, they were decidedly non-heroic.

"Huh?" I said.

"You are Byx of the dairnes?"

"What?"

"Byx. Are you not called Byx?"

"Yes, but—but—"

The red-haired man tore off his helmet and grinned a wide, gap-toothed smile. "Well, that was easier than we'd expected. The Lady will be pleased!"

"The Lady?" I mumbled.

"The Lady," he repeated. "The Lady Kharassande."

"Kharassande of the Donatis?" I asked, too stunned to accept the obvious.

"She no longer calls herself that. She is now styled the Lady of Nedarra. I am called Varis. I was Varis of the Corplis for all my life, but I'm now Varis of Nedarra, lieutenant in the army of a Free Nedarra, sworn to serve the Lady until the end of days."

A smaller, older man trotted up, helmet off, smiling through a bushy gray beard. "Captain Sagari," Varis said, "I present Byx of the dairnes."

I stifled a sob, straightened my shoulders, and gave a nod.

"No," I said. "Not Byx of the dairnes. I am Byx of Nedarra."

56
Pathfinders

Captain Sagari's troops soon captured the Murdano's men who'd been pursuing us. As I was scanning their bitter, exhausted faces, I noticed a horse with a blanketed bundle on its back. Two soldiers carefully lowered it to the ground and began to unwrap it.

I swung off my horse and ran.

Ran to find Maxyn—alive, but horribly hurt.

Lieutenant Varis tried to stop me. "Delay a moment, Byx. He's been badly treated. You may not wish to see—"

I pulled away and fell to my knees beside Maxyn. His hands were wrapped in bloody bandages. His face was swollen. And his eyes, when they opened, seemed empty and lost.

"Maxyn," I said, stroking his forehead.

He blinked, shook his head slowly, and muttered, "Byx? Is any of this real?"

"It's real, Maxyn. You're safe. You're with me."

We had no wagon, so Tobble kindly suggested letting Maxyn ride with me. "I'll ride with one of the soldiers," he said as I mounted Havoc.

"Ride with me, little wobbyk," Lieutenant Varis suggested. He leaned over, grabbed Tobble's paw, and swung him onto his saddle, where they towered over Havoc and me.

With the help of gentle hands, we managed to get Maxyn seated in front of me so I could keep him steady.

"I'm sorry, Maxyn," I said softly as we started our ride to Khara's camp.

He didn't respond, and I understood why. After what he'd gone through, there would be no forgiving. I didn't deserve it.

Maxyn jerked his head, and I realized he must have been sleeping. "What did you say?" he asked weakly, his words muffled by a swollen jaw.

"I said I'm sorry. For everything you've gone through."

With effort, he turned to look at me. A deep cut, from ear to muzzle, oozed pearly blood. "Don't ever say that to me again, Byx. You're my leader, and I'm proud to serve you." He attempted a smile, although it wasn't entirely successful. "Although you *can* be a bit of a nag."

It was early evening before we neared the camp. The sight took my breath away.

White tents, sheened with moonlight, seemed to stretch on forever. Cooking fires blazed. Soldiers moved purposefully, stacking supplies, caring for horses, and cleaning their weapons.

Someone was singing a sprightly tune, accompanied by a lute and recorder.

It was a massive undertaking, one that underlined the dark reality of the war that lay ahead. And yet there was something oddly cheerful, even heartening, about the scene.

They were here. Somewhere, in the midst of all this, Khara and Renzo and Gambler awaited.

We dismounted. Maxyn, with his arms around two soldiers, was able to limp along beside us, while Sabito circled overhead. Varis, acting as our escort, led the way to a center tent, no larger or grander than the others.

Tobble and I looked at each other, smiles overtaking our faces. He gestured toward the tent.

"After you," he whispered, but before I could move, the tent flap opened.

Khara and Gambler appeared before us.

They looked weary, but otherwise unchanged. Their eyes glistened in the creamy light.

I took a shaky breath. "Byx of Nedarra, reporting for duty."

Tobble gave a little bow. "Tobble of Nedarra, reporting as well."

Khara's lower lip trembled. "Well met, dear friends. You have arrived just in time."

"In time?" I asked.

Khara held out her palm, revealing the stone I'd given her before we'd separated.

She passed it to me, clasping my hand tightly in both of hers.

"Time, my fellow pathfinder," she said, "to stop a war and save the world."

From behind us came the sound of someone approaching. We turned to see Renzo, shaking his head. He had an anteleer drumstick in one hand and a silver mug in the other. Dog was trotting beside him.

Renzo sent Khara a knowing smile, then turned his gaze to us.

"Well, it's about time," he said. "What took you so long?"

Acknowledgments

Endless thanks to my amazing editors, Tara Weikum and Chris Hernandez, as well as Ann Dye, Renée Cafiero, Sarah Homer, Barb Fitzsimmons, Alison Donalty, Jenna Stempel-Lobell, Patty Rosati, Andrea Pappenheimer, Suzanne Murphy, and all the other folks at HarperCollins who've helped bring *Endling* to life; and to my wonderful agent, Elena Giovanazzo, at Pippin Properties, Inc.

The Endling series by
KATHERINE APPLEGATE

When one is endangered, all are in peril!

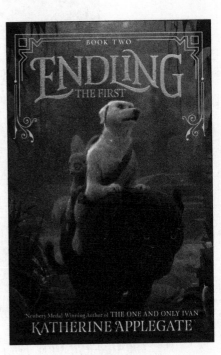

Book One

Book Two

The last of her kind.
The first to lead a revolt.

HARPER
An Imprint of HarperCollinsPublishers

www.harpercollinschildrens.com
endlingbooks.com

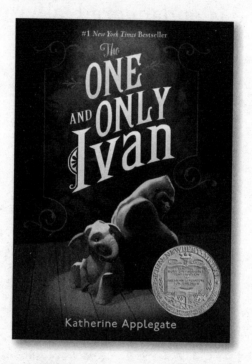